QUEEN OF NOTHING

For Sam Courtney,
Here goes nothing!

QUEEN OF NOTHING

T. A. PRATT

T. A. Pratt

The Merry Blacksmith Press

2015

Queen of Nothing

© 2015 Tim Pratt

Cover design by Jenn Reese
www.tigerbrightstudios.com

Interior art by Zack Stella
www.zackstella.com

For information, address:

The Merry Blacksmith Press
70 Lenox Ave.
West Warwick, RI 02893

merryblacksmith.com

Published in the USA by The Merry Blacksmith Press

ISBN—0-69259-132-X
978-0-69259-132-1

DEDICATION

For Aislinn

Three Days Late

"**WELL *THAT* THEORY DIDN'T PAN OUT,**" Rondeau said.

"I confess I had little faith that it would." Pelham nudged the undisturbed patch of sand at the back of the cave with his toe. The dusty, cool air smelled of canned beans, and, as an inevitable corollary, farts.

Rondeau sat down on a dusty cooler and leaned his back against the cave wall. "I don't know, it seemed sort of… mythic. She didn't come back to life on schedule, so I thought maybe if we waited three days, *then* she'd resurrect. We're in a cave. She's a god who's also a mortal. I thought that's how these things were done."

"We don't even have a stone to roll back, and I don't think Mrs. Mason's godhood is particularly related to Christian mythology."

"Oh, sure, but the rule of threes, that's a thing, right?"

"In comedy, as I understand it."

Rondeau scowled. "In magic too, Pelly. Triple goddess. Three-fold law. Junk like that. We could keep waiting, but I'm not a big fan of desert camping under any circumstances, especially indefinite ones. It looks like Marla isn't coming back from the underworld to spend a month on Earth as a mortal like she usually does. So… do we have theories? Is her failure to appear more like forgetting to go to the dentist, or like being kidnapped by a murder cult?"

Pelham wandered away from the plot of sand where, in the past, their mutual friend and intermittent employer Marla Mason, part-time goddess of death, had returned to the mortal world, typically rising up naked and sand-caked and cranky. "There could have been some sort of… mythological emergency. Something that required her attention as a god, and delayed her return to mortality?"

Rondeau hrmphed. "You'd think she'd at least answer our calls then." The underworld didn't have phones, or eat least not ones mortals could

1

reach, but there were certain procedures in place to send Marla messages: writing notes and burning them on a fire made of rotten wood and animal bones, lighting black candles and chanting in a circle of salt, yelling into open graves, things like that. She very rarely *answered* those messages—when she was in goddess-mode, she paid as little attention to the goings-on of mortals as Rondeau did to insects buzzing around a porch light—but surely if she knew she was going to be late she'd make an exception, and send an apparition of a flaming dog skull to bark her new schedule at them, or something. Rondeau would've settled for an entirely non-eldritch email.

Then again, maybe it just hadn't occurred to her. Even mortal Marla wasn't the most considerate when it came to valuing other people's time, and when she was in Bride of Death mode, she was about as warm and thoughtful as a bad case of hypothermia. But…. "It's possible she's just being an inconsiderate asshole," Rondeau said. "Maybe even probable. But we can't rule out the idea that she's in trouble."

Pelham nodded. "Indeed. But what sort of help can we possibly offer, if she is?"

"I could summon an oracle." Rondeau shuddered at the thought. "There are old wild spirits all over this valley. I could find one and ask it what's going on."

"Hmm," Pelham said. "The last time desperation led you to summon an oracle, we were nearly killed, and we *were* exiled from Las Vegas. If Marla hadn't convinced the Pit Boss to let us return, we would still be homeless."

"There's that. There's also the problem that gods don't usually like people asking questions about them. If I summon an oracle and ask it to reveal secrets about a being of immense power? It would try to answer, because they always do, but the price for that answer could be more than I'm willing or able to pay."

"It is Mrs. Mason, though," Pelham said simply.

"Yeah. It's Marla. I know." Rondeau suddenly perked up. "Hey, hold up. I'm not the only guy on this side of the Rockies who can summon oracles anymore. Bradley Bowman is in San Francisco now. He's got all the same powers I do, *and* he knows a hell of a lot more about how to use them properly. He's got a lot more experience."

"He also diligently studies and applies himself."

"Yeah, I know." Rondeau shook his head in wonderment. "Some people are so *weird*."

"Shall we call him?" Pelham said.

"Huh." Rondeau stood up and began to pace around. "I don't actually have his number. I mean, B wasn't even living on this plane of reality until recently. Do autonomous fragments of multiversal collective meta-gods even *have* phones? I could get in touch with Perren River in Felport, and she could probably find me a number for Sanford Cole in San Francisco—all the chief sorcerers know how to reach each other, more or less—and Cole would know where to find B, they're working together again...."

"But Perren would ask questions," Pelham said. "It may be better, perhaps, if people don't realize Marla Mason has failed to return to Earth."

Rondeau nodded. "Trouble in the realms of gods is the sort of thing sorcerers are interested in for all kinds of reasons, most of them bad. Maybe it doesn't matter, but I don't want Marla getting pissed at me for talking out of turn. Cole's part of her inner circle, and B's like a kid brother to her, so they're safe to loop in on this.... We could just start driving, and we'd get to San Francisco in eight or ten hours, depending on traffic. Once we get there, I know where Cole hangs out, we can do this face-to-face, old school."

"Do we dare leave this place unattended, though?" Pelham said. "What if Mrs. Mason arrives tomorrow, or the next day, and laments our absence? I would worry less if she had cultists here to greet her...." He trailed off. The existing cult of the Bride of Death had been slaughtered by an ancient otherworldly monster they'd discovered in the caves below Death Valley, and though Rondeau and Pelham had expected more weirdo zealots to drift into the valley, drawn by mysterious compulsions, no one had shown up yet. Which, in retrospect, was kind of ominous in itself.

"We could park her motorcycle in the cave," Rondeau said. "Nobody's going to wander in here, the place is magically concealed, so it should be safe. We'll leave the suitcase with her clothes and stuff. There's food and water. Hell, we'll even leave a note, and her phone, so she can call us if she *does* come back. If Marla's anything at all, she's self-sufficient."

"I admit, I grow anxious just waiting, and it would be pleasant to take action, of whatever sort."

"Yeah," Rondeau agreed. "Forward motion is a good way to distract yourself from being scared as hell."

THEIR RV LOOKED LIKE a battered piece of junk, but it was ensorcelled to run perfectly, and after recent upgrades it could even drive fully autonomously, with an illusory figure—who looked like an old man who got his fashion advice from the golf channel—in the driver's seat to keep people driving past from freaking out. (They could have cast a look-away spell on the vehicle, of course, to keep people from noticing, but that was a bad idea, unless you *enjoyed* being rear-ended and sideswiped by other drivers who simply didn't notice you there.)

Rondeau piloted the RV out of Death Valley himself rather than engaging the auto-drive, because even though he loved sloth and indolence almost as much as he loved runny cheese and oral sex (albeit not in combination), at the moment he wanted to feel like he was *doing* something. They rolled down a bumpy dirt road, through the scrub and sand and surprise patches of wildflowers, and as usual didn't see another living soul… except one.

There was a woman in oversized sunglasses relaxing in one of those folding poolside lounge chairs, improbably sitting in a clear patch of sand, no vehicle or camping gear in sight. She wore a skimpy red bikini that matched her bright red hair so perfectly it was like they'd been dyed to be identical, and she was so pale that Rondeau winced at the thought of what the sun was doing to her: the woman was courting melanoma. She was probably late thirties or early forties, and he vaguely noted that she was pretty, though these days he lusted after boys almost exclusively. What was she *doing* out here, though? Who came to Death Valley to sunbathe?

She raised a hand and waved at him lazily as he went past, and he waved back, out of bewildered politeness. Oh well. People were weird. He didn't think of the woman much after that… until later, when he had good reason to.

ONCE THEY HIT THE HIGHWAY Rondeau and Pelham mostly hung out in the RV's living area and let the vehicle drive itself. They played desultory hands of gin rummy, took naps, and read as they cruised along the freeways. Since they had food in the cupboards and a toilet in the back and enough room to stand up and stretch their legs as required, they didn't even stop for pee or food breaks. Rondeau had spent most of his life on the East Coast, and it was still strange to him that you could spend so many hours driving and still be in the same state. California had a surpassing bigness about it.

They arrived in San Francisco right in the thickest part of evening rush hour, reduced to crawling through the congested streets. No amount of magic could make their progress any faster, at least not without flinging the obstructing vehicles out of the roadway, which was probably beyond their capabilities anyway, and would in any case get them in trouble with the same local magical authorities they were hoping to ask for help. Eventually they got to the right block and Rondeau took the wheel, then found a nice big stretch of red curb in front of a fire hydrant not far from the tiny bookstore in North Beach where Sanford Cole currently held court.

"I think I have a look-away charm." Pelham patted the pockets of his jacket. "To keep us from getting a parking ticket."

The fact that Pelham wasn't fretting over the unlawful transgression of parking illegally demonstrated real progress in his moral flexibility, something Rondeau appreciated. "Nah, don't worry about it. I'm friends with the sorcerer who runs the city. Save the charm for an emergency. It's not like we can get towed." The anti-theft charms on the RV were more than sufficient to prevent its removal by legal means, too.

"I feel terribly grubby." Pelham attempted to smooth out his old-fashioned suit, which to Rondeau's eye looked not even remotely rumpled. Rondeau grunted. He was dressed in a blue vintage '50s bowling shirt and brown corduroy pants. He usually made more of a sartorial effort, but a few days waiting in a cave in the desert had dinged his enthusiasm for fashion.

The used bookstore was a small storefront squeezed between an artisanal toast restaurant on one side and a cell phone store on the other. The glass door had gold leaf lettering that read Singer's Books. Under hours it just said "Variable," but the hanging sign in the window read "OPEN." A bell rang when they pushed their way in. The shop was deep and narrow, or at least it *seemed* narrow, with floor-to-ceiling shelves on all the walls and freestanding as well, forming a maze of book-lined aisles that were barely wide enough to squeeze through. The cashier's nest was practically a fort made of shelves surrounding a beaten-up wooden desk. A young woman with dreadlocks and ostentatiously chunky glasses sat on a stool, marking her place in a trade paperback copy of a volume titled *Final Girl* with her finger. Her smile was distracted but genuine. "Help you?"

"I'm looking for a quaint and curious person of forgotten lore," Rondeau said. "Sanford Cole?"

She frowned, and she was no longer at all distracted. "Sorry, I don't know who that is."

"My name's Rondeau. What's yours?"

She kept frowning, and he thought she wouldn't answer, but she shrugged and said, "Tessa."

"Good to meet you, Tessa. Cole knows me. I hear these days he's hanging out in the back room of this shop. If he's not around, I can wait." He glanced around. "There's plenty to read, anyway. Way better than most waiting rooms."

"You might as well wait for Godot, because I don't know anybody named Cole. But there's no law against browsing." She went back to her book, but the tension in her posture was obvious. Rondeau wondered if she was an apprentice or a full-fledged sorcerer. Maybe a bibliomancer. He hadn't seen her push a button or send a signal, but that didn't mean she hadn't communicated his presence in some way. He could get insistent, but he was tired after the drive, so he figured he'd give it some time.

Rondeau sauntered through the shop with Pelham. This seemed to be one of those bookshops obsessed with taxonomy, with divisions and sub-divisions of category noted on the shelves with handwritten labels. Like, they didn't just have "Children's Literature," they had "19th-Century Children's Literature" and "Picture Books by Author-Illustrators" and "Weird Creepy Old Children's Books" and so on. Pelly oohed over a shelf featuring old books on etiquette, full of sample letters for writing to monarchs and cardinals and ambassadors, and guides to formal dining traditions in Austria-Hungary, and sumptuary codes. Rondeau's interest in books began and ended with crime and mystery novels, and there was a pretty good selection here, including a couple of old McBain's he hadn't read yet, in a section marked "Police Procedurals." The adjacent section on "Amateur PIs" probably deserved a look too.

In an adjacent aisle a woman laughed, a raucous but not unpleasant sound, and it somehow tickled the back of Rondeau's brain. He didn't recognize the laugh, exactly, but hadn't he known someone who laughed *like* that, if in a different voice?

A middle-aged redhead appeared, wearing a blue and white dress in a shifting optical-illusion sort of pattern, clutching a copy of the *Principia Discordia* and chuckling to herself. She caught Rondeau's eye, winked, and vanished around a shelf. She definitely looked familiar... or was it just that bright red hair, so much like the woman he'd seen sunbathing in Death Valley? Could it be the same person? It was hard to tell—the sunbather had been wearing sunglasses, and rather less clothing—but maybe. Were they being stalked? Or, no, the woman had been here before they arrived, or they would have heard the bell over the door ring when she came in, so... reverse-stalked?

Rondeau didn't dismiss the idea that he was paranoid, but he also didn't reject the possibility that he wasn't. A few moments later he heard the bell tinkle, and leaned out of the aisle to see the woman disappear out the front door, carrying a paper bag with her purchase. Hmm. Just what he needed. More things to worry about.

A moment later, the clerk turned the "Open" sign to "Closed" and walked over to him. "So, uh—Rondeau, was it?"

"That's me," he said cheerfully.

"So that's Mr. Pelham?"

"You're two for two, Tessa."

"Sorry for earlier, I just had to check, and then I needed to make sure there was no one else in the shop." She took a particular book down from the shelf she was standing beside, then put it back in, upside down. She gave Rondeau a smile and walked away.

Okay. That was a weirdly inconclusive interaction. Rondeau turned back to the shelf of mysteries—and instead of the shelf, there was a door, standing partially open, but not wide enough to reveal much of the space beyond, except the presence of more bookshelves there. Definitely not just a secret door; this wasn't a bookshelf on hinges. This was a magically concealed entrance, and one hidden well enough that even Rondeau's illusion-sense hadn't tingled in its presence. (Bradley probably would have seen right through the glamour, but he preferred to see the world as it truly was, while Rondeau cultivated a certain amount of willful blindness; it made the world a prettier place.) Rondeau whistled, and Pelham hurried over to join him. "A half-open door, Pelly. Would you call that an invitation?"

Pelham cleared his throat and rapped his knuckles on the door.

"Come in!" a familiar voice called.

Pelham pushed the door open the rest of the way and stepped through, and Rondeau followed. The door swung shut behind him with a definitive click, and when Rondeau looked back, there was no door visible at all, just a shelf of books... showing not the spines of books but the reverse edge, as if Rondeau had wandered around the back of a bookshelf. He turned back, and suddenly there was Sanford Cole, white-whiskered and diminutive, sitting behind a desk piled high with volumes, peering at an old newspaper through a magnifying glass.

The room was surprisingly bright, with rectangular windows high up on the walls, above the ten-foot-high shelves. There was no sunlight at the moment in San Francisco—it was very nearly night—so that light was coming from elsewhere. Rondeau reached out, tentatively, with his supernatural senses, and decided they were in a pocket dimension, a bit of carved-up and snipped-out space created by a powerful sorcerer for use as a refuge or study.

Cole put down the magnifying glass and gave them a mild smile. "Ah, Rondeau, and Pelham. Always a pleasure. What brings you to my city?"

Rondeau suddenly felt underdressed. Cole was dignity personified. "Sorry to barge in, sir. We're really looking for B, I mean Bradley, but we weren't sure how to find him, or even if he was, ah, still around. Like, on this mortal plane or not."

Cole nodded. "He is, and from what he's told me, he intends to stay indefinitely. Apparently independent existence suits him, and he is in no great hurry to rejoin his collective. I'm afraid Bradley is not in the city now, though—he's out on one of the sea islands with his apprentice, Marzi."

Rondeau raised an eyebrow. "I thought Marzi was going to be *your* apprentice?"

Cole's smile was a flash, there and gone. "So did she, and Bradley, too. But I told Bradley he was certainly experienced enough to take on his *own* student at this point. He is, after all, a tiny fragment of the intelligence that oversees the integrity of the multiverse itself. I have, of course, been happy to help and offer my guidance as needed."

"Having a student helps keep Bradley tethered to our world, too, huh?" Rondeau said. "Gives him something to do, so he doesn't take off and get re-absorbed into the godhead, or whatever."

Cole's smile was warmer now. "Marla always insisted you were more astute than you liked to let on, Rondeau. Yes, that angle did occur to me. It is pleasant to have Bradley back. I understand the burdens of responsibility, and the inescapable call of duty, but if Bradley can find a way to do his great work while still allowing some part of himself to dwell among friends, that is the most desirable of all possible outcomes. Why are you looking for him? Not more trouble, I hope, like that dreadful business with the Outsider?"

Pelham said, "Mrs. Mason was supposed to return from the underworld three days ago."

Cole nodded. "Oh, I know. I keep her cycle marked on my calendar. It's good to know when Marla Mason is abroad and walking up and down in the world." He laced his fingers together on his desktop. "But I note you say 'was supposed to.'"

"She never showed." Rondeau looked around for a place to sit, was disappointed, and settled for leaning against a shelf instead, arms crossed.

"We waited three days... it seemed like a mythic interval, I don't know... and then we started to get really worried."

"She *is* a god," Cole said. "I can't pretend to know what the lives of such beings entail—I have avoided consorting with such forces whenever possible, beyond a few ill-considered youthful forays—but I imagine her existence is quite complicated. Perhaps she's simply dealing with a matter of some importance?"

Rondeau chewed his lower lip for a moment. "I dunno, Cole. Her bargain with her husband was, she'd spend a month in the underworld, and a month living as a mortal. One on, one off. She was pretty clear about that, and I get the idea that when gods make a deal, they stick to it. That their laws are less like contracts and more like gravity. It's not like Marla is the only god of death. It's a whole duality thing. Her husband could step in to cover her, right?"

"Unless something happened to Mr. Mason, too," Pelham said quietly. "If something happened to Death himself."

"You decided against summoning an oracle to ask after Marla?" Cole said. And then: "Ah. You want *Bradley* to summon an oracle instead. To take the danger and burden of repaying the oracle on himself."

Rondeau almost ducked his head, but he settled for a shrug. "It's half cowardice, sure. You heard about the thing that happened with the Pit Boss? The last oracle I summoned stole all my money and kicked me out of Las Vegas."

"I understand that is because you made an ill-advised bargain with the creature."

Rondeau lit up. "Yeah! Exactly! It was a *terrible* bargain! I have the same powers to summon oracles that Bradley does, but he's got more experience, and a better natural sense, and, hell, he's just *better* than I am. Me and Bradley are both driving high-powered sports cars, but he knows how to handle his. I just flip mine over and end up in a ditch."

"It's true that you've received no formal training in the use of your powers," Cole said. "Though I gather you haven't been interested in pursuing such studies?"

"I'm a lazy hedonist, Cole. I'm happy sitting around in my suite at the hotel playing video games and eating lobster. I don't *want* to be a crazy powerful sorcerer. I wouldn't even be here right now, except...." He shrugged. "Marla."

Cole nodded. "Marla. She does inspire a certain loyalty. It isn't easy to become her friend, but once you do, it's forever. She's demonstrated a willingness to destroy the fabric of reality itself to help a friend. You know she'd do anything for you."

Rondeau snorted. "I dunno if I'd go *that* far. When I fuck up she's pretty happy to let me twist for a while."

"Don't be uncharitable." Pelham's voice was sharp. He thought Marla Mason hung the moon, and the stars, and probably the space station and satellites and most of the planets besides. "Mrs. Mason intervened with the Pit Boss and returned you to your position and status in Las Vegas. She just wanted to make sure you had time to learn from your mistakes first."

Rondeau nodded. "I did learn. I haven't summoned an oracle for anything important since."

Cole said "Mmm. It's up to Bradley, of course. But have you considered attempting conventional divination?"

"We know enough about divination spells to find a lost set of keys, but that's about it," Rondeau said. "Besides, I mean… she's a part-time *god*. She can't be easy to find."

"Divination magic is a specialty of mine." Cole rummaged in the drawers of his desk and drew out a roll of purple velvet cloth. He opened it on the desk, revealing a small brass bowl and a clear glass tube full of small sticks with dark heads. "Lucifer matches, from 1829. They were swiftly made redundant by the invention soon after of phosphorus matches. But I bought these, and enchanted them. Now, let me see, where is my special inkwell…." He opened another drawer, removing a quill pen, a ragged scrap of hand-pressed paper, and a black inkwell. "Ink mixed with my own blood, and a charm to prevent coagulation." He dipped the quill and scrawled something on the paper, then opened the tube and carefully removed a match. Cole didn't strike the match, just stared at it, and the head burst into flame with a sudden flare and accompanying chemical stench. He held the paper to the match and when it began to burn, dropped the flaming scrap into the brass bowl.

The smoke that rose up was copious and thick, mostly black but streaked with gray threads, and weirdly odorless. Cole stared at the smoke, grunted, and then waved his hand through the smoke, dispersing it. "Marla Mason is nowhere in this world, or if she is, she is hidden so well even I cannot discern her position. Such concealment is certainly within the power of a god. Has it occurred to you that, perhaps, she doesn't wish to be found?"

"What, that she found some other route to re-enter the world besides her sandbox in Death Valley and she just didn't tell us?" Rondeau scowled. "That she ditched us? I mean, maybe. Last time she was on Earth, after we beat the Outsider… things got kind of fraught at the end. We were all pretty surprised when Marla teamed up with Regina Queen and froze Nicolette into a block of magical ice for all eternity."

Cole nodded. "I heard about that. Bradley was very disappointed in Marla. He thought her refusal to recognize Nicolette's redemption and transformation, her dedication to leading Felport, was a regrettable lapse in judgment. Small-minded and spiteful, I believe he said."

Rondeau nodded. "Also nasty and vengeful, and I say that as someone who hated Nicolette from guts to garters. Marla's been going on and on for months about how she's trying to do better—she even has those words tattooed on her wrist! And then when Nicolette actually gets her shit together, and helps us capture the Outsider too, Marla turns on her. I couldn't understand it."

"I'm sure Mrs. Mason had her reasons." Pelham was loyal, as always, but even his voice had an edge of doubt.

"Didn't she task the two of you with… getting rid of Regina Queen?" Cole said.

"You mean did Marla tell us to murder the person she used as a tool to stop Nicolette? She sure did." Rondeau shuddered. "Like we're assassins now? I mean, yeah, Regina Queen's as evil as the sun is bright, but still. I'm not a killer if I can help it, though. We made a deal with the new boss of Felport, Perren River. She put those lunatics Squat and Crapsey on her payroll, to keep them from causing trouble—better to have them inside the tent pissing out than outside pissing in, that sort of thing. She sent the deranged duo after Regina Queen, with their expedition funded by a hefty contribution from my personal coffers. I hear they got the job done."

"An elegant solution, in its way," Cole said. "I'm sorry Marla put you in the position to come up with it."

"Yeah. I guess maybe Marla's off somewhere sulking because we all got mad at her, but…." Rondeau shook his head. "What if she's in trouble? If we find her and she tells us to fuck off and leave her alone, that's one thing. But I'm not going to stop looking if she might need help."

Cole nodded. "Bradley and Marzi will be back tomorrow. Perhaps he'll have better luck tracking her down than I did. In the meantime, do you have a place to stay?"

"We're open to recommendations," Rondeau said. "We're not picky. Any of the best hotels in the city will do."

Oracular Emperor

BRADLEY BOWMAN, OFTEN KNOWN AS B to his friends, sat in the window of the Borderlands Café in the mission, sipping a strawberry lemonade and watching people stroll by on the street. Rondeau and Pelham were late, which wasn't surprising. Rondeau was often *calamitously* late, and Pelham was always scrupulously on time, so when the two of them joined forces, they split the difference, and were usually only moderately tardy.

B had spent the night on a rocky island decorated mostly with the shit and eggs of sea birds, teaching his apprentice how to transform into various interesting animals, and how to read omens in guano and the patterns of flight, and how to survive comfortably in inhospitable circumstances. Just before dawn he'd crept away from her sleeping form and taken their boat, leaving her to make her own way home however she could. She'd be pissed at him, but she'd shown some serious leaps in ability whenever she got annoyed or backed into a corner, and he was exploiting that quirk. Being a teacher meant being kind of an asshole sometimes, but he was a soft enough touch that he'd make it up to her when she got back.

He'd returned to find a message from Cole, about Marla maybe being missing, and Pelly and Rondeau being worried. Well, they were still on her staff, or whatever—in her service—so it was their job to be worried. She wasn't Bradley's problem. He wasn't sure where he stood with her anymore. He'd always thought people were too hard on Marla, honestly. She was uncompromising and tough, and could be sharp-tongued, but she was also loyal, and devoted to doing what was right, no matter what the cost. But the way she'd teamed up with Regina Queen... even by the logic of the ends justifying the means, that was a terrible idea, and the ends in this case had involved stealing Nicolette's chance at redemption. Even so, he would have talked things out with Marla, let her explain herself, but she'd just straight-up ditched him that night. She was supposed to come to the hotel after she froze Nicolette, to join him and Marzi on their trip to San Francisco, but she'd never shown up, never got in touch, and they'd made the journey without her.

For the first time, misgiving stirred in him. Had Marla gotten in trouble that night? He'd assumed she was just pissed-off at his disapproval, that she'd decided to stomp off and do her own thing, but what if something had happened to her? Had *anyone* heard from Marla after she froze Nicolette? She should have had a couple more weeks walking the Earth after that night, before returning for her month in the underworld, and now she hadn't returned from *that*....

Had Marla been missing for more than a month without anyone realizing it?

Rondeau and Pelham arrived just then, and there were hugs and effusive greetings and annoyed glares from some of the people working on laptops nearby. They all sat around the table, and B dove right in. "Guys, did either one of you hear from Marla after that night she froze Nicolette?"

They exchanged glances and Rondeau shook his head "No. We argued, because she wanted to make *us* responsible for Regina Queen, so we took off."

Pelham nodded. "We returned to Las Vegas. Wasn't Mrs. Mason supposed to meet you that night?"

B nodded. "Yeah... but she never showed up."

Rondeau whistled. "Whoa. Do you think she's.... I mean... I know she's half god, but there *are* things out there that can kill gods. I helped kill one myself, once. You were there, B. Or a version of you was, anyway."

"Mrs. Mason is not dead," Pelham said. "I would know."

Rondeau frowned. "I know you were, like, magically bound to serve her, Pelly, but didn't she absolve you or whatever? Set you free?"

"Some bonds cannot be broken. If she died, I would feel a pain, here." He put his hand over his heart. "A very particular pain. Those of my family line sometimes succumb to death themselves, when that pain touches them, and they realize their principal is gone."

"The rich *are* different," Rondeau said. "Okay, so she's alive, at least. But where is she?"

B shrugged. "Still in the underworld, just working overtime?"

Rondeau shook his head, with a stubborn and determined expression that seemed out-of-place on his face. "I don't buy it. She made a deal to spend every other month in the underworld, and alternating months on Earth, living as a mortal, except for the bit where her husband gave her physical immorality, anyway. Those deals can't just be broken, right? Mythology is full of gods getting fucked over because they made a promise to a mortal and had no choice but to stick to it. I figure one of two things happened. The first is, Marla came back to Earth on schedule, and we missed her arrival because she used magic to hide from us, or changed her point of entry to avoid us. In that case, she doesn't want to see us, and okay, I can respect that. That's Cole's theory. I hope it's true." Rondeau leaned forward. "Because option two is, *something happened*, something that broke her deal, in which case, she could be in bad trouble."

"So we summon an oracle and find out," B said. "That's why you wanted to see me, right?"

"It is," Pelham said.

"Also because we wanted to bask in your glory, movie star," Rondeau said. "But, yeah, basically. I'd do it myself, but I've had some bad experiences with the whole oracle-summoning business. I think I'm starting to get a phobia. Especially when it comes to summoning something big enough to tattle on a god."

"It's not a small thing," Bradley agreed. "The divinities value their privacy. But, okay. Let's do it." He rose.

Rondeau's eyebrows went up in alarm. "Right now?"

"We're not all lazy millionaires with time to kill, Rondeau. Soonest begun, soonest done, and all that. I think I know where we can find a potent oracle. I sensed it a few days ago, and did a little research. Could be just the thing for us."

They summoned a car with a ridesharing app, and a gray SUV driven by a man with elaborate facial hair topiary showed up not long after. The journey, less than four miles from the Mission to the edge of the Financial District, took twenty minutes, because if the city of San Francisco was a beating heart, the streets were its clogged arteries. They disembarked at the corner of Grant and California, before a stately brick church.

"Old St. Mary's Cathedral," Bradley said. "The cornerstone was placed in 1853. When the structure was finished, it was the tallest building in the state." The church now stood in the shadow of skyscrapers.

"I do so love old things," Pelham said approvingly.

"We're not going to talk to God, are we?" Rondeau said. "I mean, is there a God? Like, *that* God? The big beard in the sky one?"

B shrugged. "If so, I haven't met Him. There are powers of varying degrees, and some choose to appear in different guises, so who knows? No, we're here to converse with a ghost. I figure, if we want to find out what happened to the ruler of the land of the dead, why not ask someone who's probably spent some time there?"

"That makes as much sense as anything," Rondeau said. "Who's the stiff?"

"His Imperial Majesty Norton the First, by the grace of God Emperor of these United States and Protector of Mexico. His twenty-one-year reign ended when he collapsed and died in front of this church in 1880."

"Ah, this was the madman who declared himself a sovereign?" Pelham said. "And the city humored him, by accepting his currency and printing his proclamations? I've read about him."

"He was more than a madman," Bradley said. "Which isn't to say he *wasn't* a madman. But he was also a sort of natural-born Fisher King, as I understand it, with a powerful magical link to San Francisco and its people. He once stopped a riot by standing between two angry mobs and reciting the Lord's Prayer, and he spun more powerful glamours than that, on occasions that weren't as well documented. His death was the result of a powerful magical assault on the city."

"Sanford Cole was his court magician, right?" Rondeau said. "Playing Merlin to Norton's hobo King Arthur."

B nodded. "Cole doesn't talk about Joshua Norton much, and when he does, it's usually with as much exasperation as affection, but there's no denying the emperor had a strange power—majesty born out of adversity."

"Not unlike Mrs. Mason herself," Pelham said.

"Now, now, Marla never declared herself Empress," Rondeau said. "She just *acted* like one."

"Let's see what his majesty has to say." B tapped Rondeau on the arm. "No making fun of the emperor, if I manage to call him up, all right? Norton was pretty serious about his imperial dignity." B sat down cross-legged on the sidewalk, leaning his back against the wall of the cathedral. He opened himself to the world, and sensed the same wisps and vibrations and tremulations in the air he'd noticed before: something unsettled dwelled here, or at least this spot was a point of contact for that unsettled things multi-faceted existence.

Bradley's most potent power—and Rondeau's too, not that Rondeau had bothered to learn how to use it with any delicacy—was oracle generation. He could call into existence creatures of mysterious provenance, which took the forms of ghosts, demons, demi-gods, or monsters, and ask them questions or give them tasks (though the latter was especially dangerous, as Rondeau had learned to his dismay). There was always a price, and the depth and danger of that price varied depending on the magnitude of what you asked. The ability to generate oracles was rare, and poorly studied, and there was great debate in the sorcerous community about exactly what the oracles even *were*. One prevailing theory was that the creatures summoned up had no true, external reality of their own: they were simply visions conjured by powerful psychics as a way to access information their supernatural perception couldn't make sense of directly. Like a mentally unstable character in a movie talking to a hallucination, learning truths they couldn't confront without the illusion of distance: according to that theory, oracles were just a way of talking to yourself.

Bradley had gradually come to believe in the other theory, though: that oracle generators lent their psychic strength to real supernatural creatures that otherwise hovered below the level of perception, giving them depth and heft and, sometimes, a terrible autonomy. Rondeau was right to be afraid of his power. It could conjure up dangerous things.

Ghosts weren't usually dangerous, though. They were sometimes fragmentary, stubborn remnants of a deceased individual's strong emotion—not the soul itself, but the soul's fingernail clippings, its blood stains, or the echoes of its last screams, retaining the shrapnel of a personality. Other ghosts were the remnants of people strong-willed (or unhinged) enough to avoid entering the underworld at all, stuck dwelling in an Earthbound purgatory of their own making, and generally driven mad by the experience. Still others were like shadows cast from the underworld into the material world, projections of larger-than-life figures who'd passed on: those ghosts belonged to sorcerers of extraordinary power, mostly. This ghost felt like the latter sort to Bradley. Emperor Norton was in the underworld, but his connection to the city he'd loved was still powerful, and his attention could be drawn at the site of his death. B thought the emperor could project his form here, with the proper encouragement.

"Your majesty," Bradley said. "Could I have a word?"

The air before Bradley flickered. Rondeau grunted, but Pelly didn't react. Whatever was happening was below the level of non-psychic perception, apparently, at least so far. That was good. Bradley sitting down on the sidewalk hadn't drawn so much as a glance from passers-by, but a truly visible ghost would. Something inside his head *tugged*, like a fishhook was embedded in his frontal lobes, and Bradley exercised mental discipline to grab that line and pull it. Slowly, slowly—

The shimmer in the air snapped into focus. Emperor Norton, a dignified old man in a uniform of his own making (something between that of a drum major and a doorman) and wearing a battered top hat, stood on the sidewalk, looking down at Bradley. He had a doleful and distracted air. Bradley rose shakily to his feet, beads of sweat popping up on his brow. Calling up oracles was purely mental work, but it took a physical toll.

"I am always happy to hear the entreaties of my subjects." The Emperor's voice seemed to come from a long way off, filled with echoes and sonic tribulations.

"Your majesty, I seek news of the underworld."

The Emperor shook his head slowly. "That is a realm where my rule does not reach, young man."

"I need only knowledge, not action, sir. Can you tell me the whereabouts of the Bride of Death?" Marla always seemed more amused than irritated by the name her cultists had chosen to give her. It was accurate, after all: she was a god by marriage.

"The Dread Queen," the Emperor murmured. "I—" He turned his head, frowning. "The walls of my palace tremble, young man. This is not information to be lightly given."

"Then name your price." Bradley had learned long ago to never give an oracle carte blanche, but to always define the terms of the bargain up front. Usually the oracles didn't want anything *too* difficult: things that took time and effort, actions to honor or soothe, or to make small changes in the physical world that the oracles couldn't manage themselves.

"I—there is a power greater than myself here, you understand. I am an emperor, but I serve at the pleasure of the sovereign of Hell."

"You deny me?" Bradley felt the hook in his mind wriggle, and almost pull free, but he held it tight. Sometimes oracles couldn't do as he asked—their levels of knowledge and power varied—but he'd never encountered one that *wouldn't*: usually they just set a terribly high price if they were reluctant, and then it was a question of how much Bradley was willing to pay.

"It is not I who deny—"

A hand appeared, skin the color of bronze, resting on the emperor's shoulder. There was a wrist attached, but that was all—the limb was cut off beyond that, like it belonged to someone else, reaching into the frame of a shot in a film. The emperor turned his head, looking at the unseen figure, and the stricken expression of terror on his face was so total and bleak that Bradley shrank back in sympathetic fear. The emperor nodded, as if agreeing with some unheard comment or command, then turned his face back to Bradley. "You must accept my apol—"

Bradley screamed and fell to his knees as the hook was *ripped* from his mind, and Norton vanished. Bradley thought, *Shit, am I lobotomized, would I even* know *if I was lobotomized, does wondering about it mean I'm* not—

Rondeau helped him up, and Pelham pressed a handkerchief against his forehead. There was some healing magic soaked in the cloth—Pelly was full of little tokens like that—and a soothing wave of relief washed through Bradley's head, taking the pain away. He leaned against the wall of the cathedral. A couple of concerned passers-by were asking if Bradley was all right, and Rondeau said, "Just a migraine, he'll be okay, we'll take him home."

Though the pain of having the oracle ripped away was gone, Bradley was still terribly unsteady on his feet. Rondeau and Pelham supported him, one on either side, like he was a drunken guest of honor at the end of a bachelor party. A woman stopped in the middle of the sidewalk: a tall redhead in oversized sunglasses, a form-fitting dark blue dress, and heels so high the sight of them gave Bradley vertigo. "You look like a mess!" she exclaimed. "You poor dear. Isn't it a little early to be quite *that* drunk?"

"It's only early if you didn't start last night," Rondeau said. "Didn't I see you in a bookstore yesterday?"

"Who reads books anymore?" She patted Rondeau's cheek. "It's too early to try and pick up women on the street, too, sweetie." She glanced at the cathedral. "Oh, good old Emperor Norton. He was really my kind of guy. One of my people, you know?"

Bradley lifted his head, with some effort, and looked at the woman, *hard*, with his full-spectrum vision… but she just seemed like an ordinary woman, on the near side of middle-aged, with a grin that wanted to eat the world. Which meant she either *was* an ordinary person, just one who'd made an improbably well-timed non-sequitur… or she was something so powerful she was able to hide her power even from a psychic as perceptive as Bradley.

"Wait," Rondeau said. "How did you—"

"Toodles, gents." She sauntered off.

"Should I follow her?" Pelly said.

"Yeah. Though don't worry much if you lose her." Rondeau's voice was grim. "I think *she's* following *us*. I'm ninety-eight percent sure that's the woman I saw sunbathing in Death Valley, and a hundred percent sure she was in the bookshop yesterday."

Pelly frowned, nodded, and set off after the woman. It was hard to imagine the small man as a capable operative when it came to tailing someone, but from what Bradley had heard, Pelham was a man of many talents, and came from a long line of people trained from birth to be perfect assistants and helpmeets to sorcerers.

Bradley straightened away from Rondeau's support, testing his ability to hold his own weight. He was wobbly, but not so unstable he expected to fall over.

Rondeau looked down the street, watching Pelham disappear around a corner. "We should ask Cole about local redheaded sorcerers, because she's clearly taken an interest in us."

"Yes," Bradley said. "But first take me someplace where I can eat a hundred eggs. Calling up that ghost took a *lot* out of me, and we didn't get much at all in return."

"Sure we did," Rondeau said. "You didn't notice? You're supposed to be the perceptive one."

"What do you mean?"

"Well, who in the underworld can tell a dead soul to shut up, and actually pull him out of your summoning spell?"

"I don't really have a complete understanding of the underworld—I've only been there once—but… Death could, I guess, or Marla."

Rondeau nodded. "That sure wasn't Marla's hand on the emperor's shoulder. And it wasn't Death's, either. Every time I've seen that guy, he's had a ring on every single finger, flashing a different gemstone in each one. That means there's someone *else* down there bossing people around. I think something's rotten in the state of Hades, B."

"I don't know. They're gods, they can look like whatever they want."

Rondeau shrugged. "Yeah, sure. I could be crazy wrong. But I'm curious. Summoning up an oracle didn't work. Maybe it's time to appeal to a higher power."

"Like who?"

"Like your boss, or brother, or dad, or other self, or whatever," Rondeau said. "The all-seeing Big B."

A Terrible Tipper

MATT LEANED ON THE COUNTER, looking at the sun shimmer on the lack of cars in the parking lot. The diner was in a deeper-than-usual mid-afternoon lull, with no customers in the place at all excepting a redhead in a back booth who hadn't taken off her sunglasses.

The new waitress, Mel, was keeping busy anyway, marrying ketchups and refilling napkin dispensers. He wasn't sure what to make of her. She had some kind of trouble behind her, that was for sure—probably on the run from an abusive husband, if he had to guess—but she was tough as hell, no-nonsense, and a hard worker. He was pretty sure she'd work out. She was in her early thirties at the outside, so still plenty young enough to make a new life out of the ashes of whatever she'd left behind. A little too severe to be called pretty, but she was hardly homely, and she could catch a better man than the one she'd run away from, Matt figured, if that was her inclination. Though she didn't much seem like she needed a man, or anyone at all, for that matter.

The redhead lifted a hand, and Mel headed over to her booth. "You need anything else?"

"Not at all." The redhead dabbed at her lips with a napkin. A plate of fluffy scrambled eggs and link sausages sweating grease sat nearly untouched on her plate, though she'd eaten about half the toast. "I am delighted with your service. You remind me very much of a woman I used to know. Have you ever been to Hawaii?"

"Waiting tables doesn't pay quite that well," Mel said. "Besides, who needs Hawaii? I don't like swimming, and when it comes to sand, there's plenty of that right here in Arizona."

"Mmm. The woman you remind me of… I owe a lot to her. I owe my *life* to her, if I'm entirely honest."

"Honesty's the best policy, so I'm told."

"I wouldn't go quite that far—Mel, is it? Here. Take this. You can start saving up for a trip to the islands." The redhead passed something to Mel, then rose and sashayed out of the diner like she was walking on a fashion-show runway someplace. Now *she* could get any man she set her sights on, Matt reckoned, even if she was pushing forty. Hell, age was no drawback in this case. You couldn't sway like that without years of practice.

"That's a woman who could make you forget your vows," Matt said. "I don't believe I can even remember my wife's name right now."

"You're a sexist pig, Matt." Mel didn't put much acid into the comment, though. She was looking down into her hand. "She left me a hundred dollar tip on a twelve-dollar check."

Matt whistled. "That makes up a bit for how slow it's been today, I reckon."

"There's that. Something funny about her, though."

"Anybody who drops a hundred dollar bill on the table in a place like this is funny *somehow*."

Mel tucked the tip unselfconsciously into her bra and went to greet a handful of customers who rushed in all at once, and the next half hour was pretty busy, with Matt back behind the grill and Mel running around hard enough that he considered calling in one of the other girls to pick up the end of a shift.

When a lull came, and Mel stepped into the back to take a slug from a bottle of water, she suddenly gasped and reached into her bra. "What the *hell*?" she said. She held out a handful of wet, torn leaves. "The money's gone, and there's *this* mess instead!"

Matt blinked. "That," he said after a moment, "is just about the shittiest magic trick I ever saw in my life."

The Limits of Omniscience

RONDEAU SAT SIPPING ESPRESSO on the edge of the bed in his hotel room, even though caffeine always made him too jittery. Bradley was at the table, sticking sensibly with decaf, and Pelham sat on an armchair in the corner, fretting. He'd followed the redhead for a while the day before, but had lost track of her when she went into a shop and never came out, at least as far as he could determine. On several occasions Pelham opened his mouth, as if to say something, and then didn't. Pelham had a way of radiating his anxiety but keeping other feelings to himself. Rondeau knew if whatever Pelham was mulling over mattered, he'd come out with it eventually, once he'd examined it from every direction first.

"So do we light black candles and chant?" Rondeau said. "Or burn DVDs of your old movies?"

B shook his head. "It shouldn't come to that. Those kind of rituals are ways for mortals to get the attention of larger forces that aren't usually aware of them on the individual level. Big B is already aware of me, the way you're aware of your little toe, anyway, which is to say, you probably don't think about it much unless you stub it on something." He sighed, rolled up his right sleeve, and extended his hand over the table. Then he carefully tipped the cup of decaf coffee over, spilling a scalding stream onto the flesh of his forearm. B hissed at the pain, and the television clicked on: "Whoa, hey, self-mutilation is a *really* rare characteristic among us Bradleys, what's the big idea?"

Rondeau rose and approached the TV screen. Big B's face was too close to the camera—though surely he wasn't actually using a *literal* camera?—and they mostly had a view of him from the eyes down to just above his chin, filling the screen. "Sorry, big man," Rondeau said. "Just wanted to get your attention."

B wrapped a napkin around his forearm and nodded. "I yelled at the mirror for ten minutes this morning but you never appeared."

Big B snorted. "Yeah, well, *busy*, here, and there, and everywhere, and since there are no looming existential threats in your branch of the multiverse, you'll forgive me for not popping in for a chat."

"We're worried about Mrs. Mason," Pelham said. "She's vanished, and we fear some terrible fate has befallen her."

"Or else she's just pissed off at us and doesn't want to hang out," Rondeau added. "We'd like to know which one it is for sure, though."

"What do you say?" B asked. "Want to take a peek into our universe and let us know if you see Marla? Believe me when I say we've exhausted the other obvious avenues of research."

"I'm flattered you guys think so highly of my capabilities," Big B said. "But it's not that easy."

B frowned. "Dude, you're omniscient and omnicognizant. Right? You're all-seeing, as long as you bother to look?"

Big B sighed. "How soon they forget. And by 'they' I mean 'autonomous buds of my overarching consciousness,' by which I mean, you, Little B. Yes, I can look through the multiverse, and see what's happening anywhere in any given universe. I can even get a sense of probable futures in any particular universe, though that's mostly a case of looking into adjacent universes where events proceeded more quickly, and seeing how things turned out *there*. But you have to think about the scale of what I'm talking about here, guys. It's really, really hard for me to focus on the micro level and look for a specific person in a specific universe. You're asking a park ranger to locate one very particular leaf in a vast wilderness area, you know? Sure, I can do it, in theory, but what a pain in the ass, especially when there are other things to deal with, like bear attacks and lost hikers and parts of the forest being on *fire*."

"You're talking to us right now without any trouble," Rondeau pointed out.

"Ha. What do you know about me and my trouble? I can focus on Little B pretty easily, because he's part of *me*. Likewise, Rondeau, you've had some success calling my attention in the past, but that's because you're presently inhabiting a body that used to belong to me—we've got a serious sympathetic connection going there, you know? Me and Marla have history, sure, but I'm not, like, *magnetized* to her in that way. But, total truth time, sure, I probably could task a non-trivial fraction of my consciousness to looking for an individual person in a specific branch of the multiverse, and locate them. But Marla's not a person. She's a *god*. She plays at being mortal every other month, but she's still a god."

"So?" Rondeau said. "Marla told me you outrank gods. That you are to Earthly gods as gods are to humans."

Big B chewed his lip for a moment, then spoke. "That's true, as far as it goes, but it's not so much about 'rank' as it is about 'power and responsibility.' I have a *much* bigger chunk of reality to look after than your terrestrial gods do. Even the gods of death, and they're major players, are just in charge of everything that can live and die. I have to be in charge of *everything*, in an ever-expanding multiverse. And, yes, I have a lot of power... but I'm only supposed to use that power to do my job. You remember the last Possible Witch?"

Rondeau nodded. She'd been a creepy creature that looked like a woman except for her glittering, faceted eyes. Marla, in typical Marla fashion, had once threatened to beat her up.

Big B said, "Right. The reason she got fired, by which I mean, *ceased to exist*, is because she strayed past the boundaries of her job description. She opened a portal to another reality, and then pretty promptly disintegrated, because instead of protecting the integrity of reality, she damaged it instead." Big B stared at them each, hard, in turn. "The laws I'm bound by are laws of nature, guys. The realms of gods—and, I admit, the private pocket dimensions of two or three sorcerers of sufficient power—are not clearly visible to me, not the way mundane reality is. Think of me like a cop. I can absolutely kick down the doors to any godly realm or wizardly pocket dimension... but only if I have a good reason to do so. Until Marla or her husband Death do something to mess up the fabric of reality, I can't barge in and ask them what's going on, you know?"

"So you can't help us?" Rondeau said. "You could've led with that."

Big B sighed. "I'm more trying to set expectations here, okay? What I *can* do is make a courtesy call. I can sort of... send a message... to the underworld, and ask what's going on, but the beings that dwell there are under no obligation to answer, and if Marla isn't in the mood to talk to you, she might not talk to me, either." He looked away from the camera for a moment, then looked back, his expression troubled. "There is one weird thing though. I've glanced into nearby realities adjacent to yours, and Marla is around in most of them, doing her thing, kicking monsters, causing trouble—she's even trying to bother *me* in a couple of them, asking me to intervene in things I have no business getting involved with, just like you are here. But... the only realities where Marla's missing are ones that branched off from the universe where the Outsider was running loose. So her disappearance might have something to do with *that* creepy disaster."

"Wait," Rondeau said. "You're talking to *lots* of versions of us right now?"

"Right now, and five minutes ago, and probably five minutes from now, yeah. In one universe you stabbed yourself in the hand with a fork, Little B, to get my attention. It's gonna leave a mark."

Little B frowned. "I know we're blowing Rondeau's mind with the apprehension of the infinite and everything, but back to the Outsider— what could it have to do with Marla's disappearance? We beat that thing hollow, we bottled it up, it's totally contained—right?"

"That's an affirmative. The Outsider *is* a threat to the fabric of reality, and if he was loose again, I'd know it. You sealed him up good, and he remains sealed in every branch of the multiverse."

"So if he didn't do anything lately," Rondeau said, "maybe he did something *before* we sealed him up? Something that Marla found out about, that led her to go off the grid?"

"Being a detective sucks," Little B said. "I thought I was good at it, but it turns out, I'm just psychic."

"Usually that's enough," Big B said. "Look, I need to go, there's a technologically advanced version of Earth where scientists have built a device to generate something they're calling a Seagroves-Raschke bridge, which basically connects adjacent parallel realities, and I kind of need to squish that before they turn my beautiful multiverse into scrap metal and screaming and monsters. I'll send a ping to the underworld of your reality, though, and let you know if I hear anything back." The screen turned black.

"What even is the *point* of having omnipotent friends if it turns out they can't do anything for you?" Rondeau complained. "So what now?"

B shrugged. "Now I go back to teaching my apprentice, and we wait for word from Big B." He said distracted farewells and let himself out.

Rondeau looked at Pelham. "How're you holding up, man?"

Pelly gazed at nothing at all. "My existence has been centered on Mrs. Mason. Even in the months when she was away, I have endeavored to make things go smoothly for her return. If she is somehow lost to us... what will I do?"

"Have champagne brunch with me forever?"

Pelham shook his head. "I require purpose in life, Rondeau. I have been trained to provide support for those doing meaningful work. A life of hedonism would be, for me, a life of despair."

Rondeau pushed his plate away. "When you put it like that, it doesn't sound so appealing to me, either."

A Divine Visitation (or Two)

PELHAM SAT ON A PARK BENCH, throwing popcorn to pigeons, who squabbled even in the midst of his great largesse. It was hard not to view their bickering as a metaphor. Pelham felt he owed Mrs. Mason everything. He'd pledged himself to her service after a lifetime of training in arts practical, martial, and social. Pelham had been *created* to serve, but Marla had refused to use him simply as a valet or bodyguard or errand-boy. She'd grown to trust him, and treated him as a friend. She'd even sent him out to travel the world, to find his own way and have his own experiences, to live as something more than an extension of her will—to find his *own* will.

He was so grateful to her for offering him freedom that he'd become even more devoted to her as a result. Pelham did have his own life, now, independent of Mrs. Mason, but he would always be there if she needed him, and he couldn't imagine an existence entirely absent of her presence and influence.

He was afraid he might have to learn to imagine better.

A bearded old man in a dirty trenchcoat dropped down onto the bench next to him, smelling of cheap cigars and feculent body odor. "Hello, Pelham." He spoke in a voice Pelham imagined was roughened by years of swallowing bad things and often vomiting them back up.

Pelham believed in politeness whenever possible. "I'm afraid I have forgotten the circumstances of our prior acquaintance, sir."

"Last time we met, I looked a little different. My name's Reva."

Pelham bowed his head. "The god of the exiles and the wanderers. Yes. I understand the Outsider tried to devour you. I am pleased you escaped unharmed."

Reva nodded. "I never thought I'd see Marla again, after she told me to stop meddling in her life back in Hawaii, but then she appeared just in time to save me from being eaten by the Outsider. I owe her."

"Do you know where she is?" Pelham couldn't keep the hope out of his voice. "She is one of your people, an exile from her home city—can you find her?"

"She's an exile, but she's also a god. Trying to find her is a bit like trying to capture fog with a butterfly net. Either she chooses to hide herself from me—and we know she values her privacy—or some other magic, beyond my own, seeks to conceal her. When I sensed you were in the city, I knew you would be worried about her absence, and thought I should come talk to you, and tell you what I know."

Something deep inside Pelham's chest ached. "You sensed me. I am one of yours, then. An exile. Because Mrs. Mason is my home, and I do not know where to find her."

"I'm sorry. But yes. Pelham, after the Outsider tried to eat me, tried to take on the power of a god, and failed… it went in search of another meal. One even richer than myself."

"Oh, no. No. Not Mr. Mason?"

Reva whistled. "You call the god of Death 'Mr. Mason'? Well, I can see that. Yes. The Outsider devoured Death. That's why the Outsider was so much more powerful than before when you all fought him Felport, and sealed him away—it was fat with the powers of Death."

Pelham frowned. "Then…. Mrs. Mason, is she in the underworld? Is that why she hasn't returned? She is too busy running the business of the afterlife, without her late husband's help?"

Reva shook his head. "I don't think so. You know how Marla used to travel magically, during her months as a mortal—she would step from this world into the underworld, take a shortcut, and then emerge somewhere else on Earth?"

"Yes, I recall. A harrowing way to travel. While in transit, in the land of the dead, Mrs. Mason… changed."

Reva nodded. "All the godhood that was suppressed during her month on Earth came rushing back to her then. She became the Bride of Death for those few steps—Dread Queen Marla, beautiful and terrible. When I found out the Outsider had killed her husband, I waited in her realm, in her throne room, because I didn't want her to be alone when she realized she'd been widowed. When she stepped from the mortal world, she realized something was wrong, that her domain was out of alignment, and she came to the throne room. I told her what I knew, what the Outsider had done… her rage and pain were terrible to behold, Pelham. I tried to console her, but she sent me away. She told me she was too busy for grief, that she had a world to tend, and no one to help her do it. I wasn't sure what would happen next—if a new god of Death would rise, or if she would need to seek a new consort, because the god of Death is a dualistic god: not just the killing frost but the rising sap, death twinned always with rebirth, you know?"

"What did happen?" Pelham said.

Reva shook his head. "I don't know. I tried to go back, later, to see how Marla was holding up. There are passages gods can use to reach the underworld, ways that would kill mortals—they lead through volcanoes, or pits deep in the Earth—but all the paths to the underworld were closed to me, sealed by a magic far greater than mine. I reached out in every way I could, but the underworld is a black box now. I have spoken to some of the other gods, and while there have been rumors of some great disturbance and upset in the underworld, no one knows what's happening there, not for sure." He sighed. "You haven't heard from Marla, obviously."

"No, but knowing she was widowed seems a crucial piece of the mystery," Pelham said. "Thank you for telling me."

Reva rose. "I have to minister to my flock—San Francisco is booming now, and it's full of strangers who've moved here for jobs and opportunities… and displacing longtime residents who can no longer afford to live in their home. *All* of those are my people, and some need my help."

"You have a purpose," Pelham murmured.

"I *am* my purpose," Reva said. "That's what it is, to be a god. People think it's power, but it's not. It's duty, personified."

"I have a duty to Marla. To help her if I can."

"I know. If I hear anything, I'll let you know."

Pelham nodded, and watched Reva walk away, scattering the pigeons briefly as he went. Then Pelham took out his phone to tell Rondeau what he'd learned.

BRADLEY WAS IN A DANCE STUDIO with Marzi, teaching her mirror magic. They focused on scrying and spying, mainly, but Cole had recently told him about a way to travel from mirror to mirror, and they were talking over the principles of that, too, though in some ways it was even riskier than traditional teleportation. A motion in the mirror startled him, and he turned his head to see his reflection raise its hand in a wave that Bradley hadn't initiated.

Marzi fell back, raising her hands in preparation to weave a net of defensive magic, but Bradley put his hand on her shoulder. "No, it's not a feral reflection, don't worry—it's my boss."

"You wound me," the reflection said, though how an image in glass could speak audibly was a question Bradley hadn't been able to satisfactorily answer. Big B crossed his arms and scowled. "I'm not your boss. I'm more like your big brother."

"Do you have any words of brotherly wisdom?"

Big B sighed. "Look at this shit." He waved his hand, and the mirror changed, becoming something like a movie screen instead, showing entirely different images: a shadowy cave, lit by torchlight.

"Whoa." Marzi stepped forward, tilting her head. "That's a nice trick. How's he do it?"

Bradley shrugged. "*I* would do it with either a light-bending illusion, or by psychically pushing the image into the viewer's mind. I have no idea how *he* does it."

"Duh," Big B said. "I do it with *magic*. Now look. This is what happened when I tried to get in touch with Hell. I found a nice gloomy cavern full of skeletal remains and sent a query."

"I don't see you in this image," Bradley said.

"That's because it's a reconstruction of what I saw through my eyes, or what you might as well call my eyes. Think of it as a first-person shooter with no shooting."

The image shifted, taking in gloomy stone walls, and, yes, there were fragments of white bone scattered around. A hand appeared in the field of vision—Big B's hand—and snapped its fingers. A large fire burst into light, hovering inches above the cavern's uneven floor, flames burning yellow with occasional flashes of blue. "Person-to-person call, the overseer of the multiverse to the gods of Death, please."

The fire flickered, then grew, flames rising nearly to the ceiling, and then an oval of darkness grew in the midst of the flames. A figure appeared, not stepping through the fire, but hovering just back in the doorway. He had the body of a man, skin bronze and bare chest criss-crossed with scars. He wore loose pants of pale fabric, held up with a belt of rope, but something about his bearing struck Bradley as more penitent than hillbilly.

The newcomer had the skull of a cave bear where his head should have been, all yellowed bone and oversized fangs. The head tilted, and in the eye sockets, motes of red light rose and vanished in a stream, like burning cinders wafted upward by the breeze of a campfire. "There is only one god of Death in the underworld, just now." The cave bear's mouth opened and closed, though a lipless mouth couldn't have really made all those sounds, and the voice was deep, echoing, sepulchral. "What business do you have with me, watchman?"

"I'm curious about the whereabouts of an old friend, Marla Mason. Last I checked, she was one of the gods of Death."

"Much has changed. Marla Mason neither dwells in my realm, nor rules it."

"Do you mind if I asked what happened?"

"Is this universe in danger? Do you have some cause to ask these questions, beyond mere curiosity?"

"No, I just—"

"I am busy, watchman. If that is all, I will go." The thing with the bear skull—the new god of Death?—waved a hand, and the dark oval in the fire narrowed until only flame remained.

The view of the cavern disappeared, and Big B was back in the studio's reflection, sitting cross-legged on the floor. "That was all I got. Other attempts at contact were ignored." He shrugged. "Unless he was lying, Marla's not dead, but she's not running things anymore. Knowing Marla, it's hard to imagine she went willingly, and even harder to imagine that she hasn't tried to do anything about it. Maybe she got dumped on Earth and she's in a coma or something, shielded from magical divination."

"Gods. What happened to the *old* Death?" Bradley asked. "What, was there a coup?"

"For the really important gods, the universe abhors a vacuum," Big B replied. "Gods *can* die, and if something killed the old god of Death, the universe would have called up another one."

"Okay, but I thought Marla was married to the office of Death, not to any particular incarnation. Shouldn't she *still* be the Bride?"

Big B shrugged again. "Maybe Skullbear wanted a divorce."

"Can they divorce? Isn't marriage among gods one of those law-of-nature things?"

"If so, maybe Skully had to settle for a separation. I can't do much more for you, B. I'm starting to feel myself fray a little just meddling to *this* extent. There was black mold on the wall of my house this morning and all the tomatoes in the garden are full of these tiny biting worms—Henry was pissed. I need to tend to my own business. Marla's probably not dead, though, which means she's out there, which means maybe you can find her. Take care, and good luck. Call me if you get bored on the mortal coil and want to rejoin the collective." Big B shimmered, and then he was just Bradley's ordinary reflection again.

"Damn," Marzi said. "My boyfriend and I were talking about getting married in a year or two. Maybe I should reconsider. That shit seems fraught."

"Every unhappy marriage is unhappy in its own way, I guess," Bradley said. "I'd better call Pelham and Rondeau and tell them what this new dead end looks like."

RONDEAU STOOD ON THE BALCONY overlooking the bay, phone to his ear, and when Bradley had finished talking, he said, "Wow. Pelham just called me—he got a visit from Reva." He relayed what Pelham had learned, and there was a long moment of silence.

"Well, shit," Bradley said at last. "Putting *those* pieces together makes a picture start to form, huh? The old god of Death died, and a new one rose up, and I guess he didn't get along with Marla."

"She can be difficult," Rondeau said dryly.

"So Skully did *something* to Marla. Maybe he couldn't divorce her, so he kicked her out of Hell?"

"First she gets exiled from her job as chief sorcerer of Felport, then ousted as co-regent of the underworld," Rondeau said. "Her résumé is kind of a mess."

B ignored him. "So where is she, and how do we find her, if she's not reaching out and the god of Death doesn't want her found?"

"I mean… maybe she's making a new start," Rondeau said. "She was never too thrilled with being a god of death, right? She felt like she had too much to do here on Earth to spend all her time among the dead. So… maybe she saw her chance to start over, and took it. I hate to think she'd leave us all behind, but we didn't part on super good terms. Maybe she's just clean-slating things."

"It's a possibility. But as much as she used to complain, there's nothing Marla takes more seriously than her duty. You think she'd just give up her responsibilities in the underworld?"

"I dunno," Rondeau said. "I mean… maybe she thought Skully could do a better job than she could."

There was a moment of silence. Then Bradley said, "Have you ever known Marla to think anyone was more qualified than her to do *anything*?"

"True words," Rondeau conceded. "But what happens now? How do we find her?"

B sighed. "I'm starting to think the better question is, how do we learn to accept that maybe we *can't* find her?"

Going On

"I KNOW, PELLY, but what are we even doing here?" Rondeau zipped his bag closed. "We've been waiting around for weeks, and nothing's happening. I know I don't seem to do much back home, but I am the co-owner of a hotel and casino, and they need me around occasionally. I could fly back and forth from here to Vegas, but San Francisco is a pretty damned arbitrary place for us to be anyway."

"Is that it, then?" Pelham sat in the corner, head bowed. "We just give up on Mrs. Mason?"

"I'm not giving up, because I'm not doing anything anyway, not personally. I have private investigators out looking, circulating Marla's photo all over the country, and in a few other countries, too. Cole's hooked into the sorcerous community. Bradley is doing the psychic thing every chance he gets. If Marla pops up anywhere, we'll hear about it. In the meantime, I'm just sitting here, and while I like sitting around, I'd rather do it at home."

"I feel so helpless, Rondeau. I don't know what to do."

"You say Marla's alive," Rondeau said. "Skully told Big B the same thing. Can you take comfort in that?"

"What is she is in danger? What if she is in captivity, walled up in some terrible place?"

"Then I feel bad for the terrible place, because Marla will tear it down to the foundations. There's nobody tougher or more capable. You know that. Are you sure you won't come home with me?"

"Las Vegas is not my home. Mrs. *Mason* is my home."

Rondeau nodded. "Pretty much what I thought, and I get it. I'm going to miss you, buddy. Cole said you should come see him, if you're looking to keep yourself occupied. He says a man of your talents could be, and I quote, 'a great help to my great city.' Like San Francisco's so great. It's cold in the summer and damp in the winter. Give me Vegas any day."

"I suppose it would be good to have some useful work, to occupy my mind," Pelham said. "And being close to Mr. Cole means I would hear quickly if he receives any news about Mrs. Mason."

"There you go." Rondeau picked up his suitcase. "Take care, Pelly. Everything will be all right. We're talking about the unsinkable Marla Mason here, you know? And in the meantime… life goes on."

Rondeau made it all the way downstairs and into the back of the limo waiting to take him to the airport before he allowed himself to cry.

"Ah, Marla," he whispered into his cupped hands. "Ah, shit. Where did you *go*?" If she'd died, they could have had a funeral, or at least a wake. They could have toasted her, and recalled her great moments, without necessarily forgetting her less-than-great ones. They could have laughed, cried, cursed, emptied themselves out… and then let themselves get filled up by life again, in time. If Marla had decided to leave the Earth forever and fully take on the mantle of a goddess, that could have been softened by some ritual, too: Rondeau could have thrown the greatest imaginable Bon Voyage party, a masque to put the Red Death to shame. But instead, there was just this uncertainty, this unresolved chord, this somehow aggressive inaction.

There are few words as heartless, and as entirely bereft of comfort, he thought, as "life goes on."

A Woman with a Past, Presumably

"**You don't look much like a Mel.**" The road-tripper made a big show of squinting at her name tag, though mostly he was staring at her tits. Some of the younger girls wore their uniform shirts too tight or partly unbuttoned to entice bigger tips, but thirty-something years into her bumpy life Mel was too old for that nonsense. Some guys plowed ahead without any encouragement at all, though.

Still, she didn't go straight to nasty. Her boss, Matt Lefkowitz, had asked her to tone it down a little. ("If this was a little tourist trap in some small town, having a mean-as-hell waitress could be a selling point, people would line up to get insulted. But we cater to the highway trade here, and what with online reviews and all, try to take it easy.")

"Huh." She put the plate of scrambled-too-hard eggs and streaky bacon before him. "You'd better take it up with my mother. She's the one who named me." (The name on her driver's license was actually Melody, but she didn't like that. She was unsure of many things, but she knew she was not *melodic*.) She kept her voice bland and pleasant, even though she hated road-trippers. The truckers were fine (unless it was the late shift and they were hopped up on something), and the bikers were almost always polite as long as they were indoors, but people from California or New Mexico passing through on their way to somewhere else seemed to think the rest of the world was unreal, something on a sound stage, props in their exciting life story: or else they just figured they could be assholes because they'd never been here before and never would be again.

"I've got your name already, so how about your number?"

Mel raised an eyebrow and regarded him coolly. He was maybe twenty-five, with a stupid self-satisfied face and the kind of sideburns he'd clearly spent a lot of thought and time cultivating. "Sorry, son. Turn left on the way out and head for Nevada where the brothels are legal, they'll take care of you."

She started to turn away, and he grabbed her wrist. A voice spoke in her mind, some piece of advice from who knows who or when—"If someone grabs you, hit them"—but punching this guy in the face for something so minor would probably get her fired; Matt liked her, but not enough to carry her through a battery charge. Instead she twisted her wrist and pulled away with enough strength to break the guy's hold easily—one douche's hand was no match for her body weight, especially when he was sitting and she was standing, with all the leverage in her favor. She said, "Grab me again and you'll pull back a bleeding stump, kid," and made sure to say it loud enough for the truckers at the counter to turn and look at them.

She should have left it there—he probably would have just slunk out of the diner, embarrassed—but some imp of the perverse made her reach out and pat him on the head like he was a little kid. "Now eat up, you're a growing boy."

That was too much. Nothing is more fragile than the ego of a healthy young white male in America. "You bitch," he said, rising and reaching out to shove her.

Something whispered in her mind—*wait*—and she let him push her, an awkward half-assed push since he was still rising from the booth. She stumbled back, more dramatically than the push warranted, then set her feet and delivered a straight punch to his face. She could have broken his nose, or possibly even his teeth, but she aimed for his cheek instead, and sent him sprawling back into the booth with a howl. She kept her fists up, waiting for a counterattack, but he just gaped at her. He'd probably never actually been punched before. She remembered vaguely that the first time was always something of a shock.

Matt came out of the kitchen, a dishtowel draped over his shoulder, and a large knife in his hand. He was well over six feet tall but thin and storklike, somehow avoiding the rotund physique that should rightly come with endless access to the greasiest foodstuffs known to man. He glanced around. "That sure looked like self-defense to me. She warned the boy first and everything. You gentlemen agree?"

The truckers at the counter chorused yeses.

"Do we need to call the police?" Matt said.

Mel shook her head. "No, I don't want to press charges. Assuming he leaves a good tip, that is."

The guy got out of the booth, eyeing Mel warily, and started toward the door.

Matt cleared his throat. "Son, we *will* send the police after you if you dine and dash."

The guy reached into this pocket, took out his wallet, and sullenly tossed bills on the table. Mel glanced down. More than enough. "You want change, honey?" Making her voice sweet as the whipped cream on a milkshake.

He opened his mouth, probably to insult her, then thought better of it and fucked off out of the diner.

"He's gonna leave us a terrible review on the internet, Mel," Matt said. He could make even good news sound doleful, and bad news always came out positively sepulchral.

"Yeah, but the rest of these guys will leave good ones. 'Come to Matt's Hash House for dinner, stay for the unlicensed underground boxing matches.'"

Matt chuckled. "Need any ice for your hand?"

"Nah. Hitting someone once doesn't really hurt if you do it right."

He grunted. "Where'd you learn to throw a punch like that anyway, Mel?"

She tried hard to keep the bleak shadow that question summoned inside her from showing on her face. "Oh, you know. You pick things up, here and there."

"I bet you do. You need the afternoon off? Something like that can shake you up."

Mel knew he meant it sincerely. He was a good boss. She paused for a moment and examined how she felt. The result was… fine. Like that kind of violence barely rated on her personal scale for traumatic experiences. That was kind of alarming thought. "Nah, I'm all right."

"Best tend to your other tables, then. I bet they're gonna be real polite now."

They were, and a couple of them even wanted to high-five her, which she tolerated. She refilled coffee cups and took orders and made chit-chat when necessary, but inside her head, Matt's question kept rattling around: Where had she learned to throw a punch like that? Where had she learned how to do *anything* she knew how to do, apart from waitressing, which she'd mostly learned on the job? Mel had no idea.

She didn't have any memory of her life at all prior to a few months ago, when she'd awakened in a nearby motel room with nothing but the clothes on her back and a purse that contained an expired Arizona driver's license that read "Melody Sendall," a bent stick of gum, a cigarette lighter (but no cigarettes, and she didn't crave them), and several grand in cash, some of the bills strangely water-stained.

She'd used as little of the money as possible in case it was stolen and could somehow be traced, but whatever bad business she'd been involved in hadn't come back to hurt her yet.

Matt had hired her soon after she was "born," and giving her a job without asking too many questions about her past was clearly his good deed for the year. She was paid just like the undocumented dishwasher: without an excess of paperwork. She was pretty sure Matt thought she was a battered wife on the run. Maybe he was right.

She couldn't remember a husband, but she had awakened with a small gold ring, hanging on a simple chain, around her neck. It could have been a wedding band, but it just as well could have been some kind of family heirloom. She had no idea.

At first she'd been consumed with a desperate need to find out who she was, and where she'd come from, and what had happened to her, and she'd searched the web for her own name, checking out lists of missing persons, but all without success. She'd considered going to the hospital, telling some doctor her woes, but what if she was mixed up in bad trouble and the cops found out about her? Interacting with anything that left a record seemed like a bad idea.

Then the dreams had started. Bad dreams, full of shadows and dark water and shouting and drowning.

The first time she woke from one of those dreams, she decided the past was probably better left buried.

Lady Luckless

THREE MONTHS AFTER MARLA FAILED to arrive as scheduled in Death Valley, Rondeau sat in the security room at his casino, watching the monitors. The guys on surveillance were more vigilant when the boss popped in at random moments to make sure they were doing the job right, a management trick he'd picked up from Marla during her days as chief sorcerer of Felport. Rondeau had originally been a much more hands-off investor, content to spend his days on sex and sloth, but recently he'd taken a greater interest in the day-to-day running of operations, because even the most elemental of pleasures paled when they became repetitious and uninterrupted. Now that he worked a little, the free hours were that much sweeter.

In the bustle of the casino floor, the sudden cessation of movement drew the eye more than movement itself, so when a woman stopped dead in the middle of the carpet, looked up at the camera, and waved, Rondeau noticed. People mugged for the cameras, sometimes—and sometimes they even did it to distract from confederates who were doing more subtle things in the background—but in this case, Rondeau recognized the woman: bright red hair, white dress patterned with red diamonds, shark-eating smile.

"Get eyes on that woman, and watch where she goes," Rondeau said, and one of his security guards relayed the instructions to the employees on the floor. Rondeau hurried out of the security room, down the unglamorous corridors that supported the dream of glitter and loss in the public areas of the casino, and emerged through a door tucked away behind a potted plant near a double line of slot machines. He wished for a super-spy radio earpiece, but settled for calling the security room on his phone. They told him the woman had walked to one of the hotel's restaurants, the cheap one that looked like a '50s diner, and taken a booth in the back. Rondeau walked calmly—running in a casino didn't create a good impression—toward the diner, pushing in through the chromed door. The hostess and servers recognized him—he had a weakness for the mint chocolate milkshakes here and stopped by a couple times a week— and he gave an affable nod. Everybody tried to look busier now that the boss was present, which wasn't hard, as they were plenty busy anyway. After you'd just lost a lot of money, settling into a red vinyl booth and digging into an order of cheese fries and imaginary nostalgia could be a great comfort.

He went to the booth in the back, where the redhead sat stirring a spoon in a cup of coffee with the deliberation and focus of a monk spinning a prayer wheel. He slid into the booth across from her. "Haven't seen you in a while," he said.

She took the spoon out of the coffee, put it in her mouth, looked him in the eyes, then drew the spoon out slowly and set it on the table beside her cup. "I got bored waiting for you all to do something. I get bored easily. It's an occupational hazard. So I went and did some things myself, and came back, and found out you all did… nothing much at all while I was gone."

"Lady, who even *are* you? And what are you talking about? And why were you everywhere I looked a few months ago?"

"I'm hurt you don't remember me, I'm talking about finding your missing friend, and because I was watching you, dumb-dumb." She leaned over and patted his cheek. "Sure, I had a different face the last time we met, and I'm sure my voice sounded different, but the hair was the same, more or less. This is my real look, by the way." She made a face and stuck out her tongue. "Or, at least, the way I looked right before I stopped being human. The first time. My biography is a little complicated."

Rondeau stared, and something clicked in his mind, and he tried not to whimper. "You're dead. Marla killed you."

The redhead sipped her coffee. "No, Marla killed the *body* I was inhabiting. And then she dispersed my disembodied consciousness into the sea, diluting me throughout a pretty large portion of the ocean. She neutralized me. I don't die that easily." She leaned forward, showing some freckled cleavage. "Go on. Say my name."

"You're Elsie Jarrow." Rondeau closed his eyes, but then he was sitting across from Elsie Jarrow with his *eyes closed*, which did not seem like a smart idea, so he opened them again. Jarrow was the most powerful and notorious chaos magician in recorded history. During her active years she'd been a cross between a fairy godmother and a wicked witch: you never knew if she'd curse you, kill you, or make your wishes come true. She was a creature of whim and whimsy, a bearer of black swans and bad tidings, a reverser of fortunes. She'd eventually become such a potent force of disorder that anyone who came near her developed cancer, their cells driven mad by her proximity, and then Jarrow's *own* body succumbed to the emperor of maladies, and she left the flesh behind to become a creature of pure will, bodiless. Unfortunately, giving up your body had documented negative effects on the mind, and it hadn't improved her disposition. It wasn't so much that Jarrow was malevolent, any more than radiation was motivated by malice, but her very presence meant death, and being untethered from her body made her even more unpredictable than she had been before: and even then she'd been a sorcerer who took power from the unexpected, disorder, and disaster. Eventually Jarrow had been captured and imprisoned in a special cell at the Blackwing Institute, wrapped so tightly with spells of binding and order that she was barely even conscious most of the time... until Marla's enemies made a bargain with her, providing her with a body that could stand up to the carcinogenic properties of her consciousness and setting her free in exchange for killing Marla.

The fact that Jarrow had failed to carry out the murder-for-hire was testament to Marla's pure stubbornness and ingenuity, but the victory hadn't been without cost. In order to stop Jarrow, Marla had been forced to make a bargain with Death himself, becoming a part-time goddess who spent half her year serving in the underworld as co-regent of Hell.

Now, it seemed, the bargain had proven insufficient, because Jarrow was back.

"What do you want?" Rondeau said.

"I want you mopes to find Marla and restore her to her glory, such as it was," Elsie said.

Rondeau shook his head. "Okay. *Why?*"

"Professional courtesy. There aren't that many gods who started out as ordinary humans, so I figure we should stick together."

Rondeau leaned back in the booth. "You always had a high opinion of yourself, Elsie, but—a god?"

"Oh, yes. I used to say I was like unto a god, and at my mortal peak I think I could have gone toe-to-toe with middling divinities like Reva and

Ch'ang Hao, though probably not against Death or some of the other heavy hitters. But I've changed. I got upgraded. I'm a deity, now, all uplifted. My own nature used to be poisonous to me, my devotion to chaos destroyed my body and, I'll admit it, thoroughly deranged my mind—but now I'm hooked into the superstructure of reality. Look: I made this body from memory, and I don't have even one tiny tumor, not a speck of melanoma. Magic I could just barely do before, with all the power at my disposal, is now trivial. Oh, there are new constraints on me, sure—I can't act against my nature, and if I make bargains I have to stick with them… or at least find clever loopholes to wriggle out of, which is more my style. But, all in all? Godhood agrees with me."

Rondeau licked his lips. "What are you a god *of*?" He was terribly afraid the answer was "cancer," that she was seeding his marrow with little engines of death just by sitting there.

She laughed. "I'm a trickster god, Rondeau. There are lots of us, waxing and waning in power, but I have to say, I'm feeling pretty ascendant these days. Coyote and Kokopelli and Loki are all still around, but they're shaped and tethered by some old ideas, and I'm the trickster of the moment. I'm the god of layoffs and winning lottery tickets, of finding your soul mate on an online dating site and getting murdered by internet trolls, of sentient algorithms and disruptive technologies. I'm the god of the singularity, the unevenly distributed future, climate change and private space flight. I'm the god of the edge, Rondeau, where everything teeters and everything bleeds."

"But—*how*?" Rondeau had known two other humans who became gods: Bradley, who was uplifted to fill a vacuum when the old overseer of the multiverse broke her own laws and ceased to exist, and Marla, who married into godhood. "Did you, like, kill and eat the old trickster god?"

"Strangely enough, Marla helped me become what I am today—but how about we let *her* tell you that story. Your curiosity about my ascension will give you an extra incentive to find her."

"Last time you and Marla crossed paths, you were trying to murder each other. Why should I help you find her? How do I know you don't just want to finish the job?"

"You are the dumbest of all possible dumb-dumbs, sweetie. I don't want to hurt Marla. I could say I feel gratitude to her, because of how she helped elevate me, but the truth is, the world is just more interesting with her in it, stomping around trying to fix everything and making stuff worse half the time in the process. Anyway, I already *know* where Marla is, and why she hasn't reached out to you. I could just tell you… but that's not very tricksterish, now, is it? I will give you a little hint, though. It won't help *you*, but if you tell your friends, one of them might figure it out. Here's how I found Marla, despite the new god of Death's best attempts to hide her: first, I found Marla's brother." She drained her coffee cup and stood up. "I'll see you soon."

"I can't say I'm looking forward to it."

Elsie left the diner, and a few moments later, Rondeau followed. She was already out of sight, but he could see the path she'd followed, because every slot machine she'd passed was flashing jackpot lights and dumping torrents of coins. A little farther along he passed a blackjack table where everyone stared, dumbfounded, at their hands: every one of them had 21, including the dealer, which counted a win for the house, at least. Then his phone began to ring, and he had to run around dealing with the consequences of Elsie's presence, and outraged or elated customers: a roulette wheel where only red numbers had come up for the past half hour, a poker table where four players had all been dealt pat royal flushes, a craps table where nothing but snake eyes appeared no matter how many fresh dice were broken out, and more.

Rondeau smoothed feathers and talked people down, using a few persuasion spells when reason failed, and normal odds and order soon reasserted themselves. He briefly worried that he'd take a financial hit from the trickster's passage, but in the final analysis, the outrageous and impossible wins had been balanced by staggering losses, and the accountants had informed him, dumbfounded, that the day was a perfect push: the house had lost *exactly* as much as it had won.

"Right on the edge," he muttered, and went to call Bradley.

BRADLEY WAS WITH COLE, Marzi, and Marzi's boyfriend Jonathan on the grass in Dolores Park, on a hill up above the children's playground. Cole like the view of the city and the bay, and the vibrancy of the young people drinking, smoking, sunbathing, dancing, and making out in the grass, so he often took lunch here. They all sprawled on a big red-and-black checked blanket, eating from the enchanted wicker picnic basket Cole called his "cornucopia," which held a seemingly inexhaustible supply of fruits, meats, cheeses, and assorted beers and wines, all at the perfect temperature. Bradley didn't know if the basket connected to a pantry somewhere, or if it contained its own pocket dimension, but Cole assured him the food was real, and not just conjured; food produced my magic might taste delicious and make your belly feel full, but it was no more nutritious than eating lumps of salt clay.

Cole delicately smeared pate on toasted slices of baguette while Marzi and Jonathan snuggled and murmured together in low voices. Bradley was thinking of giving Marzi the night off for some R&R; he'd noticed she was much easier to teach if she'd gotten laid recently, but then, that was probably true of almost everyone.

His phone rang, and the screen said "Rondeau." He grunted. He hadn't heard from his friend since he headed home to Vegas. Had he gotten word from Marla? "Hey, man, what's the word?"

Rondeau was never the most linear thinker, and his account rambled a bit, but eventually Bradley got it all straight. After about three seconds of silence, during which Bradley tried to synthesize some pretty surprising facts, Rondeau said, "Well? What was Elsie talking about? Do you think Marla's brother Jason knows where she is?"

"I can't imagine why he would. They're not exactly close, what with all the murdering and scamming he's done, right?"

"Sure, but they made peace, sort of, when we were all in Hawaii—or at least decided to call things even and stop trying to kill each other. She said she might send him a Christmas card sometime, and I think they talked when their mom died. I know Marla had Pelham send flowers to her funeral, anyway. It's worth a try, talking to him."

"I'll see if I can track him down," Bradley said.

Through the Mirror

"HE DOESN'T HAVE A PHONE?" Marzi asked.

Bradley shook his head, then adjusted the angle of the full-length folding triple mirror minutely. "Nope. Jason's off the grid, and changing locations every day or two, doing his best to be a ghost. According to Cole's divinations, tonight he's in a derelict farmhouse in western Pennsylvania. The place doesn't even have running water, as far as we can tell, or electricity, or any other amenities beyond a roof and walls, and those probably have holes in them. I'd fly in to find him, but there's no reason to think he'll be there even a few hours from now, and I'd rather not chase him all over the countryside. The direct approach is best. Besides, I've been wanting to try this for months." He glanced toward the corner, where Pelham sat, hands folded in his lap, expression alert. The small man was dressed impeccably as always, in a suit with a waistcoat, and not a strand of his thinning hair was out of place, but Bradley was perceptive, and he could see Pelham was wound as tightly as the innards of his own antique pocket watch.

"I thought Jason was some kind of smooth operator?" Marzi arranged small white candles on the carpet, referring often to a diagram Cole had drawn. "Shouldn't he be living in a penthouse and scamming old ladies?"

"If I had to guess, I'd say he's probably hiding out from the consequences of a recent job."

"He is no gentleman," Pelham murmured.

"Right. You guys think maybe he's hiding out with Marla?" Marzi took a box of wooden fireplace matches, struck one, and began to light the candles.

"The thought has crossed my mind. Hard to imagine the two of them being all buddy-buddy, but I have it on good authority that families are weird." Bradley stepped back, cocked his head, and nodded in satisfaction.

The candles, arranged in a complex asymmetrical pattern, were all reflected in the central mirror, and the mirrors on either side were angled to double, triple, and quadruple those lights in their own reflections, creating the illusion of an infinite series of corridors. An illusion that could be turned into reality, if he did this right.

"You sure you don't want me to go?" Marzi said.

Bradley shook his head. "I don't even want *Pelham* to go. Travel by mirror is so risky that even people brave enough to teleport tend to avoid it. If you're unlucky with teleporting, you get maimed or you die. If you're unlucky with travel by mirror, you just *wish* you were dead. And sometimes, the person who comes out of the mirror isn't the person who went *in*. Cole says my natural ability to see through illusions should keep me relatively safe, but for anybody else, it's very easy to get... lost. You don't need to come, Pelham, really—I can handle it."

"If there is a chance that Mrs. Mason is on the other side of that glass, then I am going." Pelham was the definition of unflappable, so Bradley shrugged.

"Okay then. Marzi, kill the lights. Keep the candles burning while we're gone, all right? And Pelly, stay close to me."

Pelham rose and joined him, putting a hand on his right shoulder. Bradley stared into the mirrors, letting his eyes blur, looking past his own reflection and into the lighted depths: a sky full of stars, a sea full of luminous fish. He didn't let himself blink, and as his eyes watered, the view before him softened further. Bradley took one deliberate step forward, and then another, and then another, until he passed the point where he should have crashed into the glass.

As a little kid, he'd seen a cartoon about a little boy who walked through a mirror into a world on the other side. It wasn't an adaptation of *Through the Looking Glass, and What Alice Found There*—it had definitely involved a little boy, and not a girl, though Bradley couldn't remember much else about it, certainly not what the world beyond the mirror had been like. Despite occasional attempts at research on the internet, he'd never been able to track down the name of the show, either because it was too obscure, or because his unreliable memory muddled the details too badly. The program had made a big impression on him, though, or at least one moment had: the boy, reaching out, hands touching the glass, which rippled like water, and let him pass through. Bradley had spent a lot of hours trying to push through the mirror hanging on the back of his mom's bedroom door, always frustrated, desperate to discover a magic that eluded him. The failure of that mirror to yield was his earliest, purest memory of disappointment.

And now, he was through the looking glass. There was no magical world on the other side, though. Just a hall of mirrors, the walls reflecting him and Pelham, and countless candle flames, though the actual candles were no longer in evidence. He looked behind him, and felt a flutter of panic, because there were just more mirrors and corridors back there: no sign of the hotel room, or Marzi, or anywhere else. The candles seemed to brighten, and he narrowed his eyes, growing lightheaded.

"Mr. Bowman." Pelham squeezed his shoulder, hard. "I believe we should proceed forward, and to the left."

"What?" Bradley blinked, and some of his reflections blinked too, though others laughed silently, and others snarled, and one pounded on the glass with bloody fists like a prisoner trying to escape a transparent cage.

"I will show you." Pelham stepped around Bradley, taking his hand, and leading him seemingly at random. *His* reflections all behaved themselves, merely mimicking his calm progress, though Bradley's reflections continued to twist, writhe, cavort, and bellow voicelessly. Some of them bent to blow out candles, or snuffed the flames between fingertips, plunging whole infinite sections of the hall of mirrors into darkness. Somewhere in the distance came the crash and tinkle of breaking glass and falling shards, but Pelham continued plodding along, choosing corridors and crossings with barely any hesitation, moving them along.

Something touched the back of Bradley's neck, and he spun around, only to come face-to-face with himself—but this version of him smiled, showing teeth that were shards of broken mirror. The mirror-fanged Bradley reached out and closed his hands around Bradley's throat, smiling as he throttled him—but then Pelham was there, reaching past Bradley to punch the mirror-monster in the face. The blow might have broken a human's nose, but the monster's face *shattered*, and where the creature had been, there was only a scattering of silvered glass on the dusty black floor.

Pelham grabbed Bradley's hand and pulled him, dragging him through the hall of mirrors, until they reached an open window set halfway up the wall, revealing a derelict bathroom beyond. "Go!" Pelham whispered, pushing him toward the window, and despite his fuzzy head, Bradley obeyed, clambering through the waist-high square and falling onto a filthy tile floor beside a cracked toilet. He looked up at the mirrored medicine cabinet he'd passed through, the glass miraculously intact.

A moment later Pelham *leapt* through the mirror, landing inelegantly beside the clawfoot bathtub. Bradley staggered to his feet and looked at the medicine cabinet. Three versions of himself stood behind the glass, snarling with mirrored teeth, but then they shimmered, and it was only his own reflection, wide-eyed and dazed-looking.

Pelham rose, took a handkerchief from his pocket, and began binding up his left hand.

"Are you all right?" Bradley said.

"One of them slashed me across the palm," Pelham said. "But it is a minor wound, of no consequence."

"I don't know what happened in there." Bradley sat on the edge of the tub, still feeling shaky, but more lucid now. "Cole told me it was a place of illusions, and he thought my ability to see clearly would protect me, but I guess he was wrong."

"I believe Mr. Cole underestimated the other element of your power," Pelham said. "You act as a catalyst, to intensify magic, isn't that right? In your presence, ghosts sometimes gain material substance, and you can summon oracles to manifest even when they possess only the most tenuous of links to our reality."

"Shit. So those creatures of reflection behind the mirror became more than light and shadow in my presence—they became more real."

"I believe they wished to take your reality for their own, yes."

"How did you manage to lead us, though?"

Pelham shrugged. "I was there when you discussed your plan to travel by mirror with Mr. Cole." Pelham had been working as Cole's private secretary, and was apparently so adept at his job that Cole already couldn't imagine running San Francisco's magical underworld without him. "He said the key was to remain focused on one's destination, because there are many mirrors in the world, many reflections, and it is easy to become lost. I am... very good at remaining focused."

"I owe you, Pelly." He looked around. "So this is where Jason's holed up, huh?"

Jason Mason stepped into the doorway, a pistol pointed at them. "That's right. And it's where I'm going to dig a hole to bury you two. Or, wait, maybe I'll get you to dig the hole. Less work for me then."

Bradley sighed and stared hard at Jason, who blinked and swore, swinging the gun to and fro, looking around the room wildly. Bradley put a finger to his lips, then stood up and stepped to one side, preparing to slip around Jason's flank.

Pelham was faster, though, darting forward and grabbing Jason's gun hand, twisting, and taking the gun from him. Jason grunted and tried to run, but Bradley tripped him up, and Jason fell in a heap. "God *damn* it," he said. "I hate magic. Turning invisible? You fuckers don't play fair."

Bradley released his pressure on Jason's mind. "We weren't invisible. I just made it so you couldn't see us." Tricks like that were almost useless against sorcerers—even the greenest apprentice knew how to shield her mind from such psychic attacks—but for all his formidable qualities, Jason had no defenses against magic.

Pelham stood over him, gun held loosely at his side. "Mr. Mason. We're looking for your sister."

Jason sat up. "Yeah, I figured. Mind if I stand?"

"I think you're good on the floor."

Jason grunted and leaned against the wall. He was as handsome as ever, if a bit wolfish, and his usual cocksure smirk was already reasserting itself, but he'd clearly been living rough: his shirt was stained, his jacket rumpled, his hair sticking up, his jaw blued by stubble. "You know, I was *just* about ready to come out of hiding?"

"Your sister, Mr. Mason. Where is she?"

"I don't know, Pelham. You don't still hold a grudge about that time I held you hostage, do you? I ask, because it seems like our roles are reversed now, and I'll remind you, I was pretty good to you."

"You did not treat me unkindly," Pelham said. "I will give you the same courtesy, if you answer my questions. If not..."

"Who knew tiny butlers could sound so threatening?" Jason said. "Look, it's just like I told Elsie Jarrow when she came calling—I don't have any idea where Marla is. I haven't seen her since she came to visit mom in hospice, right before she died, and that was months ago. I thought you guys *killed* Elsie, Pelham. I nearly shit myself when she showed up on my doorstep. I was afraid she was going to drag me on another murder road trip or something, and I've been hiding ever since, afraid she'd find me again."

"You can't hide from people like us," Bradley said. "You just don't have the resources."

"Yeah, well, it makes me feel better to try, all right? Now that you've found me, and been disappointed by my total lack of information, how about you get lost?"

"Look, Jason, Elsie visited us, too. She said if we wanted to find Marla, we should find you first. Now you're saying you haven't seen her? You don't know anything about her location? What did you tell Elsie?"

Jason rolled his eyes. "I told her *nothing*, all right? Look: Elsie shows up a couple few months back. She tells me she wants to find Marla, I figure because she wants to finish the job she started in Hawaii, to kill her. I didn't have any information, and believe me, I would have spilled if I did—being Elsie's traveling companion once was enough. Me and Marla mended fences a little bit, but I'm not gonna die to protect her. Elsie says, what was it—she says, 'It's okay, blood always tells.' Then she takes out this silver knife, like a scalpel, and I thought I was dead, but she just told me to hold out my hand. Said she could pluck a hair from my head or a breath from my mouth, but that blood was more traditional. She cuts my palm, and catches the blood in a little bowl, and then she just walks off. I packed up my stuff and started hiding after that."

"Hiding *after* Jarrow finds you is kind of a barn-door-post-horse-theft idea, Jason."

"I don't need your advice on how I should practice self-care." Jason scowled. "Can I do anything *else* for you two?"

"Yeah," Bradley said. "Some blood and hair will do it."

Jason groaned.

Familial Tendencies

THEY CALLED MARZI TO RELIEVE HER of mirror-watching duty, then flew home on a plane, having had their fill of unconventional travel. The next afternoon Pelham and Bradley stood in Cole's workshop. It was a cross between a modern chemistry lab and an ancient alchemist's lair, sophisticated glassware and equipment mingled with fire-blackened cauldrons, antique brass instruments, and hazy crystals.

Cole took the vial containing a drop of Jason's blood and held it up to the light of an oil lamp. "Miss Jarrow is really quite ingenious," he said. "I'm sure some other sorcerer has thought of this approach, but it's not a technique I've ever heard of."

"You lost me." Rondeau covered a yawn. He'd just arrived from Vegas. "What are we doing and how are we doing it?"

"You know how Big B has no trouble finding me, because my body is *his* body?" Bradley said.

Rondeau nodded. "Sure. Sympathetic magic link. The thing is the thing, the thing calls to the thing, A equals A, all that."

"Right. One basic form of divination is blood magic, but really anything that carries DNA will do the job—hair, flesh, whatever. If you have a drop of someone's blood, you can create a sympathetic magic link, and use the blood to locate the rest of the body."

"But you already tried that method, along with so many others," Pelham pointed out.

Cole nodded. "Yes. Some powerful magic—which we know now to be the work of this new god of Death—obscured Marla from us, rendering direct methods of divination ineffective. But *indirect* ones...."

"Wait," Rondeau said. "This is like DNA testing, right? Like, paternity tests—you can compare the kid's DNA with the dad's and find out if they're related."

Bradley nodded. "A familial link. The DNA isn't identical... but it's similar enough, and you can examine the similarities to find out if people are siblings, or parents, or whatever."

Cole placed a small blue glass bowl on the wooden lab table, uncapped the vial of blood, and let the sample drip inside. "So we modify the traditional divination method. Instead of using this blood to locate its owner, we attempt to locate people *related* by blood to its owner: close relatives of Jason Mason. As I said. Ingenious." He poured a clear fluid from a beaker into the bowl, then used a wire whisk to mingle the substances. "The atlas, please?"

Bradley took a heavy leather-bound volume of maps, which had undergone its own magical preparations, and placed it on the table, closed. Cole murmured a few words, then poured the contents of the bowl onto the cover of the atlas.

Instead of resting on the cover, the fluid was absorbed into the atlas, like water disappearing into sand. Cole counted under his breath, then opened up the book and stepped back. The pages of the book began to flutter, then flip by themselves, and stopped on a two-page spread of the United States of America.

Bradley and the others crowded around. There were three drops of blood on the map: one in Pennsylvania, one in Florida, and the last in Arizona. Bradley grunted. "The one in Pennsylvania is Jason, probably. But why are there two others? Jason is Marla's only sibling, and their mom died a while back. I think we would have heard if Marla had ever had a kid. I guess Jason might have fathered a child, though. He's got 'deadbeat dad' written all over him."

"Humans are traditionally born of woman *and* man," Cole said. "Could one of those be Marla and Jason's father?"

Rondeau whistled. "I always assumed her old man must be dead, but I don't know why I assumed that. I'm actually not even a hundred percent sure her and Jason have the same father. I got the sense their mom was a little bit, uh, let's say, less than discerning when it came to romance. Among other things."

"We've got two leads to check out, anyway." Bradley flipped through the atlas to more specific entries for Florida and Arizona, and both were marked by red droplets, narrowing the geography further. "Huh. Hey, Cole, is there any of that blood left? I've got an idea...."

Desert Recon

PELHAM AND RONDEAU FLEW TO FLORIDA, while Bradley and
Marzi headed for Arizona. They drove in a sleek, black, low-slung sedan,
which happened to be sentient, self-driving, and mysteriously magical:
the car called herself Sierra, and she liked Bradley and Marzi because they
were psychic enough to hear its nonverbal voice. (To communicate with
other people, Sierra was pretty much limited to honking in Morse Code.)
The three of them had been through battles together, and road-tripped
out west from Felport after the fight with the Outsider, and had formed
a pretty tight bond in the process. Sierra had been languishing, bored in
one of Cole's garages, and was happy to get out, take the air, and go on an
adventure.

They set out first thing in the morning, and Sierra was adept at eating
up the miles. Bradley had used Jason's blood to magically infuse both his
phone and his apprentice's: their map apps now showed a steady red dot
where their target waited, in a little place that was less a town than a series
of freeway amenities for truckers and road-trippers.

For the first few hours of the journey they'd chatted about Cole's
idiosyncrasies, Marzi's training, and what she might want to do in her
magical career once that training was done—Sierra wanted them to
drive around the country as freelance monster-hunters and supernatural
problem-solvers, which had a certain appeal. As they drew nearer their
target, though, the conversation turned inevitably to Marla.

"You think we drew the lucky straw, or Rondeau and Pelham did?"
Marzi said.

"That depends on whether Marla's hiding out willingly, or being held
captive. If she's trying to avoid notice, then I'd say Florida's more likely.
She crawls out of the ground in Death Valley after she returns from Hell,

and she's spent a lot of time in the Southwest lately as a result. I don't think she'd hide out so close to a place where she's been operating. But if she's being held against her will… well, I imagine it's easier to keep Marla captive if you don't have to transport her too far. I'd put our odds at about fifty-fifty, honestly."

"I wish I'd gotten to know her better," Marzi said.

"Maybe you still will."

"She's so badass, it's hard to imagine *anyone* holding Marla captive, you know?"

Bradley nodded. The thought had occurred to him, too. "I know. If we find her, and she's not in trouble, and she tells us to buzz off, we will. Maybe being kicked out of the Hell was the best thing to happen to her, and she's happy. But we need to know she's okay."

"She can't be all *that* captive, if she's our red dot." Marzi poked at her phone. "She's moving around. Looks like she left a trailer park and… went to a diner by the interstate."

"Good. I could use some lunch anyway." They covered the ground to the appropriate exit in another forty minutes, and Sierra slowed to get off the freeway. There was nothing in the dusty vicinity but a cluster of fast-food restaurants, gas stations, a big truck stop, and a diner, clearly the oldest building in the area, set a little bit apart. The parking lot was half full, drawing those passing customers who wanted to sit for a while instead of hitting a drive-through or settling for eating a gas-station-adjacent burrito while they fueled up.

Sierra parked herself in a corner of the lot. *Don't leave me here long,* she said in Bradley's mind. *I'm a bird of paradise among sparrows here.*

"We'll be mindful of your dignity," he said aloud. "Well, ready to see Marla? Or possibly a weird old man who fathered her? Or her totally unknown niece or nephew?"

"Can't wait."

They got out of the car, pushed through the diner door, and looked around. There was a tall, cadaverous guy behind the grill, a pretty young blonde waitress flirting at the counter, and an older waitress taking an order from a family of four in a booth—

"Marla." Bradley's heart surged, ripples of elation flooding his body. He rushed across the diner toward her, calling her name, but he stopped three feet away when she turned her head and looked at him with eyes entirely bereft of recognition. He knew her well, and he was supernaturally perceptive, besides, and it was clear that Marla wasn't just pretending not to recognize him—she had no idea who he was. "Sorry," he said. "I, uh, thought you were somebody else."

She narrowed her eyes—that look of suspicion was *pure* Marla, her essential self shining through despite the superficial changes: longer hair, red lipstick (had she *ever* worn lipstick before?), the pencil tucked behind her ear, the yellow waitress uniform. Her nametag read "Mel," which was just close enough to right to make his heart break. "Have a seat anywhere," she said. "Someone will help you in a minute." She turned back to her customers.

Bradley retreated to a booth, where Marzi was already sitting. She raised an eyebrow at him, and he leaned forward. "She doesn't know me."

"So what do we do?"

"I... I don't know." He'd been prepared to rescue Marla from danger, or to endure the sharp side of her tongue and be driven away, but to have his former teacher and longtime friend—the one person who'd had the single biggest impact on his life—look at him with a total lack of recognition wasn't an outcome he'd considered.

"Let's eat while we think about it, then," Marzi suggested.

Bradley smiled despite himself. His apprentice might have pink hair, but she had a practical streak Marla herself would have admired.

Marla appeared, notebook in hand. "Something to drink? Know what you want to eat?" Her tone was brusque, but whether that was because of the way he'd greeted her or just her natural mien, he couldn't tell.

Marzi ordered coffee. "Just water for me," Bradley said. "What's good here?"

Bored, now. "Everything's about as good as everything else."

They ordered fries and burgers, and she went behind the counter to put in their order.

"Maybe she's in, like, supernatural witness protection," Marzi said.

"Something was done to her mind." He frowned, looking at Marla with his psychic vision. Her inner landscape was full of mists, blind alleys, locked doors, dead ends. "Something pretty extreme."

"Can you fix it?"

"Mmm.... given sufficient time, probably, but I don't know if she's going to sit still while I poke through her mind."

"So squeeze her brain a little and make her pass out."

"When someone's got psychic trauma, inflicting *more* psychic trauma isn't an ideal first step. I think... let's keep an eye on her. She has to sleep sometime, and when she does, I can see about breaking down some of the blocks in her mind—maybe we can get her to remember enough that she'll remember who I am, and let me finish the job properly."

"Stake out!" Marzi said.

BRADLEY CALLED RONDEAU from the parking lot to let him know they had eyes on Marla, and to convey what he'd learned of her condition.

"Oh, good," Rondeau said. "We were about ninety percent sure this old man drinking in the middle of the day in the most horrible bar in the world wasn't actually Marla in disguise, but it's good to have confirmation. You want us to join you?"

"If you like," Bradley said. "I still don't know exactly what we're dealing with, but maybe having more familiar faces around will help."

SOME HOURS LATER, they sat in Sierra in the parking lot of a convenience store and the adjacent laundromat, across from the trailer park where Marla—or "Mel"—apparently lived. They had a view of her trailer, which she'd entered about an hour ago after finishing her shift at the diner, and they were just waiting for the lights to go out so Bradley could poke at her dreams.

Marzi yawned, exhaling cheese puff-laden breath into the car. "Stake outs are boring."

"Yeah, they go a lot faster when you see them in the movies. Though filming them is pretty dull, too, as I recall. Then again, filming just about everything is pretty dull, in the aggregate."

Marzi shifted her feet, moving around the litter of candy and chip wrappers at her feet. She'd attempted to combat boredom with snacks, with only temporary success.

You'd better clean all this up, Sierra said. *I don't fill your bodies with garbage.*

Marzi nodded. "Sorry, Sierra. I've gotta take a leak anyway." She gathered up the trash, stuffed it in the biggest of the empty potato chip bags, and Sierra opened the door. "Call me on the ol' brain-link if anything exciting happens, B." She disappeared around the back of the convenience store, where the bathroom was located. The store itself had closed at eleven p.m., but the lock on the bathroom door was busted anyway, so it didn't inhibit access.

Bradley fiddled with the radio, keeping his eyes on the lights still burning in Marla's trailer, as two minutes became five became ten, and uneasiness set in. Maybe Marzi was having intestinal distress due to the diner main course followed by junk food dessert, but… "Sierra, can you reach Marzi?"

Direct mind-to-mind communication was tricky, and Bradley couldn't speak to Marzi psychically without some preparation, but Sierra could hear both of them as long as they were within a hundred yards or so of the car, so his apprentice should have still been in range.

She doesn't answer, Sierra said.

Crap. "I'd better check on her."

You realize it's a trap?

"I had roles in a couple of thrillers back in the day. I know how it goes. I'll be careful." He got out of the car, and cautiously circled the convenience store, reaching out with all his psychic senses, feeling for signs of life and active minds—and there *was* something, a blur of bad energy, in the bathroom.

Marzi just woke up, Sierra said. *She's panicking about something, she says someone grabbed her.*

He went to the door, pushed it open, and saw Marzi, bound and gagged with rags and clothesline on the filthy floor by the sink.

Uh oh, he thought, but before he could turn around, he felt something cold press against the back of his neck. *Now* he could sense the other mind behind him, cool and controlled: all the mental blocks and barriers erected in her mind served to mask her general psychic signature, especially with Marzi's panic jamming his frequencies.

"Why are you two watching me?" Marla said. "Who are you?"

Bradley swallowed. "I'm pretty sure the question you really want to ask is, who are *you*? I can tell you, if you want. But I promise, we don't mean you any harm. We're your friends. At least, we used to be, back when you remembered us."

The cold thing against his neck didn't move. "I don't know why I can do these things. Sneak around in the dark. Set an ambush. But I can. As soon as I saw the threat, as soon as I met you in the diner, I knew just what to do." She patted him down with her free hand as she spoke, but didn't find anything but his keys and phone and wallet—she took them all away. She stepped back. "Turn around."

He did. She'd changed out of her uniform into dark gray sweats, perfect for hiding in shadows. She pointed a gun at him, and *that* was bizarre, because Marla had never bothered much with guns—in a world of magical warfare they were about as much good as a pointy stick. "Pick up your friend. We'll go somewhere and have a talk."

Bradley knelt beside his apprentice. She looked dazed. "What did you do to her?"

"She's fine. I just came up behind her and put her in a sleeper hold. I knew how to do it—how to cut off her blood supply without crushing her throat. I'm full of surprises. Pick her up, come on."

He heaved Marzi up over his shoulder, though his spine protested, and she grunted. "Ugh. I should work out more."

Marla directed him out of the bathroom and told him to start walking into the darkness behind the convenience store. There was nothing that way but flat land, scrub, and the dim shapes of distant, unlit buildings. He had the terrible feeling he was being marched toward a grave.

"Your name is Marla Mason," Bradley said, though carrying his apprentice was using up a lot of his breath. He should have prepared some spells of strength and endurance. "You—"

"Shut up." That offhand voice, expecting to be obeyed: that was pure Marla, too. After a few minutes of silence, she said, "There are pictures of me on her phone."

Bradley grunted. "You guessed her lock code? Or did you beat it out of her?"

"Ha. She was looking at her phone in the bathroom when I crept up on her. I get the sense you two haven't done this sort of thing too often before. These pictures. When were they taken? How long have you been watching me?"

"Why don't you look through *my* photos?" He told her his code.

Another silence, and then a long hiss. "You're in pictures *with* me."

"We hung out a few months back. We hadn't seen each other for a while. I wanted a few snapshots to remember the occasion."

"Stop, and don't turn around," she said. He obeyed, and a moment later heard a few hard *cracks*.

"Did you just break our phones?" he said.

"Phones are just fancy tracking devices. I don't like tracking devices. Keep walking."

They moved on for a while longer, until she said, "Here is fine."

"Here" was nowhere in particular, just a couple of big stones surrounded by scrub brush. "Sit on those rocks."

Bradley put Marzi down carefully on the larger, flatter rock, and she blinked up at him, pulling herself unsteadily into a sitting position.

"Take out her gag," Marla said.

Bradley unbound the rags and tossed them on the ground.

Marzi smacked her lips. "Ugh," she said. "Damn, Marla, amnesia makes you cranky."

Marla was standing out of rushing-and-grabbing distance, gun pointed between them. Her face was hidden in shadow, so Bradley improved his night vision, but it didn't help: her expression seldom gave much away anyway.

"So we're just going to let her hold us at gun point?" Marzi said. "That's a thing we're letting happen?"

"I'm trying not to spook her," Bradley said.

"The things I know, the things I can do... I must have been some kind of spy." Marla didn't sound like she was asking; more like she was musing aloud. "Maybe even an assassin."

"You've killed a few people," Bradley said. "But always in self defense, or in defense of others, as far as I know." Sure, in her position as a god of the underworld Marla been involved in countless other deaths, in an official capacity, but it hardly seemed like the time to go into all that.

"How can you know that about me, unless you're spies, too? But you're *terrible* at being spies. You couldn't even watch or follow me properly."

"In our defense, we were expecting more of a reunion with a friend, and less of a hostile operative situation." He coughed. "Anyway, you're not a spy. Not exactly. Though you are good with secrets. You've had lots of jobs, and 'mercenary' was one of them, but that was a long time ago. Lately you've been more of a... freelance do-gooder." That sounded more plausible than "monster hunter," but only just.

"Do you know what happened to me?" she said. "To my memories? Was I drugged? Operated on? Or did I just hit my head like in some stupid movie?"

"We're not sure. You disappeared. Your friends have been trying to track you down. But we think we know who did this to you. You were in charge of.... what's the best way to put it...."

"An underworld organization," Marzi said.

Bradley nodded. "Yes! Exactly. But your partner got killed, and then a rival came in and took over your business while you were distracted. He decided to get rid of you, but for whatever reason, he didn't want to kill you. Instead, he wiped out your memories, and dropped you in the desert."

"That *should* be the stupidest thing I've ever heard," Marla said.

"Do you believe us?" Bradley said.

"Her, I don't really know." She gestured at Marzi with the gun. "But something about you... I don't know what it is... I feel relaxed around you."

"We're old friends, Marla. We've been through the wars together."

"Marla. Marla Mason." She shook her head. "That doesn't mean anything to me. What are you here for?"

"We were just trying to find you, but now that I know why you haven't been in touch... I think we can help you recover your memories. We can try, anyway."

She nodded. "Can you do it at gunpoint?"

Bradley sighed. "Marla, if we wanted to hurt you, we would have done it already."

She snorted. "You're amateurs. You couldn't take me on my worst day and your best one."

"Not if you were in full possession of your faculties, no, but... Can I show you something? Promise you won't freak out?"

"I don't know much about myself, but I'm pretty sure I'm not the freaking-out type."

"Marzi? Do you mind?"

She nodded. "Hmm. Banana?"

"Banana is traditional, yes. Or snake, but banana is less startling."

Marzi stared hard at Marla, then muttered to herself and made a gesture.

Marla swore. "What the *hell*?"

"She turned your gun into a banana," Bradley said. "You weren't a spy, Marla. You were a sorcerer. So are we. In a fair fight, with all your resources, you'd turn *both* of us into tatters of meat confetti, but since you can't remember anything...." He waved his hand, casting a bug-in-amber spell, and Marla grunted, held in place, the air around her from the neck down transforming into a transparent solid. Bradley walked toward her, then waved again, releasing her.

She rolled her neck on her shoulders, scowling at him. "I *want* to kick you in the knee, and then knee you in the face as you fall down, but that's just the impotent rage talking. Magic? Are you fucking kidding me?"

Bradley shrugged. "The world is strange. It wasn't drugs or surgery that messed with your mind—it was sorcery. But I'm good with minds. Let us try to fix you?"

She looked at the banana in her hand, then peeled it, and took a bite. She chewed thoughtfully, then swallowed. "Pretty good. All right. Let's go to my trailer."

BRADLEY SENT MARZI back to the car, so Sierra wouldn't worry and come roaring through the trailer park, smashing into things. He accompanied Marla to her place, which was all ancient faux-wood paneling inside, and as Spartan as her usual living accommodations. She sat on the edge of the small bed in the back of the trailer and looked at him frankly. "Hey. Bradley, right? Let me ask you something: do I *want* to get my memory back? Or would I be happier if I never remembered?"

Bradley opened his mouth to answer, then paused, thinking the question over. The Marla he knew had never worried much at all about happiness; she'd worried about duty, and about ensuring the happiness of others—in the sense that people were happier when there weren't monsters trying to eat them or steal their life energies, anyway. She'd taken satisfaction in doing important work. Possibly she *would* be happier, for some values of "happy," if she stayed a waitress at a diner in the middle of nowhere instead... but assuming her essential self was unchanged, she would never be satisfied with that kind of life. Finally he said, "The Marla I knew would want to take back anything that was stolen from her, including her memories. But I won't lie to you: your life is going to get exponentially more complicated if I can help you remember. You won't want to work at the diner anymore, I'm guessing."

She nodded. "I'm sick of my hair smelling like bacon grease anyway. Let's do it."

He sat cross-legged on the floor, on the thin and scraggly no-color carpet. "Okay. Just lay back and relax."

"Was I the relaxing type, in my old life?"

"Well, no. But it's never too late to try new things."

Marla lowered herself back on the bed, arms crossed over her chest, feet dangling off the end of the mattress. Bradley decided that was as mellow as she was likely to become, and closed his eyes, reaching out for her mind, projecting himself into her mental landscape. There was a bright, crystalline kernel of consciousness there, like a lattice of white light, surrounded by mist and thickened shadows.

"I'm going to help you sleep, now," he said.

"You're the psychic surgeon. Do what you do. You've already proven I can't stop you anyway."

He reached out with his conceptual hands and caressed her consciousness, soothing it, and heard her breath change, becoming slow and regular. Now she wouldn't be as likely to unconsciously fight his psychic prodding. First, he blew away the mist and illuminated the shadows in her mind, revealing her constrained inner world. The courtyard that held her consciousness was small, and surrounded completely by towering walls, pocked and pitted, the color and texture of ancient bones. Knocking the walls down one at a time would be exhausting and piecemeal. They hadn't been erected that way, surely, bit by bit, so maybe they could be taken down more efficiently, too. Perhaps there was a keystone, a load-bearing wall, one spot he could knock down to cause the rest of the walls to tumble in turn....

He let his psychic body rise over her inner landscape, hoping for an overview of the terrain, and gasped (or did the purely psychic equivalent). The walls surrounding her spark of consciousness weren't walls at all, but dikes. The rest of her mind was submerged in dark water, a vast sea of oblivion, brackish and bleak. If he'd knocked down a single wall, the waters would have rushed into the protected courtyard, dousing Marla's last spark of consciousness entirely. She would have become an emptiness, still breathing, but bereft of anything resembling a human mind. If he'd been less careful, Bradley could have rendered his friend brain dead. This was a nasty trap, set to erase Marla entirely if anyone tried to restore her memory.

Bradley gritted his imaginary teeth. He was the greatest psychic in this reality, probably, or at least the greatest one who wasn't hopelessly insane. Mental landscapes were malleable, expandable, *manipulable*, and he gestured, opening a sinkhole beneath the stillness. The dark waters roiled, and then swirled, and a whirlpool began to twist. He gestured again, and opened another hole, and again, until three maelstroms swirled, and the level of water began to recede all over Marla's mind.

As the waters fell, shapes were revealed. A mountain of gold. A mountain of ice. A mountain of glass. The Whitcroft-Ivory building, a landmark in Marla's former home city of Felport. A castle carved in obsidian, with jagged towers brushing the belly of the sky. The waters continued to swirl away, and smaller structures were revealed: a tree house, a train car, a trailer (even more dilapidated than the one she currently inhabited), a bookshop, the forbidding walls of the Blackwing

Institute, a forest, a pier, Marla's old apartment building. Her inundated mental landscape gradually became the city it should have been all along, a hodgepodge of places metaphorical and remembered. Figures flitted and dashed and moved in that landscape, and fires burned, and armies clashed, and candles glowed, and musicians played, and porch swings swayed. Some of the images he recognized from experiences he'd had with Marla, or stories she'd told, but most things, he didn't. In fact, he began to feel like an invader, and so as the last of the waters trickled away, he closed up the sinkholes (he'd drained the waters to sunless reservoirs in the depths of her mind). He took the gleaming core of her consciousness and set it in the sky, making it a sun to dry the last of the puddles and illuminate the memories below. He could sense her mental imbalance shift into accord.

Bradley departed her mind, opening his eyes, and fell over on the carpet. He was so thoroughly drenched with sweat he might have been submerged in those dark waters himself.

Marla groaned and sat up on the bed. She looked down at him, then nudged him with her foot. "Shit. Bradley. Shit. *Shit.* You gave me back *all* my memories."

"Good," he croaked.

"Yeah. Good. *Great.* Except there were a couple of memories I'd deliberately sealed off myself, years and years ago, and now I'm having to cope with those, too, damn it. *And* I remember things about being a goddess, things that were always closed to my mortal mind before. Holy Hell, Bradley. I remember everything. I remember every… little… thing."

"What can I say," he said. "I'm the best I am at what I do."

"You're too good. I remember every conversation I've ever had. Every line of every book. Every scrap of knowledge, every overheard snatch of song, every whisper, and when you can see everything, the connections are so clear. Just a second." She leaned over the bed and vomited on the carpet, then just held herself still, her hair a lank curtain hiding her face. "Okay. I think that's all the barfing I've got in me right now. Did you know I killed my one true love when I was a young mercenary sorcerer? I didn't, either, until you uncovered the memory. Ha. I hung out with his eternal spirit just a few months back in the underworld, too. Daniel. The god part of me hid that from the mortal part. I'm all intermingled now."

Bradley watched the puddle of her vomit spread. It was getting too close to him, so he sat up, though it took an effort. "Sounds like we have some catching up to do."

"First, tell me this—how did you find me?" Marla said.

"Well, it was complicated, but—"

"Did Elsie Jarrow help you?"

"Uh. Yeah. Wow. How'd you make that leap?"

"She visited me in the diner a while back. I didn't recognize her at the time, of course, but in retrospect…. I'm not one hundred percent sure why she wanted you to find me, though I have some ideas." She sighed and stood up. "We'd better get going. We've got a lot to do."

"We do?"

"Sure. You knew if you gave me back my memories, life would get complicated." She held out a hand and helped him to his feet.

"Oh, good. Complicated. Where do you want to go?"

"Is Rondeau settled back in Vegas? That's as good a home base as any. I've got some preparations to make… and a story to tell, I guess. Maybe two."

"Rondeau and Pelly are on their way here, actually, but I'll tell them to re-route."

She nodded, then surprised Bradley by embracing him. Marla was never much of a hugger. Trust her to get all touchy-feely when her breath smelled like sour vomit. "Hey. Thanks, B. I owe you, and I already owed you *anyway*."

"We're friends. You don't owe me anything."

"Doesn't mean I won't repay you, though." She paused. "Assuming we all survive the next week, anyway, which is maybe not super likely."

The River Lethe

THE NEXT NIGHT RONDEAU, BRADLEY, AND PELHAM sat on couches in the conversation pit in Rondeau's suite in Las Vegas, watching Marla, waiting for her to spin a tale. She wasn't quite sure how to begin.

Marla hadn't talked much on the drive from Arizona to Vegas, busy collating her own thoughts, putting things together, feeling out the possible paths to the future. Her goals were clear. How to achieve them less so. The *consequences* of achieving them were pretty clear to her, too; she just didn't like thinking about them. In some ways, the only thing worse than failure would be success.

"You sure you don't want Cole here?" Bradley said. "And Marzi. She's still an apprentice, figuring her shit out, but she could be helpful, too—she held her own against the Outsider when the time came."

Marla shook her head. "I can't ask them to help me with this. Cole's a friend. Marzi's an acquaintance. You're…." She scowled. "Are you going to make me say it?"

"You're my family, too," Rondeau said. "Anything you need, always."

"That was uncharacteristically earnest and sincere," Marla said.

He shrugged. "I thought you were lost forever. Turns out that's the way to make me miss you."

"Even so, guys… you should know my ultimate goal here. I want to overthrow the new god of Death and take his kingdom away from him. You're family, okay, but I can't even ask *you* to do that. Which isn't to say I won't take volunteers."

"I have followed you to Hell before, Mrs. Mason," Pelham said. "I will do so again."

"I'm not sure the 'Mrs.' applies anymore, since my husband died."

"Widows are addressed by the same title they used when their husbands were alive, Mrs. Mason."

"Suit yourself." She relaxed into the couch, or tried to. Her muscles still ached from the months of working in a diner, being on her feet day after day, and even a long session in Rondeau's palatial shower this morning hadn't washed all the kinks away. She could have used magic to soothe the hurt, but she wanted the reminder of all the time she'd lost. She tried not to think of the collective hours of suffering her period of amnesia had caused the denizens of the underworld.

"I'll go, too," Bradley said. "I've only really been to the underworld once, and I didn't get to see much of the place."

"You know I hate to be left out," Rondeau said. "Count me in."

Marla smiled. She'd expected them all to say yes, but it was gratifying to be right. "Thanks. With your help, I'm only facing almost certain defeat, instead of absolutely certain defeat. I should tell you what happened, after I saw you all last. How I went from the reigning monarch of the land of the dead to the queen of nothing. After that business with the Outsider in Felport, I was supposed to meet Bradley and Marzi at their hotel. I decided to take a shortcut through Hell, because it's safer than teleporting and faster than walking or taking a cab. But when I opened the door to the underworld..."

MARLA STEPPED THROUGH the office door, leaving her angry friends behind. They disapproved of how she'd dealt with Nicolette, freezing the witch into a lump of magical ice, keeping her in stasis forever—they thought Nicolette deserved her chance at redemption, but Marla had made the hard decision, and done what she thought was best, just like she *always* did. If they didn't like it, they could fuck off.

Her mind was a seething mass of misgivings, doubts, and even a treacherous thread of something that might have been regret—

But when she stepped through the door, cool serenity descended as always, and the part of her that fretted about the opinions of mortals receded into a tiny unilluminated portion of her mind. Her intellect became cool, vast, and not even remotely amused. Marla Mason was no more: she was the dread queen of the underworld now, the Bride of Death, and it was just a shame there was still time left on her mortal month in the world, because there was so much *work* to be done here below. Still, a bargain was a bargain, and had to be upheld.

The queen paused in the foyer that wasn't really a foyer at all. The walls were cracked, the ceiling a moldy ruin, the floor pitted and splintered. She'd noticed the disarray the last time she passed through the underworld, but hadn't thought much of it—the underworld's appearance was just a convenience, after all, because it had to look like *something*. Now, though, she could sense a deeper wrongness. Something about her realm was... broken.

She looked around, and the walls dissolved, shimmered, and became her throne room, a cavern of obsidian, onyx, and black marble. There were two chairs there, carved of sapphire and emerald. Once upon a time, one chair had been smaller than the other—the smaller chair belonged to Death's consort, a mortal raised to godhood to rule beside a creature more purely divine, to temper the cold reign of death with a spark of human warmth—but the queen had put a stop to *that* nonsense. She and her husband were co-regents, equal halves of a whole....

But Death wasn't here, now, and his emerald chair lay toppled on its side. She reached out for him, tried to sense him, which was normally as easy as sensing the position of her own left arm.

Nothing. Where could he be? Was *he* out, walking the Earth, for some reason? He'd come to Earth to help her, during the battle with the Outsider, but what other business did he have among the living?

She realized the compulsion to return to Earth, normally so overwhelming when it was time to fulfill her bargain and spend a month as a mortal, was gone. She felt no pull toward the mortal realm at all—as if the deal she'd struck to spend six months of each year on Earth had been broken. The bargain she'd made with her husband, Death. But what could break that arrangement?

"Marla."

The queen spun. There was another god here. That happened, sometimes: they could reach this place more easily than mortals, by passing through certain places that meant death to humans. Volcanoes, trenches in the deep oceans, miles-down caves teeming with blind monsters. The other gods came for favors, or to socialize, but Death and his queen routinely turned them away, too busy with their business overseeing the world's cycles of death and rebirth—without which there would have been no gods at all.

"I don't have time," she began, and then recognized him. "Wait. You're Reva. The god of the lost and displaced."

Reva bowed his head, not that he had a head, exactly. His form was purer, here, than when he appeared on Earth, and he was a man-shaped fog of mist and longings. "I am. I was… not friends with your husband, exactly… but acquaintances, certainly."

"You *were*? You aren't any more? Did you have a falling out?"

Reva shook his head. "Marla. The Outsider… when Death opened a door from this realm in the Outsider's presence, on that beach in San Francisco, the monster could sense the path to this place. The Outsider could find the passageways, and pry them open, and pass through. After I encountered the Outsider I could sense his actions, you see, because he was an exile himself, one of *my* creatures, as far from home as it is possible for anything to be. I felt him come here, and I pursued, to warn your husband, but I was too late." Reva sat down on the stony floor and put his head in his hands. "I'm sorry."

The rings. In Felport, fighting the Outsider, she'd noticed it wearing ostentatious, ornate rings. The monster hadn't worn jewelry in their earlier encounters, but she'd thought the rings were merely an ornament, a refinement of its human costume.

Her own husband, when he chose to appear in human form, often appeared wearing rings, each holding a precious stone from the wealth below the surface, each gem imbued with strange magics. The Outsider's increased power, its new abilities, in the final battle… It had stolen those powers from Death, consuming the god and gaining his strength.

"He is dead?" the queen rasped. "My husband is dead?" She touched the necklace at her throat, where her wedding ring dangled.

Reva didn't raise his head. "You're the only god of Death, now, Marla. I'm so sorry. This realm is yours alone, now… and it's incomplete. I don't know what happens next—if you should take a mortal consort, or if another Death will rise to replace your husband, or—"

In the back of her mind, the mortal part of Marla, the part that still longed to do good in the world, to care for her friends, to make amends, to make a difference, to kill monsters, to *do better*, howled in agony at the loss of her husband, and in fear at what the uncertain future might bring.

The greater part of her, the part that was now the only ruler of the land of the dead, howled in agonies of her own.

The agony of being cut in half, and left alone, to reign in Hell.

She snarled at Reva. "*Go!* Begone from this place!"

"There's no need to kill the messenger, Marla—"

"Don't call me that. Marla is a seed. I am the tree that grew from her. Her time is gone. New burdens have been laid on me, and I no longer have the luxury of bothering myself with mortal concerns. Begone, or I *will* kill you."

Reva held up his hands. "If there's anything I can do to help you, just let me know."

"You are the god of exiles. I am not an exile. I am *home*." She turned her back on him, and he wisped away, back toward the volcanic vent or undersea cave he'd used to come here.

The queen trembled, clenching her fists, her diamond-sharp nails drawing blood. Where the droplets fell, dark red flowers sprang up from the floor, and she howled and stomped them into the stone. Her husband

had always handled the rebirth parts of their reign: he was the one who brought back the sun and raised the flowers from their slumber. She was the black-tongued destroyer, bedecked with a belt of skulls, bringer of ice and winter. But now, flowers grew for her, because she was the only one, because she was the *all*.

She gestured, summoning the shade of a necromancer named Ayres who'd once thought to command the dead, and even made demands of Death himself. He appeared as an old man in a black undertaker's suit, head bowed, duly deferent. "You have my sympathies on your loss, majesty," he murmured.

"Your sympathies are unnecessary. What is the state of my kingdom?"

"The dead are uneasy in their afterlives, but nothing has fallen apart; the center holds. An untended garden does not turn immediately to wilderness, and the same is true here. The realm you and your husband built is strong."

"You will be my steward, for now," the queen said. "You are duly empowered. Set to right those things that have fallen out of true, and if you encounter something beyond your powers, tell me."

"Yes, majesty." She could sense his glee at the newfound responsibility and the powers that came with it, but she'd chosen him because he'd been a man of little imagination, and death had not changed him: he would do as he was told and wouldn't dare try to exceed his remit.

She looked at the toppled chair, and tears of blood welled in her eyes. She dashed them away. There was no time for mourning. She gestured, and the chair settled itself upright again. Let his throne be a memorial. Another gesture, and the cavern became blackness in all directions, full of stars, each star a mortal life. Some burned bright, and others guttered. She and Death had largely automated the process of death, and the migration of souls had continued even in the brief absence of a guiding mind. There were always complex situations, though: snagged souls, troubled passings—and she spent an interval setting those problems to right, easing paths, unsnarling tangled lifelines, and knocking down the flimsy magical structures of a few sorcerers who believed they'd found ways to confound, or capture, or elude death (the cessation of life) and/or Death (the deity who oversaw those processes).

When all the lights were taken care of, she brought back the throne room, and collapsed onto her own chair. She and Death used to take turns decorating their palace, expressing their will to create surroundings decadent or severe, Gothic or whimsical, as the mood struck. Now her unconscious mind (for even gods have hidden seas of thought) had decorated her throne room for a funeral, with red curtains, shrouded mirrors, black-blossomed flowers, and scores of candelabras.

She put her face in her hands and sobbed, allowing herself a few moments of wracking, ruined release. Death. Her Death. She thought of the first time she'd seen him, a swaggering tough, newly birthed from the primal womb of chaos where the gods grew. He'd come to threaten the mortal Marla Mason, to take her dagger of office, which unbeknownst to her was actually Death's terrible sword, won from a previous incarnation of Death by a sorcerer long years before. The Walking Death, they'd called him then, because he walked in the world. He'd worn his rings, and his sharp suit, and his blade of a smile, and he'd threatened her city, casually exerting cruel power to make her bend to his will.

But Marla Mason didn't bend, and had a streak of the contrarian as wide as the river Styx. She'd resisted, and so Death had exiled her from Felport, and taken over the place as his own, holding an entire city hostage. Rather than meet his demands, Marla had chosen to invade Hell, taking her friend Pelham to the underworld with her, planning to seize control of the underworld and hold *it* for ransom instead. An audacious plan, and one that didn't work out at all the way she'd intended. Before their fight was done, she found herself married to Death himself, and transformed into a god-by-proxy, because she needed access to that level of power. Then she'd used Death's terrible sword, a blade capable of cutting through time and dreams and abstract concepts, and performed surgery on the smug new god: she'd cut away the Walking Death's cruelty, his caprice, his savagery, and left behind only the parts of him that were *good*: his mercy, his sense of duty, his sense of humor, his flirtations, his gift for dry understatement. She'd carved him into a man she could love, and into a god fit to rule the land of the dead.

Who said you couldn't change a man? You just needed the right metaphysical tools.

What began as a marriage of magical necessity turned into a love match, in time. Death had sometimes joined her in the mortal world for travels and adventures. She'd learned the ways of gods in the underworld with him. They made love as mortals did, and as gods did, and if pressed, she couldn't have said which she preferred. Both the mortal Marla Mason and the dread queen of the underworld were closed-off creatures, unwilling to let anyone come too close, devoted to protecting themselves so they could better protect others. But Death had been the greatest exception to that, the only one to truly breach her defenses. He had become the home of her heart.

Now he was gone. She was a widow. A jagged half of a broken circle, with a realm to rule alone.

Ayres appeared before her, and she rose from her throne in alarm. One of his eyes was swollen shut, a gouge in his cheek bled, and he held one hand, twisted and withered, against his chest. His undertaker's suit was singed and torn. "Majesty," he said. "There is something terrible rising, in the depths of the primordial chaos."

The queen scowled. She'd gone into the depths during her last month in the underworld, to kill a monster that had invaded her realm and fed on the souls of the dead... though in the end she'd been unable to kill the beast, and had been forced to make an accommodation with it instead. "Not that *dragon* again?"

"No, majesty, she departed as promised, and has not attempted to return. This is... something new. I questioned him, and he struck me. He is rising through the sea of afterlives now. He says he is coming here. He says he is coming for *you*."

The air shimmered, and the queen suddenly wore elaborate armor made of bones, and ice, and precious metals. The terrible sword of Death appeared in her hand, glittering and envenomed. "Some monster thinks I am weak now, because my husband has died? He tries to strike at me because he thinks I cannot strike back? He will learn otherwise."

"I am no monster, woman." The voice reverberated through the cavern, booming and vast.

Ayres whimpered and crouched, squeezing his eyes shut.

A figured stepped into the light cast by the candles, and with every step he took, the throne room changed around him: the stone walls became bare rock, the candles smoky torches. He dragged a more primitive realm into immanence with him, and he seemed better matched to life in a cave than a palace: muscular, bronze-skinned, bare-chested and scarred, wearing rough-woven pants with a belt of rope, and no shoes on his feet. His body was that of a man, but his head was an immense bird's skull, perhaps a vulture's. Red lights glowed and streamed in his ocular cavities, like embers rising on warm updrafts.

The queen brandished her sword. Whether she felt fear or misgiving was unimportant: she had her duty, and she would defend her realm. "How dare you come to this place uninvited? Those who do so often find it impossible to leave."

He stopped a few feet away from the huddled form of Ayres, the edges of his cave shimmering against those of her palace. "I have no intention of leaving. Travel to the mortal world is a corrupting influence. I wish to remain pure." He glanced at Ayres. "You were a horrible man, weren't you? Avaricious, selfish, petulant, petty. You would have done even more damage than you did, if you'd had a stronger mind. Your afterlife has not been pleasant, I see, dwelling in a little world shaped by your own failings and fears… but it is not harsh enough for justice. You deserve a worse Hell. Go to it." He gestured, and Ayres vanished.

The queen widened her eyes and tightened her grip on the sword. She tried to call her steward back, but though she could sense Ayres, she could no longer reach him. He was back in the bubble of his own afterlife, which—like all the afterlives of every soul in this place—was shaped according to his own expectations, decorated and populated from the jumble of his living memories and the vestiges of his living mind.

Or, at least, it had been. Now the interior of his bubble was full of fire, screams, pursuits, knives, and more terrible things: punishments inflicted on him by demons. She tried to reach through the barrier, to bring him out of that place of torment, but the permeable borders of his afterlife were solid as iron now.

She screamed and launched herself at the skull-headed interloper, but he merely crossed his arms, and the ground beneath her feet turned to mud, then solidified again around her ankles, holding her in place. The reality of his cave spread like ink through water, encroaching on her palace, overwriting the red velvets and dark walls with damp, unhewn stone.

He sat cross-legged on the ground before her, head cocked, and when she swung the sword at his head from her fixed position, he caught the flat of the blade between his palms, twisted his wrists, and wrenched the sword from her grasp. Her armor fell to pieces around her, bone and ice clattering on the cave floor. She stood in a shift of white cotton, and she trembled.

"There," he said. "That's better." He adjusted his legs, sitting in the lotus position. "I am the new god of Death. The universe sensed the absence of the old god, and drew me into being. I floated in the dark at the bottom of the primordial chaos for a time, growing to understand the realm I was made to rule. I watched your return, and your attempt to set the ruin to right. I admit you are competent, in your way, but your fundamental principles are soft and corrupt. They simply won't do."

The queen frowned. "*You* are my new husband?"

He shrugged. "Technically, I suppose—"

"There is nothing technical about it. I am married to Death. That means I am married to you."

"Traditionally, the mortal consort of the god of Death goes into oblivion with the god."

"Traditionally, the god of Death and his consort rule for centuries or millennia, and pass on naturally, according to cycles of death and rebirth that are beyond even our understanding, *husband*. Traditionally, death isn't murdered by a monster from another universe. I'm not sure what good relying on *tradition* will do us here, and anyway, I'm not going anywhere. I'm not the hurl-myself-onto-the-funeral-pyre type." She scowled hard at her feet, exerting her will, and the floor released her feet. Rather than aim a kick at her new husband's face, she sat down across from him. "We're going to be working together. Frankly, I could use the help. Let us find a way to move forward, for the good of this realm, and the world beyond."

He shook his head. "You *stink* of mortality, woman."

"That mortal core is the whole *point* of me, husband. Death takes a mortal consort because his business is mortality, and it's useful to have a reminder of what the living are actually like. I don't like mortal-me all that much better than you do—she's irrational and pig-headed and always thinks she's right—but she serves an important purpose. Circumstances here can become a bit too rarefied and removed from the reality of the living."

"Pig-headed? Always thinks she's right? It is not only your mortal form that exhibits such qualities, woman. I have reviewed your tenure. You attacked my predecessor with his own blade, and altered his personality."

"He was unpleasant. I made him better."

"You *diminished* him. How do I know you won't turn on me some day, and cut away those parts of myself you find objectionable?"

"I can make a promise. When gods promise, they stick. Though to be honest, you seem rather unpleasant, too. Are you sure you wouldn't like a trim? I'm a deft hand with a magical scalpel."

He crossed his arms over his chest. "You do not amuse. You, a creature born of man and woman, dare question, dare *change*, beings born of infinite possibility?"

"Who are you to question me? Who's got more experience ruling Hell? You were *literally* born yesterday. Those scars on your chest are decorative. I've earned mine."

"I may be new to this world, but I came to life infused with the wisdom of my forebears, and a more basic, fundamental understanding of the nature of my role and reality than you will ever possess. You had to learn to rule Hell: I was *born* knowing how. That is why my will is stronger than yours, here, and why the nature of this place responds to my desires more readily than yours."

"You know, the old Death and I ruled as equal partners—"

"Nonsense. You were selfish. You insisted on spending fully half the year living as a mortal, leaving the old Death to shoulder the burdens of rule himself the rest of the time, juggling affairs in the underworld *and* the world above."

"The Persephone clause wasn't *my* idea. Take it up with my mortal self. I much prefer the distance and perspective godhood provides. That restriction seems to have been lifted, now, anyway, so I can stay by your side." Somewhere inside the queen, her mortal self howled, and she thought of Bradley, Rondeau, Pelham, those mortals she was so attached too, and of the strangers she thought she could help, too. But the queen could ignore her mortal self's outrage. In several decades, at most, her friends would be dead anyway, and dwelling here, as would any innocents Marla might have helped. *Everyone* came here eventually.

"I have no desire to rule beside you, woman. We have... differing ideas. You and my predecessor ran a remarkably lax realm. You truly let the dead souls organize their own afterlives?"

The queen shrugged. "Why not? They're given a little bubble of primal chaos to shape as they see fit. Those who expect flames and damnation get it. Those who expect angels and harps get that. Those with less clear expectations end up in some sort of dreamland of their own unconscious devising. Most of them don't even realize they're dead. It keeps them occupied and at peace, mostly."

He shook his vulture's head. "Such freedom is offensive. I looked in on the afterlife of a man who was a deranged killer in his life, and his realm was horrifying, continuing his Earthly activities."

The queen rolled her eyes. "Sure, but now all his crimes are committed against imaginary constructs. They're no more real than daydreams. He's not hurting anyone anymore."

"Yes, but neither is he suffering for his crimes."

"You want to punish him? Well, go ahead. I held the odd personal grudge or two from my mortal life, and made things unpleasant for some people, and improved a few afterlives, too. It's petty, but gods can be permitted a little pettiness, I suppose. There's no point in punishing anyone, though. The idea of eternal suffering as a deterrent for undesirable activity is already prevalent in the mortal world, without any need for it to be *true*—and anyway, the threat of eternal suffering is used to deter all kinds of harmless behavior, and frankly, it's a lazy way to run a system of morality. Life's hard enough for most people without making their afterlife hard, too. We aren't in the business of rehabilitating people, either. There's no point. They're *dead*. They aren't going anywhere. Why not let them stew in their own juices? It's more practical."

"There need to be consequences for those who commit transgressions in life."

"Why? Look, as a mortal I was brutal, uncompromising, and unforgiving... but I was also a pragmatist. There already are consequences for people who do bad things. They get *death*. That's not just the wages of sin; that's the wages of everything."

"We have fundamentally different worldviews. I believe in justice. Harsh, fair, and eternal."

"Okay. But I've been a god, and a mortal, and something in between, so I know what I'm talking about, and you don't. You want to torment the souls of the dead, for no reason, forever? That's just sadistic."

"That is justice. And that is how it shall be, from now on."

"Not on my watch."

"I am stuck with you as a consort, woman... but I don't really need your help to rule here. I believe my earlier incarnations allowed themselves to be distracted. Meddling in Earthly affairs, easing the passage of souls, ushering in the seasons... none of that appeals to me. The dead will die, and come here, and this is the only realm I care about. I will cede the mortal realm to you, then: we will be married, but separated. If you love the living so much, so you may dwell among them."

The queen hesitated. She would hate to give up her access to this wondrous realm, and taking on responsibility for the greening of the Earth was hardly playing to her strengths as a destroyer, but the core of her *did* enjoy life in the world above... it might not be such a terrible bargain to strike. She hardly relished the idea of ruling alongside this New Death, anyway. "What will you do with the underworld, if I cede control to you?"

"Cede? I will *take* control. I do not require your permission. As for my plans... it is time to return this realm to the classics. To the visions of Dante, and Bosch, and the nine hells of China, and the dark caves where the weeping dead eat clay and twitter like birds, and the icy caverns of

Hel. You prefer to see the afterlife shaped by human imagination? That's fine. I will look there for my inspiration as well."

She shook her head. "And what about the guiltless? The blameless?"

"Mmm. The very young, perhaps, can be spared—they wouldn't understand the terrors inflicted upon them anyway. But everyone else… no one is truly *blameless*. Even those lauded for their nobility in life held evil in their hearts." He shrugged. "I may refine my system in time, but for now, blanket torment seems simplest. It will be appropriate for more of the dead than not."

"So you want to turn my underworld of infinite variation into a scary theme park? No. It won't happen. You don't want to fight me, Death. War in Hell isn't good for anyone."

He stood up, and as he did, the throne room vanished, replaced by a gritty, ashen plane, beside a sluggishly flowing river. The terrible sword was in the New Death's hand, now, and he approached her. The queen rose and stepped backward, retreating before his slow approach, though each step took her closer to that river's banks.

"I'm not sure what would happen if I killed you," the New Death said. "I'm not even certain I can. But I can certainly rid myself of you. Send you back to Earth, and out of my way."

"You think you can just kick me out, birdbrain? That hasn't worked too well for people, historically."

"Your destiny is exile, woman. No one likes having you around." His skull shifted, the beak drawing inward, the shape of the bones shifting, and now he had the skull of some dire-fanged wolf instead. "The water behind you is another of the classics: the river Lethe, where flow the waters of forgetfulness."

"Yes, I *know*. We used to allow a little bit of Lethe water to be exported to the mortal world. There's no better potion for selective memory erasure in the world." She stopped on the shores of the river.

"All commerce with the Earthly realm will cease under my reign. Dead souls will come in, but nothing will go out. The dead will keep to themselves. No more ghostly visitations, no more oracles, no more necromancy. Which means you should take a last look around." He pushed the point of the sword into her chest, and she gasped as the icy blade pierced her. "Go. Into the water. Submerge yourself. Erase your memories. You need not be conscious of your purpose in order to fulfill it: merely being alive will suffice for the seasons to continue, for the cycles of life and death to go on."

"You want me to be a mindless Fisher King for the whole world?"

He shrugged. "Not mindless. Merely ignorant of your true nature. I will return you to Earth, to a place where you may live in peace, with resources to begin a new life. You will retain your physical immortality. These are my promises to you."

She straightened her back, raising her chin. "And if I refuse to go?"

"I wasn't giving you a choice." He lunged forward with the sword, and she dodged aside, but his attack was a feint. The waters of the river Lethe rose up behind her, given shape and form by the New Death's will: a vast bearlike creature made of water wrapped its dripping arms around her, squeezing her, and dragged her down. She screamed defiance, and threats, and rage as she went, until the waters of the river filled her mouth, and obliterated her self.

Death and Chaos

"HOLY CRAP," BRADLEY SAID.

"What a dick," Rondeau said.

"How unseemly," Pelham said.

Marla nodded. "Yeah. All that. So, here I am. Exiled from the place I pledged to serve and protect. *Again*. It's a good thing I don't believe in fate or destiny, because if I did, I'd wonder why the powers that be always pick on me. And I *am* the powers that be."

"Do you, uh… I mean… can you still do the stuff a god can do?" Bradley asked.

"You mean can I lay waste to my surroundings with fire and earthquake, survive a direct nuclear bomb blast, live forever even if I forget to eat, things like that? Yeah, sure. I've got all kinds of powers that somebody walking around in the mortal world probably shouldn't possess, and thanks to Bradley's very thorough job restoring my memory, I actually *understand* the full extent of my capabilities now. I'd make a kickass superhero, and I could probably subjugate the human race, if I were feeling more villainous. What good does any of that power do me, though? My connection to the underworld has been severed. The New Death has closed all the borders. I can't even *sense* Hell anymore. He exiled me and changed the locks. I'm surprised you were even able to summon the ghost of Emperor Norton, B. You're more powerful than the New Death realized."

"We call him 'Skully,'" Rondeau said.

Marla snorted. "Nice. And even then, Skully didn't let you talk to the Emperor long before he slammed that connection closed, too. You're strong, B, but my new husband is a lot stronger. On the plus side, I doubt he knows I got my memory back. He really doesn't seem to care at all what happens up here in the realm of the living, so maybe I have the element of surprise."

Rondeau raised his hand. "At the risk of being the dumb guy asking ignorant questions... why not take Skully's deal? Keep doing your thing on Earth. *Be* that great superhero. Help the helpless, save the innocent, live forever, and avoid your jerk of a husband entirely."

Marla shook her head. "What's the point of saving people in this world, if I know they're going to suffer forever in the afterlife? Sure, some people always had a horrible time in the underworld, but only if they believed they were *supposed* to—if that was the afterlife they imagined. Most people just spent their afterlives in a sort of hazy dream, and the more imaginative ones got to experience amazing impossible worlds, for eternity. But Skully wants every person in the world to spend forever trapped in his torture porn dollhouse universe, just because he thinks that's what a death god *should* do." She sighed. "I'm still a ruler of Hell. I have a responsibility to the souls under my care. I can't take the easy path of semi-retirement. I have to fix things."

"Yeah, okay," Rondeau said. "I withdraw my stupid question."

"Why did such a terrible god rise?" Pelham said.

Marla shook her head. "I have no idea. He's the third god of Death I've met. The first was a megalomaniacal control freak. The second, before I did surgery on his personality, was a smug, selfish jerk. This one is a sadist with a nasty sense of cosmic justice. Who knows? I think human expectations shape the nature of gods, to some degree... and humans have a pretty dark view of death, mostly. It could be worse. This is an isolationist god of death. We could have gotten an expansionist one—a Death with wings of dust and shadow, wearing a robe covered in eyes, swooping over the mortal world, killing firstborn, trying to annex Earth as a subdivision of Hell, who knows what."

"Oh, well," Bradley said. "Now I feel positively lucky."

Marla nodded. "Always happy to correct your perspective. Anyway. I have to stop the New Death and save the billions of souls that should be under my care. That means I have to somehow get into Hell, when all the borders are closed."

"I have an idea," Pelham said. "We could die." The others stared at him. He shrugged. "I didn't say it was an *appealing* idea. But if death is the only door to the underworld that remains...."

Marla shook her head. "Wouldn't work for me. I've still got physical immortality, so I can't die my way back home. I'd happily accept you guys as my mercenary goon squad, but it wouldn't work. The souls of the dead maintain continuity of personality, mostly, but they're subject to the will of the gods. The dead can shape the primal chaos of the underworld, but only to the extent that the gods of death lets them do so. If you died, you'd be at Skully's mercy, and he might even take a personal interest in you because you're friends of mine. Also you'd be dead. I don't want any of you to be dead."

"We are too young and pretty to die," Rondeau said. "Especially me."

"So what's the alternative?" Bradley said. "If the trains and portals and stairways and sinkholes that lead to Hell are all sealed up, how do we get in?"

"We find someone who's good at getting into places where she's not welcome, and ask for help." Marla sighed. "She'll probably be along any minute now."

"Who?" Bradley said, and then the doorbell rang, a loud *ding-dong.* Which was strange, because the suite didn't even have a doorbell.

"Yeah, that'll be her," Marla said. "Come in!"

Rondeau stood up. "I'll get it. The door's locked, and I've got the bolt turned and the chain on—"

The door swung open, and Elsie Jarrow walked in, dressed in a stylish black dress, wearing oversized sunglasses, with a shopping bag dangling from one slim arm. "Darlings!" she cried. "So good to see you all again. What a luscious lot you are." She dropped the bag, kicked the door closed behind her, and approached Marla, arms outstretched, fingers wiggling and beckoning. Marla consented to let the chaos witch—who was so much more than that, now—hug her. Elsie smelled of strawberries and, faintly, blood. She took a step back, but kept her hands on Marla's shoulders, gazing into her face. "Look at us," she said. "We're more like sisters than ever, hmm? Like two gods in a pod."

"Thanks for joining us," Marla said. "Have a seat."

Elsie threw herself onto the couch between Pelham and Bradley, putting her arms around them. They both tried to shrink away, and she grabbed them more tightly. "Now, now, boys, circumstances have made us enemies in the past, but now we have a common goal: to help Marla regain her throne. I'm here to help."

"Why do you want to help, though?" Rondeau said. "I get that you've been *elevated* or whatever, but why are you all the sudden on Team Marla?"

"Us girl gods have to stick together." Elsie winked at Marla. "Besides, I owe Marla a debt. She's the reason I'm the chaos goddess you see before you. Did she tell you the story of how I became so fabulous and powerful and fabulously powerful?"

Marla pinched the bridge of her nose. Being in Elsie's presence was giving her a headache. She'd better get used to the feeling. "No, I focused more on telling them about the rise of the New Death and how he exiled me from my realm."

Elsie waved her hand. "The fact that a new god arose and exiled you is pretty much all I need to know, Marla darling. No need for details. The story of how I became a goddess is much more interesting. You see, after you cruelly murdered my body and dissolved my consciousness in the ocean—"

"Elsie, please. We just *had* story time. I'd like to focus on the future right now."

That chaos god wrinkled her nose. "Oh, fine. But you have to tell them later. I get bored when people stop talking about me for too long."

Marla nodded. "Yeah, okay. I'll tell them. Partly because, in a weird way, the story of how you became a god helps explain why I was such a bitch to Nicolette, and froze her in a magical iceberg even though she was trying to redeem herself. I'd like you guys to understand why I did that."

"We just assumed it was basic vengeful nastiness," Rondeau said. "But I'm always interested in extenuating circumstances. They're probably my third favorite kind of circumstance, right after 'mitigating' and 'unforeseen.'"

Marla ignored him. "Gratitude doesn't quite convince me, though, Elsie. You're a trickster god, now, and the social contract doesn't really apply to you. Why did you help my friends track me down? Why are you here now?"

Elsie arranged her skirts over her knees, smiling like she knew all the secrets in the world. "Oh, partly I intervened just to see what your boys would do. The world is just more interesting when I meddle, and needle, and nudge. But also because I like the world with Marla Mason in it. You're too practical for my tastes, and I have a far more highly developed sense of whimsy than you do, but you never fail to shake things up. You're a walking, talking disruption of the status quo. And your new husband...." She scowled, and the room visibly darkened, all the lamps dimming for a moment. "He's no fun at *all*. I've had some lovely times in the underworld, and I'm irked that I can't go back. His closed-door policy means no more necromancers, no more zombies, no demons, no illicit trade in Lethe

water, precious little in the way of ghosts, no renegade psychopomps…
What a waste of potential strangeness!"

Marla nodded. "That sounds… halfway plausible. Can you get us
into the underworld, Elsie? I know the entryways are sealed, but if there's
anyone with a knack for wriggling through tiny cracks, it's you."

"Oh, I have an idea. I know a way in—a passageway the New Death
doesn't know about. It's surprisingly difficult to protect yourself against
those unknown unknowns. Actually getting to Hell should be the easy
part. You and I will need to make preparations for what to do *after* we get
there. We need to arm ourselves for a war in Hell. In the meantime, can
we send your boys to fetch the key to the underworld?"

"Is it literally a key?" Marla said.

"No, it's only figuratively a key. It's *literally* a sword. It's also literally in
the hands of a violent man with a ridiculous worldview named Dave. The
man is named Dave, not the worldview. Or, no, wait, maybe that's not his
name. Anyway, I *call* him Dave. He won't want to give up the sword, but
I'm sure your boys can be very persuasive."

"You're sending us to find a sword," Bradley said. "Which will somehow
get us to the underworld. Elsie, is this a joke where the punch line is you
stab us to death with the sword and we die our way into Hell after all?"

She shook her head hard enough to make her hair fly around. "It's
not that kind of joke at all! It's an entirely different sort of joke. No, this is
a genuinely magical sword, forged by a god. Or maybe not actually forged,
like with a forge and a hammer and… tongs… and things. Probably it was
just imagined into existence. I've heard it called the Blade of Banishment. I
suggested renaming it the 'Épéé of Exile' but apparently it's not an épéé and
I should have been very embarrassed about making such a categorization
error, but I wasn't, because I can't remember how to feel shame. I told Dave
it was called Night's Plutonian Sword."

"That's… not incredibly enlightening," Bradley said.

"Oh. You want advice." She put her forefinger against her lips and
went *hmm*. "First off, I'd avoid letting Dave hit you with the sword. On
the plus side, Dave is not a very good swordsman. On the minus side,
he doesn't really have to be, on account of how it's a magical sword." She
clapped her hands, once, sharply. "Do you think you can handle this
mission-critical, um, mission? Even though you're just a ragtag team of
psychics and butlers and whatever Rondeau is?"

"I'm rich," Rondeau said. "That's what I am. Maybe we can buy the
sword off Dave."

"I can make people go to sleep by looking at them hard," Bradley said. "So we can just knock Dave out and take the sword away."

"I find that most problems can be worked out if people of good will simply discuss their needs and agree to act in good faith," Pelham said. "I'm sure Mr.... Dave... will listen to reason."

"Marvelous!" Elsie said. "I'm sure *one* of those approaches will work. Dave lives in the mountains of North Carolina. Beautiful country, or so many people claim. You'll love it, assuming you like that sort of thing. Once you've got the sword, give me a call. My number's in your phones now, along with Dave's GPS coordinates. I trust you can make your own way there?"

Rondeau sighed. "I guess I'd better pack. I just got *unpacked.*" He rose and went to one of the suite's bedrooms, with Pelham and Bradley following, arguing over whether to travel by airplane or by more magical means.

"Where are *we* going?" Marla said, once she and Elsie were alone.

"To visit a few gods," Elsie said. "You and your husband were always cranky and standoffish, but me, I'm the sociable type, and I've made ever so many friends among the deities since my ascension. We should be able to borrow a few things we can use to show the New Death the error of his ways." Elsie nodded toward the bedroom. "Have you told them what will happen if you manage to win? What you'll have to do if you want to *really* secure your position as the ruler of Hell?"

Marla shook her head. "Shh. I'm waiting for the right time."

"Ooh," Elsie said. "*Secrets.*"

Night's Plutonian Sword

"**We could rent a private plane,**" Bradley said. "Rondeau's rich."

Rondeau glared at him, then zipped his overnight bag closed. "It's true that a casino is almost literally a license to print money, but when you spend a bunch of the money you printed, printing up more still takes *time*."

Bradley snorted. "Well, I'd say let's try the mirror again, but it wasn't the most pleasant travel experience I've ever had."

"I would prefer not to take such a risk," Pelham said. "I am more than content to fly commercially, however. A private plane is a needless extravagance."

"We're probably going to die in a couple of days, and then suffer for all eternity under the lash of a guy with a skull for a head," Rondeau said. "I guess we should enjoy some extravagances while we still can. Fine. I'll call my plane guy."

Two hours later they were taking off, relaxing comfortably in a lavish business jet with leather seats the color of brown butter. "I wonder what Marla and Elsie are doing right now?" Bradley swiveled in his chair, watching Las Vegas shrink out the windows.

"Probably god stuff." Rondeau popped a grape into his mouth. "Above my pay grade, which is saying something, because my pay grade is hella high."

Bradley nodded. "Right. Better them than us. So, we've got to see a guy about a sword. What's the plan?"

Rondeau gestured at Pelham. "Pelly is the tactics guy. He should decide."

Pelham sighed. "While I possess some skill at planning such operations, I lack the necessary information to make any such provisions now. All we know is a set of GPS coordinates and our target's first name, which, it seems, is likely not even his *real* first name."

"I called Cole to ask about the sword," Bradley said. "Magical blades used to be a sorcerous growth market, but they've fallen out of fashion in recent centuries. There are still a few badass mystical objects rattling around from the old days, though. Unfortunately, Cole's never heard of the Blade of Banishment or Night's Plutonian Sword. He says the latter is probably a pun on that Edgar Allan Poe line from 'The Raven,' about 'Night's Plutonian shore,' which is Poe's fancy way of describing the afterlife."

Rondeau grunted. "So it's a sword that… sends you to the afterlife? I mean, not to be an asshole or anything, but can't *non*-magical swords do that, too? Or kitchen knives? Or pistols? Or rocks?"

"Elsie says it's not as simple as killing us with the sword, though."

Rondeau nodded. "Good thing she's totally trustworthy."

Bradley sighed. "There is that."

Pelham squinted at the screen of the tablet in his hands. He often called such devices "abominable abominations," "affronts to decency," and "the death of the noble art of conversation," but Rondeau noticed he always made a point of buying the new models when they came out, and getting unlimited data plans. Pelly liked to know things, and having a world of information (including secret sorcerous bits of the darknet) at his disposal was his little addiction.

"I do find several thousand references to the phrase 'Blade of Banishment' online," Pelham said. "Most seem to reference music of a rather *belligerent* tone played by bands with an excess of umlauts in their names. There are also references to swords by that name in various RPGs, which in this context I take to mean roleplaying games, and not rocket-propelled grenades. There *is* one citation, however, referring to an out-of-print book of short stories by a pulp fantasist named Roderick Barrow. I cannot find a copy for sale electronically, and only a few used copies in print, but there are a handful of relevant pages scanned and posted to a voracious reader's personal web page. According to what I can access of Barrow's story, the Blade of Banishment is used to dispatch one's enemies and remove them permanently from the field without spilling blood or leaving a body behind—it is also called a 'sword of terrible mercies' and 'the sword of unrecoverable losses.' Instead of striking down the enemy, it simply sends them *away*, to some unspecified location from which no one has ever returned."

Bradley grunted. "You think some sorcerer—or, well, god, if Elsie's telling the truth—read that story and decided to make a version of the sword in real life?"

Pelham shook his head. "Again, I feel I have insufficient information to draw any conclusions."

Rondeau took a swig of ginger ale and belched. "So when we get to Nowheresville NC, we'll find this guy Dave, and we'll ask him. I've got a briefcase full of cash, Bradley's got a head full of brain knives, and Pelham has his gentlemanly arts, or whatever. Dave doesn't stand a chance. The sword is in the bag. Or the scabbard. Whatever it is you put swords in."

THE NEAREST AIRFIELD with car rental facilities was a ninety minute drive from the coordinates Elsie had provided, and it was already early evening when they landed. The trio deplaned directly onto the small runway, and everywhere they looked were hills and greenery, and, though it was too dark to see them, Rondeau knew there were smoky mountain peaks in the near distance; basically the opposite of Vegas. "God, what's wrong with the *air*?" Rondeau said, gagging.

"It's fresh?" Bradley said. "There's, uh, humidity?"

"I bet you can't even find a craps game out here," Rondeau said. "How about we go to a decent hotel, for local values of 'decent,' and get a good dinner, for local values of 'good,' and then grab some sleep? We can go looking for Dave in the morning."

Bradley shook his head. "Or, alternately, we could get this over with, since the fates of billions of dead souls are depending on us."

Rondeau scowled. "You know, I've gradually come around to the idea that it's worthwhile to worry about the fate of the living, but this whole worrying about the fate of the *dead* thing, that takes some getting used to."

"The dead do outnumber us," Pelham said. "The phrase 'silent majority' originally referred not to some mythical population of very quiet conservatives, but, instead, to the legions of the dead."

"That was today's history minute with Pelham," Rondeau said. "Can I at least rent a really ridiculous SUV?"

"Something with four-wheel-drive is a good idea anyway," Bradley said, gazing at the trees. "I was looking at the map, and the marked roads stop a good mile or so from the coordinates we were given."

Rondeau's black credit card worked its usual dark magic, and they acquired a dark blue vehicle that could comfortably seat six and uncomfortably seat eight, with satellite radio and GPS and heated seats and other sparkling amenities. "I wish we had time to lay some charms on the thing," Rondeau said. "It's been a while since I drove a vehicle that actually had the capacity to roll over and explode."

"In that case, I'd better drive." Pelham reached for the keys. "I believe I am the most qualified."

"I've been driving a lot longer than he has," Rondeau said, "but... yeah, he's right. He's taken classes in evasive driving, defensive driving, offensive driving, stunt driving, and who knows what else, and he's a quick study with stuff like that." He dropped the keys in Pelham's hand.

"One endeavors to give satisfaction," Pelham murmured.

"I call not-shotgun." Rondeau clambered into the back, and let Bradley ride up front. They found the Interstate, then a smaller state highway headed northwest, and the lights of the city receded into the distance. Soon they were the only vehicle in sight, a little capsule of light and life hurtling through darkness, rising into the higher elevations fast enough that Rondeau's ears popped. He looked out the window, into the dark, where the dim shapes of trees blurred past, occasionally opening into moon-and-starlit vistas that seemed to prominently feature sheer drop-offs and a notable absence of guardrails.

"Does anyone else feel like we're driving into one of those hill-folk cannibal horror movies?" he asked.

"There's definitely that sort of vibe," Bradley agreed. "We're in some kind of dead zone, for sure. The conventional phone service is non-existent here—if we weren't magically augmented, we'd be totally cut off from outside communication. I think there's a road up here on the right, Pelly—looks like that's going to get us as close to the coordinates as anything else."

Pelham slowed down, the headlights illuminating pine trees and mossy boulders, and proceeded at a crawl. Even then they nearly missed the turn-off: an unmarked asphalt road so crowded by overgrown rhododendrons that it was effectively a one-lane passage. They turned and drove slowly along the bumpy road, past the sagging remains of an old, half-demolished barn; past the burned-out hulk of an ancient station wagon; past a rusted swing set with no swings.

"I think I've played this video game," Rondeau said. "It's either zombies or demon-possessed townsfolk next."

"You need a *town* for townsfolk." Bradley swiped at his phone. "This is unincorporated land. I mean, maybe people farm out here, though how you farm this vertical-ass land is beyond me."

"I understand that operating small methamphetamine laboratories is a popular occupation in the area," Pelham said. "Also a certain amount of farming, though I gather cash crops such as marijuana are more lucrative than corn. There is also some history of militias and apocalyptic cults operating in this area, drawn by the combination of natural beauty and privacy."

"So your basic heartland kind of place is what you're saying," Rondeau said.

"Our coordinates are about a mile and half west of here," Bradley said. "Are we going to be hiking through the dark? Maybe Rondeau's whole wait-for-morning thing wasn't such a bad idea. We passed some kind of rustic cabin motel a few miles back, maybe we could turn around...."

"There's a side road." Rondeau pointed. Then he winced. "Wait, I mean, yes, Bradley's right, let's definitely do the motel room thing. That's not a side road. The side road is an illusion."

Bradley *hmmed*. "That road's not marked on the map, but it goes the right direction."

Pelham turned onto the dirt track, uneven and cratered, and they bumped slowly along. The moon had passed behind a cloud, and the darkness outside was absolute. The only sound was the low thrum of the engine and whatever noises the three of them made. After about a mile the headlights illuminated a rusty gate blocking the road, and Pelham stopped. They silently read the handmade signs hanging on the gate: "Trespassers will be shot, stuffed, and mounted"; "Down with the Secret World Government"; "This is sovereign land"; "Taxes = Slavery = Death"; "America for AMERICANS."

"Oh, Dave," Bradley said. "You're one of *those*. How does an anti-government loony get his hands on a weird magical sword?"

"Perhaps he found it hidden in some cache of ancient treasures in a local cave?" Pelham said.

"Or in the back of an antique store," Rondeau said. "Remember Marla's magical cloak? She found that in a thrift shop. It sounds like this sword is some kind of artifact, and artifacts sometimes *like* to be found."

Pelham moved the car to the side of the road and parked, and they all climbed out. The night had turned cool, and Rondeau shivered. With the headlights out, this whole place was darker than dark, the only illumination the glow from Bradley's phone. "The coordinates are about two hundred yards that way. Pretty sure we're walking into some kind of survivalist compound, so, uh, proceed with caution?"

Pelham had a backpack with him, and now he rooted through it, removing a set of night-vision goggles that he strapped to his face. Combined with his three-piece suit, it gave him the look of a very dapper insect. "I don't have your exceptional psychic vision," he said. "I must rely on other means."

"Oh, right." Rondeau blinked and squinted. He'd spent a long time learning how to tone down his exceptional senses, because seeing through every illusion and into every shadow, sensing every line of mystical energy, and perceiving every magical disturbance or quirk in the world around him, was frankly exhausting and stressful; as a result, he'd learned a kind of complacent blindness. Now he allowed his psychic senses to come online, and the view before him brightened, all the trees limned with a silvery light that indicated they were alive and thriving. He could see faint yellow-green traces in the air of past human occupation: one man, at least, had walked down this track to the gate and then back again, probably just hours ago. "Whoa," he whispered. "This psychic vision is a lot prettier in the country."

"Kind of lights up the place like the Vegas strip, huh?" Bradley whispered back. "But classier."

"Mr. Dave seems likely to possess an arsenal," Pelham said. "I believe you came provisioned against that eventuality, Mr. Bowman?"

Bradley fished a handful of chains with dangling shell casings in place of pendants from his pocket. "These necklaces are pretty much just magical Kevlar, all right? If somebody shoots you, that kinetic energy still has to go somewhere. You'll feel the impact, and it'll maybe even knock you down, but the bullet won't penetrate your body. The charm makes you stab-proof, too, so being hit with a sword won't hurt any more than getting hit with a baseball bat."

"That is nevertheless extremely painful," Pelham said.

"Yeah, but better blunt-force trauma than having your limbs lopped off." He handed a charm to Pelham, then Rondeau, and then put one on himself. "Come on. I'll lead."

He clambered over the gate, and Rondeau and Pelham followed, the latter leaping over it as adroitly as a gymnast. Pelly looked like a fussy clerk, but he was probably the most physically fearsome of all three of them. He'd been a master of bartitsu when he joined Marla's service, and since then, in his world travels, he'd picked up a few other martial skills, too. Rondeau had seen him toss a three-hundred-pound, six-foot-eight biker through a window once, without the aid of magical strength augmentation; it was all just the practical application of physics and biodynamics, Pelly said. With his physical expertise and Bradley's well-trained brain-powers, Rondeau was pretty comfortable taking the rear.

The dirt road narrowed until it became just a track through the woods, barely wide enough for one person to walk at a time. "Wait," Bradley said. "Is that a tripwire?"

Pelham wasn't looking at the ground, but up into a tree. "Indeed. There is a large log, studded with spikes, balanced above us."

"Old-school." Bradley stepped over the wire carefully. "Better than land mines, I guess."

"Thanks for that cheerful thought," Rondeau muttered.

They avoided two more booby traps on the way, and then Bradley noticed more of the luminous trails that indicated recent human passage, some distance off in the woods. They picked their way through the trees and found another, much less obvious trail, running roughly parallel to the first, about twenty yards away; *that* one seemed comparatively free of murderous surprises, and was probably how Dave and any of his patriotic compatriots went to-and-fro without risk of death by stumbling.

A short time later, the trail ended at a walled compound… though "compound" was probably overstating it a bit. The walls were roughly eight feet high, made of sheet metal nailed to wooden posts, and there was a "watchtower" on the wall that was actually just a deer stand with delusions of grandeur. The air stank faintly of diesel, and a generator grumbled somewhere behind the walls.

Pelham pointed to some protrusions studded along the wall. "Motion-sensitive lights."

"Do you have any super-spy stuff that can short out electronics?" Rondeau whispered.

"Regretfully, I do not."

"Bradley? Magic us invisible?"

Bradley shook his head. "My invisibility magics are less about actual real deal *invisibility* and more about clouding the minds of observers, so, not much good when it comes to lights."

"Well, fuck it, then." Rondeau walked out of the trees, over the protests of his friends. There was a stretch of bare dirt maybe thirty yards wide between the woods and the wall, doubtless so the survivalists could see the inevitable ATF agents begin their future raid. Once Rondeau had taken a few steps from cover, the lights came on, blindingly bright, and he shaded his eyes. "Hey, Dave!" he shouted. "My name's Rondeau, I have a briefcase full of money, and I want to buy some weapons!"

BRADLEY GROANED AND SANK back into the trees. "He's going to get himself... well, maybe not killed, but certainly hurt."

"He hopes to draw out our target," Pelham said. "We should be prepared to take action. When this Dave appears, you will be ready to render him unconscious? Then we may explore his headquarters and search for the sword at our leisure."

"Oh. Right. I guess that's not the worst imaginable plan."

They crouched and watched from the trees. Rondeau swung his briefcase back and forth, whistling, then shouted, "Yo, Dave, seriously, who has all night? I do not have all night. I am running out of night."

The gate in the wall didn't open... but a figure appeared on the watchtower above the wall. To someone with conventional eyes, he would have been a shadow behind the floodlights, but Bradley's enhanced vision revealed him clearly: he was tall, broad-shouldered, hugely bearded, dressed in Army-surplus camouflage, and holding a large and ridiculous sword in both hands. The sword was so elaborate it looked barely functional, the sort of thing cosplayers would wear to a comic book convention; the kind of sword characters with outlandish pastel hair wielded in anime. The Blade of Banishment had a curved blade etched with meaningless runes, a jeweled hilt, and a crossguard that curved and swooped and had enough spikes and pointy bits to offer more danger than protection to its wielder.

Rondeau shaded his eyes and looked up at the man. "You're Dave? Oh, hey, you've got the sword, too. Just what I wanted. Let's start the bidding at five thousand dollars, what do you say?"

"Perhaps it's best if we send Mr. Dave to sleep now?" Pelham murmured.

Bradley reached out with his psychic senses... and struck something that felt like a wall, smooth as glass, hard as diamond. He could *see* Dave's consciousness, an untidy swirl of shiny black and pulsing red and wet pus-green, but he couldn't *reach* it. "Uh oh," he said.

The man lifted the sword over his head. "I!" he bellowed. "Am! Not! Named! Dave!"

Then the man jumped off the watchtower, screaming, sword raised over his head. When he landed before Rondeau, he brought the sword down in an uncomplicated and inelegant overhand strike, like a man splitting a piece of wood—with Rondeau as the wood.

When the sword touched the top of his head, Rondeau disappeared.

Out on the Edge

THE SWORDSMAN CROUCHED FOR A MOMENT, breathing heavily, then rose and looked at the spot where Rondeau had been. "Why do people keep calling me *Dave*," he muttered before turning toward the wall and trudging to the gate. "I'm Drew." He thumped himself hard on the chest. "Drew Drew *Drew*."

"Shitting shitty shit fuck," Bradley said.

Pelham fished around in his bag. "Yes. My sentiments precisely. Where did Rondeau *go*? Do you think… did the sword send him to the underworld?"

"I don't know. Maybe Dave, or Drew, knows. But he's psychic-proof, Pelham, I mean *seriously* protected, some kind of magical force field wrapped right around his brain."

"We will see, then, if he is *everything* proof." Pelham drew a pistol from his bag.

"Whoa, wait, are you going to *shoot* him?"

"Tranquilizer dart." Pelham fired at the swordsman before he could reach the gate. Drew spun around, then groped at his shoulder, fingers touching the dart. He snarled, took a step forward, and then his eyes rolled back and he collapsed, falling on top of his sword but, fortunately (or unfortunately) not impaling himself.

"There," Pelham said. "We will disarm him, and then question him regarding Rondeau's whereabouts." He put the pistol away and walked toward the prone man, Bradley following close behind.

When Pelham got within a foot of Drew, the man rolled over and jabbed the sword into Pelham's right leg. Pelham vanished instantly. The swordsman got to his feet, grinning. "Tried to put me to sleep, but I don't sleep any more. The sword sleeps *for* me. I keep watch all the time. All the time. Who sent you? The Vatican? The UN Security Council? The Denver Illuminati?"

Bradley backed away, though it didn't help much, because Drew advanced to match him, step for step. "Uh... A woman named Elsie Jarrow sent me, actually."

That made the swordsman stop, and even lower the sword. "Elsie? I never knew her last name, but... Of course she sent you. She called me Dave, too. She's the one who gave me my sword."

Of course she did, Bradley thought.

The swordsman pressed the flat of the blade against his cheek, closed his eyes, and smiled... but then his eyes snapped open again, and he pointed the absurd blade at Bradley. "You can't have my sword back. *She* can't have it back. You won't take it from me!"

"Yeah, I get that." Bradley held up his hands in pointless placation. "Just, before you do your thing, can you tell me, where do people go when you hit them with the sword?"

Drew frowned, a look of genuine bafflement crossing his features. "Go? They go *away*."

"Gotcha. But... where is *away*?"

A look of sly delight appeared on Drew's face. "I don't know. But you know who's about to find out?"

"Oh, no," Bradley said, and then Drew hit him with the sword.

"**Hey, hey, the gang's all here.**" That was Rondeau's voice, so he wasn't dead, at least.

Bradley groaned, opened his eyes, and stared at the sky. Apparently he was on his back. Okay then. The sky was... black. Blacker than black. There were stars, bright and sharp, in unfamiliar configurations. He sat up and looked around. Rondeau sat on the gritty gray sand a few feet away, and Pelham sat beside him, sorting through his bag. There were four other people sprawled in the vicinity, all obviously dead, all dressed in the same sort of camouflage the swordsman had worn. Some of them had ice and blood crusted in their beards, and there was a general blueness to their skin that made Bradley think of death by exposure.

He looked farther away, and saw... gray, rippled ground. Low hills in the distance. This didn't look like any place he'd ever been on Earth.

Bradley got to his feet... and almost floated, rising up until his head bumped against some invisible barrier. He felt around as his body slowly settled back to the ground, and his fingers touched something smooth and curved overhead, like an invisible dome. "Wha—where the fuck are we? Why am I so *light*?"

"Pelly thinks we're on Pluto," Rondeau said. "Which, you know. Kind of makes sense. 'Plutonian Sword.'" He closed his eyes. "Man, this barely-there gravity is messing with my equilibrium."

Pelham didn't look up from the bag. "It is difficult to see how the sword would be of any use to us, as it sends its victims to the planet Pluto, instead of to the underworld. Perhaps Miss Jarrow is simply amusing herself."

"Pluto's not a planet anymore," Bradley said.

Now Pelham looked up. "It will always be a planet in my heart. Ah, here." He removed a handful of candles from the bag and set them gently on the cold ground.

"Why are we not dead?" Bradley said. "I mean, obviously: there's a dome, some kind of magical habitat, though not a very big one, judging by how I banged my head. But *those* guys, the dead friends of Dave, don't look like they had this kind of protection."

Pelham said, "I assume this dome is Miss Jarrow's doing—that she foresaw this eventuality and preferred to spare us from death."

"She gave Drew-Dave the sword, apparently, too," Bradley said. "This is *all* her way of amusing herself."

"More fun than tearing the legs off spiders," Rondeau muttered.

"All right, she kept us from dying, but how do we get *back*?" Bradley said. "I can teleport, but the odds are pretty good I'll get torn apart by the monsters that dwell in the in-between on the journey, and I can't drag you guys along with me anyway—group teleportation is an advanced skill I never learned. Normally I'd say, wait here while I go get help, but, well." He shrugged. "It's a long trip for a rescue helicopter."

"There is another way." Pelham brushed away the soil beside him, uncovering the corner of something flat and man-made. "Miss Jarrow left this, too." He lifted the edge of the object, revealing a large mirror turned face-down. Bradley helped him stand the mirror upright, propping it against one invisible wall of the dome. The mirror's frame was elaborately carved to resemble a lion's head, the reflective surface held in its jaws. "I have candles," Pelham said. "Can you prepare the ritual?"

"You guys made traveling by mirror sound so *fun*," Rondeau said. "Do we have some other alternative? Like, say, waiting for major advances in space travel and hitching a ride home on the eventual manned mission from Earth?"

"Unless the air in this dome is somehow magically self-replenishing, we have rather less time than that," Pelham said. "And if we travel by mirror… we may be able to take Mr. Drew by surprise."

"We're still finishing the mission?" Rondeau didn't bother to hide his disgust.

"Given that Elsie Jarrow sent us to Pluto when she *wasn't* mad at us, do you want to see what she'd do if we pissed her off?" Bradley said.

"Bleah. I concede the point."

Bradley set up the candles in the appropriate configuration, arrayed around the mirror. In theory, their incredibly vast distance from the Earth shouldn't matter—mirror-space didn't have a lot to do with physical space—but it was still unsettling to contemplate the journey. They were now farther from home as any human had ever been, except maybe that one 19th-century sorcerer who'd launched himself into orbit, but he was probably dead by now.

The mirror sparkled, and Bradley said. "Okay. I think we're good."

"Excellent," Pelham said. "Here are your blindfolds." He handed Rondeau and Bradley thick strips of dark cloth.

"What?"

"After our… unfortunate experience… last time, I did some research," Pelham said. "Some metaphysicians theorize the mirror creatures take strength from being seen." He uncoiled a length of rope from his pack, tied a loop around his waist, and then matter-of-factly tethered Bradley and Rondeau to the same line. "They stare into you, as you stare into them, in the hopes of switching the directionality of gaze, and turning *you* into the reflection, and themselves into the one who looks. Apparently there was a blind sorcerer who could traverse the mirror realms without fear of being attacked… though he took a wrong turn once and got lost, or so the theory goes. But you don't need eyes. You have *me*. And I have all the focus we need."

Bradley blindfolded himself, and Rondeau followed suit. A moment later, the rope tugged, and Bradley stepped forward, plunging through the mirror.

Gravity returned with a sudden downward yank, and his inner ear complained, making him lurch and almost fall.

"Gonna barf," Rondeau muttered behind him.

"*Please* don't," Bradley said.

"The way is clear." Pelham sounded perfectly calm, and began walking forward at a steady pace. The floor beneath Bradley's feet felt gritty, and sometimes bits of glass crunched under his soles. In the absence of vision, his psychic senses tried to compensate, reaching out, but the only minds were his, Rondeau's, and Pelham's. He considered tapping into Pelham's senses, and looking through his eyes, but what if that triggered the feral reflections to attack? Instead, he shuffled along in the dark, turning when Pelham murmured instructions, occasionally pausing as Pelham considered the path, and then continuing on.

After somewhere between fifteen minutes and ten thousand years, Pelham said, "We're here. I think it's safe to look. We were followed by feral reflections for a time, but they grew frustrated, I believe, and have since withdrawn."

Bradley removed his blindfold. They were at the end of a narrow corridor, lined by mirrors, and before them stood a narrow, tall window: a full-length mirror propped in the corner of what looked like a slovenly sort of barracks, bunk beds and metal footlockers, with camouflage netting hanging from the ceiling like bunting.

"I bet that's the mirror Dave poses and flexes and practices his last words in front of," Rondeau said. "Can we get out of here now?"

Pelham stepped through, and the others followed, stepping silently from the mirror realm into the squalid room. On the right side of the mirror, everything smelled of old sweat and unwashed foot stench. They untied themselves and stowed the rope, and then Pelham whispered, "Psychic recon?"

Bradley nodded, closed his eyes, and sent his mind seeking. The swordsman's distinctive consciousness was easy to find, buzzing and churning away in the next room. Bradley nodded, then eased the door open, peering out. There was something like a living room out there—it had a couch, anyway, along with many, many racks of guns and crates of ammo—and Drew was sitting in profile, hunched before a low table, furiously talking to himself and tearing pages out of a phone book. He crumpled each page into a ball and threw it over his shoulder, where hundreds of similar paper balls had accumulated. The Blade of Banishment rested across his knees.

Closing the door again, Bradley said, "Well? Ideas?"

"Mmm. Yes." Pelham reached into his bag and drew out a black, coarsely-woven sack. "Please be ready to assist me." He opened the door and crept out, moving in a crouch, making his way around the back of the couch. Bradley was sure the field of crumpled paper balls back there would rustle and give him away, but Pelham moved with such slow deliberation that the littler barely whispered, and any sound he did make was covered by Drew's grumbling and occasional curses.

When Pelham got close to the back of the couch, he sprang, bringing the black bag down over Drew's head and immediately falling to his knees and pulling the bag with him, forcing the swordsman to arch his spine and tilt his head sharply back over the edge of the couch. The swordsman shouted muffled curses and flailed his sword wildly, but he couldn't strike Pelham, or lift his head, or get any leverage to pull free.

Bradley and Rondeau moved then, spreading out to come at Drew from both sides, almost as smoothly as if they'd planned it. The swordsman was trying to tear the bag off his head, but he wouldn't let go of the sword, and with only one hand, he couldn't overcome the tension Pelham was exerting. Bradley grabbed Drew's sword hand below the wrist, leaning away from the waving blade, and Rondeau pinned the man's other arm to keep him from fighting. Bradley gritted his teeth and twisted, using all his weight and leverage to turn the swordsman's wrist farther, farther... too far. The tension became too great and, with another hearty curse, Drew's grasp popped open and the sword fell free.

The barrier protecting the swordsman's consciousness from Bradley's influence instantly vanished, and so he reached out, soothed the fiery mind, and sent the man to sleep. "It's okay, he's down."

Pelham rose, and plucked the bag from the man's head. "Poor man," he said, gazing down at the filthy face, the matted beard, the gaping mouth. "Can you do anything for him?"

Bradley shook his head. "This guy's mind is a snake pit. If I take out the violent paranoia and murderous fantasies, there won't be much of a mind *left*."

Rondeau carefully lifted the sword by its hilt, laid the weapon on a dirty army blanket, and then wrapped the whole thing up into a bundle. "You know, originally I'd planned to leave that briefcase full of cash as recompense for the sword, but fuck this guy. He killed his own friends."

"He might not have known he was killing them," Pelham said.

"Maybe not, but I doubt he would've cared either way." Rondeau tucked the bundled sword under his arm and looked around, wrinkling his nose. "Can we get out of shitland now?"

"Not just yet," Pelham said. "I have tool kit, and I'd like to render Mr. Drew's arsenal less operational. Once I've minimized the danger, I'll make a call to some of my acquaintances in federal law enforcement. If they aren't aware of this gentleman's activities, I think perhaps they should be."

"Look at us, just a bunch of do-gooding do-gooders," Rondeau said. "After *that* can we go somewhere and eat very large steaks?"

Stealing from the Gods

AFTER THE BOYS LEFT FOR THE AIRPORT, Elsie and Marla took the elevator downstairs to the casino, so Elsie could be "energized by the random," as she said. They hung out by the wheel of fortune, and Elsie *did* seem to draw some sustenance or pleasure from the environment, her eyes sparkling and her smile widening as she looked around. Marla saw mostly desperation, poor choices, and a deficient grasp of basic math in the customers here, but there was no accounting for taste. Or maybe Elsie just *liked* those qualities.

"So first we should go to Greece." Elsie slurped the cocktail onion up out of her martini glass.

"What's in Greece?"

"A small defense against our total annihilation and subjugation by the New Death, mostly," she said. "Also olives and sheep and Greek people."

"Elsie, is there any chance at all I could get something resembling an itinerary from you?"

"Oh, Marla, isn't it more *fun* when you don't know everything? I'll tell you this much: I've given your situation a lot of thought, and as you know I'm somewhat familiar with the lay of the land down in Hell, so I think I've covered most of the bases. At the very least, if we run these few errands, and if your boys come through with the sword, we'll have about a fifty-fifty chance of defeating the New Death and putting a crown back on your slightly oversized head. Can you trust me that far?"

Marla considered engaging with various parts of that response, then opted for simplicity. "How many errands are we talking about?"

Elsie scrunched up her nose. "Must you put a number on everything? Fine. We have to go three places. Well, sort of five places, or arguably six, but in terms of movement through the world of plain gross physical reality, we have three locations to visit. Three errands. Three acquisitions."

"Just going around, dropping in on gods."

"Not all of the gods. Some. The useful ones."

"Right. Hmm. I think it's going to be four errands, though. There's something I want to get my hands on, to push our odds a bit past fifty-fifty."

"Oh, *fine*, but let's do mine first. I have it all planned out, unless I change my mind, which, knowing me, you never know."

"You're nothing if not inconsistent. So. Greece. My usual method of long-distance travel is no good right now. I can't just take a shortcut through Hell, like I used to. There's teleporting, but... is it safer to travel that way for gods than it is for mortals?"

"Heavens, no. More dangerous, actually. The things that dwell in the spaces in-between are drawn to life force, and you and I are practically brimming *over* with life force, we're supercharged. Humans are kerosene and we're rocket fuel. Your boy Bradley has been dabbling with mirror travel, as I understand, but that's also more dangerous for the likes of us. We can make unreal things *really* real."

"So, what? Do we steal a plane?"

Elsie waved her hand. "Back when I was mortal a Sufi mystic taught me the secret of Tayy al-Ard, 'the folding of the Earth.' It's a way to travel without actually going anywhere. You stay in one place, and the Earth moves *under* you, and stops once your destination is beneath your feet. If you do it wrong, you get smashed against a wall or a mountain along the way, but we'll do it right instead. I'll teach you."

"I've never been the quickest study with magic, Elsie. I've always gotten along through sheer stubborn refusal to quit."

"Oh, I know, you're notorious, all grit and no sparkle. But I think you'll find certain things come more easily now that you're fully in touch with your goddess-hood, darling."

AN HOUR LATER, Elsie and Marla crouched behind an immense anvil and watched a dog-sized bronze mechanical spider pick its way across the relic-strewn floor. They were in a stone-walled workshop, lit only by low-banked forge fires. They'd traveled to Greece using Elsie's method of folding the Earth—it was disorienting, but also beautiful, seeing a whole hemisphere whip past at high speed—and they'd landed on a rocky island overlooking a night-time sea that was, in fact, fairly wine-dark. From there, they'd descended into a crack in the ground, leaving behind the ordinary world, at some point, and entering the palace of a god. Marla had paused to marvel at the decorative urns and the oversized statues of majestic figures (though it was creepy how all their facial features were smashed off, like someone had gotten drunk and angry with a hammer), but Elsie had called her a tourist and dragged her down a set of stairs into this sweltering basement workshop.

Marla elbowed her fellow god as the spider scuttled around a corner and out of sight. "Elsie. This doesn't feel like a visit."

"When I said 'visit,' I thought it was clear I meant 'burglarize,'" Elsie said. "My apologies if I was imprecise."

"Who even worships Hephaestus anymore?" Marla demanded.

"A few neo-pagans, probably. But he still has a lot of juice in popular culture. Wasn't he in a Disney movie or something? He slumbers, though, mostly. Not a lot of demand for his wares anymore, I gather, and his hot wife never visits. He won't notice if we nick a few things from his workshop. Probably. He never has before." Elsie lifted her head, peeking over the anvil. "All right, I don't see any more guardians. I'm sure they're very lazy and unobservant anyway."

"Can god-made automatons even be lazy?"

"Anything can be anything, Marla. They just have to believe in themselves."

"Every time I think I can't hate you any more, I hate you a little more."

"Shush. Hephaestus makes the most darling little helmets." Elsie scurried from cover toward a doorway, and Marla followed, trying to curse only to herself. Beyond the door was a room of seemingly infinite length, filled with gleaming racks of weapons and dark armor.

"The armory of the gods," Elsie said. "Do you like it?"

She picked up a dagger with a blade that shimmered with dark swirls of color, like oil on water. "It's starting to win me over."

"I'm going to get a helmet with wings on the side," Elsie said. "Like the imaginary Vikings used to wear. I am going to be adorable. Hmm. We're going to need, let's see, six of them."

"There are only five of us, Elsie. Me, you, Rondeau, Pelly, and B."

"So *far*. It's always good to have an extra. You never know when you'll pick up a tagalong."

"What are these helmets supposed to do for us, anyway?"

"Oh, things." Elsie wandered off down an aisle and disappeared around a corner. Marla gritted her teeth and followed. Being annoyed with her was pointless. Elsie *lived* to irritate people.

Marla put a hand on Elsie's shoulder before she could turn another corner. "I have gone along with you, with hardly any complaint, because I am an enlightened being with a widened perspective, now. But there are limits even to my cosmic patience. What. Are. The. Helmets. For."

Elsie reached out and picked up a green gladiator's helmet decorated with a motif of vines and flowers: oddly pretty, for something designed to be hit with a club. She blew a layer of dust off the helm. "The gods used to pit their champions against one another, for the proverbial shits and giggles, and these were designed to give certain mortals an edge. They make the wearer... not god-*proof*, certainly, but let's say god-*resistant*. If your mortal sidekicks wear these, the New Death won't be able to simply stop their hearts with a glance. He'll have to kill them more conventionally. I'm also *fairly* sure he won't be able to trap them in bubbles of hostile reality and wipe out their minds, though only time will tell for sure. If your new husband conjures a giant man-or-woman-eating demon, the demon could still eat them, of course. But, still, the helmets might shift this from an absurdly unfair fight to a merely horribly unbalanced fight. Wearing them will improve our own natural resistance to the New Death's interference, too. We've both got mortal cores that makes us a little less agile when it comes to shaping reality than those who are all the way god." She gave Marla a significant look. "Though I like to think we're stronger for our mortality, the way an alloy is better than pure metal."

"That was impressively lucid." Marla took the helmet from her hands. It felt light as an eggshell, but she suspected hitting it with an industrial trip hammer wouldn't even dent the crown.

Elsie beamed. "I *know*! My mind can line up the little box-cars of thought and send them chug-chug-chugging along the rails so much better since I became a deity." She took another helmet, which did, indeed, have little silver wings protruding from the sides, and slid it over her head. The helmet gleamed for a moment, as if illuminated by torchlight, then faded to transparency and finally seemed to disappear all together. Elsie thumped her knuckles against the side of her head. "There, now my skull has a skull. Try yours."

Marla hesitated. "If this thing is cursed...."

"Ooh, that's an interesting idea. I wonder if any of these helmets *are* cursed? I've had a little fun handing out magical weapons to people, just to see what would happen, but cursed armor, even better."

"What? Why have you been giving people weapons?"

Elsie cocked her head. "I was almost positive I said that out loud: just to see what would happen."

"Even now that you're a god, you don't have any *better* reason for the things you do? You used to create chaos because it gave you power—"

"Which I used to create more chaos, to get more power, and so on. My behavior was always a closed self-referential loop, Marla. Now that I'm a trickster god... I do have a higher purpose, but my approach hasn't really changed. I'm here to shake things up. Complacency is death. Somebody has to go around kicking over anthills, or else how do you find out what happens when you kick over an anthill?"

"I... yeah. Okay. We're never going to be friends, Elsie."

"Oh, you never know. You have more in common with *me* than you do with the mayfly mortals you consider your family."

Marla pulled on her helmet. It was like having her head doused with cool water. The helmet faded and vanished, and she didn't feel anything at all, except, in some peculiar way, *protected*. "I have one question, Elsie. It's important. If I take you with me to the underworld, are you going to actually help me, or fuck things up just to see what happens?"

"What did I say about how it's more fun when you don't know everything?" Elsie looked around, wrinkling her nose in disgust. "I'll scoop a few more helmets into a sack, after I steal a sack, but everything else here is a bit shit. Hephaestus never did have much of an imagination. Did you want to go find him? Maybe we could heal his bad leg, *that* would be pretty hilarious. It would mess with his whole mythic self-image."

"We should let sleeping gods lie."

Elsie groaned, long and loud. "Marla. I am *so* angry that you made that pun and I didn't."

"Even gods can't have everything. Are we done here? Where do we go now?"

"We're just going to visit one of my old neighbors."

MARLA FROWNED at the imposing brick hulk of the mansion in the distance. Even in bright sunlight, the structure was imposingly Gothic, and the bars on all the windows didn't help. Going from morning in Las Vegas to night in Greece to afternoon on the outskirts of Felport in the space of a couple of hours should have played havoc with Marla's body clock, but apparently gods in full possession of their abilities were immune to jetlag's nastier cousin, teleport-lag. "What are we doing here? You're saying there's a god in the Blackwing Institute?"

Elsie looked at a cow a few yards away in the field where they stood and whispered "Moo." Then she turned to Marla. "Well, why not? I was locked up there for ages, and I'm a god."

"Yes, but you weren't a god at the time."

"Pish. Time is an illusion. You should know that. Shall we go in? I just love coming back to visit. They're always so glad to see me."

Marla grabbed Elsie's arm before she could flit across the field. "Elsie, there are people in there. Sick people, *and* mortal staff. Sure, most of the orderlies are just homunculi grown in the basement, but since Langford took over running the place, he's brought in some of his apprentices-slash-research-assistants, and they *aren't* flesh golems who live on lavender and earthworms. I don't want any innocent people getting killed." She paused. "Or any guilty people, either. Basically any people. No killing."

Elsie shook off her hand. "The god of death is telling *me* not to take lives? That's like me telling you to be sure and use a coaster so you don't leave a ring on the table. Marla, really, you need to get past this black-and-white morality thing. Be like me, and embrace blue-and-orange morality." At her blank look, Elsie sighed. "Don't you ever read the TV Tropes website? It's great, everything you need to know about life is contained therein. Blue-and-orange morality, sweet Marla, is morality that is *alien* to your good-and-evil framework, a moral system that's totally perpendicular, or maybe orthogonal, or is it catty-corner? One of those. I'm not a human. I'm a trickster god, and I play according to rules that don't necessarily make any sense from a point of view that's not my own. So what if I kill some people? What does that have to do with anything that has anything to do with anything?"

"As usual, Elsie, I don't know what the fuck you're talking about, but it doesn't matter, so let me put this more plainly: if you kill anybody, you and *me* are going to have a fight. I know exactly how powerful you are, and you know it. I was there when you were born into godhood, and I can be there when you die out of it. You don't want me on your ass."

Elsie rolled her eyes. "*Fine.* We'll play tennis with the net up, then. Can I at least turn people into beetles?"

"As long as they get turned back to people again at the end, and have as many body parts as they started with—no fewer *and* no more…. then I guess that's okay."

"I'm Mozart, and you've taken away my piano and given me a toy xylophone, but that's fine. I can still make beautiful music. Genius flourishes under restraint, just like a middle-aged divorcee getting into kinky sex for the first time."

"Your metaphors don't even metaphor right."

"Sometimes they get away from me, but I stand by that one. Shall we just walk in through the front door? That would be pretty funny."

"Your amusement is my only goal, Elsie."

In addition to the long-distance folding of the Earth, Elsie had also shown Marla a nifty little line-of-sight variation, allowing for short hop teleports without any nasty side effects. They flittered across the cow field to the front doors of the institute, which were warded and guarded in a dozen different ways, magical and technological. Elsie smiled at the security camera and said "Oops, everything glitches." Marla had no trouble unweaving the magical protections and putting them aside for the time it took to open the big double doors and step inside.

Marla was a little alarmed by the extent of her own power; she could so easily change so many things, now. Magic that had been almost impossible for her in the past was now trivial, and she could do things she could have only imagined before. No wonder her god-self had worked to limit her understanding of her capabilities during her months in the mortal realm. A few years ago, a less emotionally banged-up, more pathologically self-confident Marla would have taken that power and set about reshaping the world to redress wrongs real, imagined, and trivial… without giving nearly enough thought to the long-term consequences of her actions. Her now-perfect memory and her expanded perceptions gave her the discretion necessary to wield that new power without causing untold disasters… so far. It was still basically like juggling hand grenades with loose pins, though.

Especially since she was running around with Elsie Jarrow, who had broadly similar powers, and used them to *court* disaster. Ah, well. Mortal life was all about compromises. Why should godhood be any different?

Elsie strolled into the marble-floored lobby and walked up to the dark wood reception desk, currently unattended. "There's no little bell to ring," she said. "I love those little bells. Oh well. I'll have to make do." Elsie took a deep breath and shouted *"Ding ding ding ding ding!"*

A young woman with flyaway hair and glasses appeared through a side door. "What—what are you doing here, can I help you, who are you?"

"Visiting a patient, I doubt it, and we are Elsie Jarrow and Marla Mason, former inmate and former patron—or, wait, matron?—of this facility, respectively. We're going to see Roderick Barrow."

The woman shook her head. "You can't just come *visit patients*, that's not how it's done here, you have to contact Doctor Langford—"

"Is my name no longer a name to conjure fear?" Elsie said. "What are they *teaching* you apprentices nowadays? What's your name, dear?"

"I'm Colette. I'm in charge of operations today while the doctor's off site."

"Does Langford really have a doctorate, or is this like a guy who buys a canoe and calls himself captain?" Marla said.

"It's probably an honorary doctorate bestowed for excellence in psychopathy and humorlessness," Elsie said. "I'm *so* glad Langford wasn't in charge of things when I was locked up here. I bet he would have bothered me all the time, with the pokings and the proddings and the evaluatings." She pointed to the apprentice. "Can I turn her into beetles?"

"Not necessary." Marla walked up to Colette and put her hand on her shoulder. "We're very dangerous people, but I'm pretty sure we don't mean any harm. When Langford comes back, tell him we visited—he won't be angry that you couldn't stop us."

The woman's hair began to rise into the air, crackling with electricity as she gathered magic for some strike. Marla sighed. "You really should sit down with the latest edition of *Dee's Peerage* and look up our names when you get a chance." Marla reached into the woman's mind with a soothing psychic touch and then caught her when she slumped, her small electrical burst of power discharging harmlessly into the air. Marla lowered the woman to the floor behind the desk. "You know, I used to be about as psychic as your average cantaloupe. Godhood is weird. I can see why so many gods are giant assholes. So much power."

"It's a good thing we can be trusted with it."

"Ha. Okay, you had your fun, you got to freak out a mortal. Let's be discreet now." Marla cast a look-away spell so no one else they encountered would notice them. "Where are we going?"

"To one of the locked basement wards, unless they've moved him." She set off toward a door and on down a corridor. Elsie knew the layout of the Institute well. This was a hospital for criminally insane sorcerers, and she'd been locked up here for ages, throughout multiple escape attempts.

Marla had been running through her mental list of inmates, trying to figure out who they might be here to visit, and she was unsurprised when Elsie led her to a basement wall made of volcanic black glass. "I used to need a special magical key to open this," Elsie said, "but, well…" She touched the wall, and a section of stone slid away. "Ooh, I love godhood."

She led Marla inside, to an incongruously ordinary-looking hallway that would have been at home in any hospital, complete with flickering fluorescent lights overhead. They walked to a window that looked in on a hospital bed, where an old man rested, unconscious, hooked up to monitors and tubes. His room wasn't entirely antiseptic, though. The skin of some brightly-striped animal, transformed into a blanket or rug, was puddled at the foot of the bed, a dented wooden shield leaned in a corner, and a scattering of gold coins and precious gems littered the floor.

"This guy isn't a god." Marla looked through the bulletproof glass and shook her head. "That's Roderick Barrow. The exothermic dreamer. How is he even still alive? I don't think he's changed a bit, physically, in all these years."

"He's in eternal stasis coma-sleep, with fancy dreams," Elsie said. "Why do you say he isn't a god? He is a lord of his own creation. You've entered his dreamworld. From the inside, didn't it seem just as real as this world? Maybe realer?"

"I went into his dreamworld a long time ago, when I was a dumb young mercenary and didn't know any better. Those memories had pretty much faded to nothing, the way dreams do, but since Bradley cleaned out all my mental blocks... yeah, I remember. Barrow saw me as an evil witch, and I stormed a haunted citadel. Being in his dream was like living in a bad movie with good special effects. What do we want with him? We're supposed to be visiting gods, not bothering insane psychic fantasy novelists."

"Mmm." Elsie put her hand against the glass. "He was better at writing short stories, really. His novels always sort of sagged in the middle. But I say he *is* a god, of a particular sort. He dreamed his vast epic fantasy world into life, and the creatures who dwell there have independent consciousness and senses of self—the things Barrow dreams about even bleed through into *this* reality sometimes, and gold coins and monster-skins are some of the more harmless apports. I consider his dream world one of my top vacation destinations."

"I remember you visited him, back when you were planning to kill me, and brought the HellHorn out of his dream," Marla said. "What did you do with that thing, anyway?"

"Oh, who remembers? I think I put it on a shelf somewhere in a dead woman's storage unit. Eventually the unit will get auctioned off and someone will find the horn, and if they blow it, oh, won't that be *interesting*? I've nipped back into Barrow's dreams once or twice since then, though, and stolen away other artifacts. There was this one spear, called Ghostreaper, I'm sure you remember it, a remarkable artifact—I brought that out of the dream and gave it to a friend of mine, to see what he'd do. It wasn't nearly as much fun as I'd hoped, though. Oh well. But *we're* going to hop into Barrow's dream and find something to help us beat up the New Death. It's like a quest! Won't it be fun?"

"Hmm. I guess going in wasn't so bad last time. Barrow was more pathetic than anything else, dreaming himself as a kind of scholar-barbarian hero combo."

"Ah, but his story has moved on, I'm afraid. These days he's no longer the wandering warrior known as Barrow of Ulthar. Now he's the Lord of the Maggotlands, Protector of the Ravenous Dead, Dispenser of Injustice, Bestower of Maladies, Emperor of the Cinderlands and the Megalith Isles, and so on and so forth. You're the one who turned him into a world-bestriding despot, actually."

"What? How is that my fault?"

"Doctor Husch told me all about it. You went into Barrow's dream to convince him he wasn't a fantasy hero destined for greatness, that he was just a man, in hopes of restoring him to lucidity, and bringing him back to this reality. You did too good a job, though. After you kicked his ass and stole his prophesied victory out from under him, he became furious, and decided that, if he didn't have a destiny, he would make his *own*. If he couldn't be a hero, he would become a conqueror. Barrow then proceeded to lay waste to every little corner of the geographically implausible map he'd drawn. He's a bit of an asshole, frankly, but he *does* dream up some good toys, and his artifacts work when you bring them into this world too."

"Unintended fucking consequences," Marla muttered. "Story of my life. How do we go in? Last time it was a whole magical rigmarole to link my mind to his."

"We are the whole magical rigmarole," Elsie said. "We go in like *this*." She seized Marla's hand, and the world changed.

The Sundered Isles

"**WELCOME TO THE SUNDERED ISLES** of the Lambent Sea." Elsie twirled around on the pale-green sand, beneath a carnivorous-looking variant of a palm tree that shook its branches menacingly.

"What the hell are you wearing?" Marla said.

Elsie looked down at herself. "Ah. Well, enter the dreamworld, get co-opted by local norms. It happens."

"Sure, but is that, like… a lizard-skin body harness bikini?"

"Mmm, basically, basically. You're so much more modest in your attire, more's the pity."

Marla was dressed in a dark cloak worn over cosplay forest ranger gear, pretty much; the knee-high boots were nice, anyway. She unhooked the cloak and let it drop to the sand, though, because the sun here was abominably hot. The cloak scuttled away across the sand and disappeared into the sea, which shone with pale yellow lights beneath the surface. "Ugh. I had enough of wearing cloaks that were secretly alive in the real world." Marla shaded her eyes and looked around. This was a rather more pleasant part of Barrow's fantasy world than the area she'd visited previously, with less in the way of dread citadels and bleeding clouds. This place was a glowing sea dotted with islands, including a few, off in the distance, that held impressively baroque structures, like full-sized sandcastles. "What are we doing here?"

"This is where old dark lords retire."

"Is Barrow here?"

"No, he's ruling from a grim fortress carved from the skull of a city-sized dragon, the usual sort of thing, hundreds of leagues away. He's not retired. He's still fighting a war with some of the other dark lords, and I imagine he will continue doing so until the sun explodes, or someone

113

sneaks into his hospital room and smothers him with a pillow, whichever comes first. We're here to visit the tomb of the late dark lord Mogrash, who began his reign in blood and fire and slavery but ended up ruling over an era of peace, prosperity, and voluntary regime change, passing control to his adopted son. Mogrash's heirs are still the main rivals to Barrow's control, or at least, they were the last time I peeked in on the place. Who knows what's going on now. Time is funny here."

"So we're tomb-raiding. What's in the tomb?"

"Mogrash's enchanted battle-axe, Trepanner."

"Like... trepanation? Drilling holes in the skull?"

"Mogrash's approach to brain surgery was a bit more *informal* than that, but, yes, Trepanner put holes in a great many skulls over the years. One of Mogrash's more bloodthirsty children inherited the weapon, but when the dark lord finally shuffled off this fantasy coil many years ago, they buried the axe with his body. His tomb is on the next island, over there. Shall we?" Elsie flickered, vanishing from sight, and Marla followed, pleased that her line-of-sight teleport still worked in this place.

Barrow's dreamworld was a bit like the underworld, in that a presiding mind controlled its shape, but anyone with sufficient will could make alterations to the fabric of local reality, to greater or lesser degrees. As long as they didn't draw Barrow's attention, they could get in and out of here without much trouble.

The dark lord's tomb took up most of the small island, and was in the shape of an immense skull, seemingly made of the same pale green sand that covered the islands. Marla thumped her fingers against it, and then swore: the walls were hard as stone, not crumbly at all.

"The local builders use sand magic. I gather if you don't pay them what they're owed in a timely fashion, they can snap their fingers and make your whole castle collapse into a heap of loose grains. But how about we use the door?" Elsie walked up to the closed mouth of the skull and made a series of mystic-looking passes. The jaws of the tomb ground open with a sound like squeaking hinges, until the mouth gaped wide enough for them to walk in without hunching over. Marla followed the chaos god down a set of stairs made of the same solidified sand, to a torchlit chamber where a giant-sized sarcophagus in the shape of a warrior in a horned helmet rested on a pedestal.

Something rustled in a dark alcove off to one side, and a rasping voice said, "I am the sibyl. I foresaw your coming."

"I bet you're just saying that," Elsie said.

"You have come to take the great axe Trepanner."

"Lucky guess," Elsie said.

The sibyl stepped into the light. She wore a ragged black dress and veil, but was younger and more handsome than the withered crone Marla had expected based on her voice.

As if reading Marla's mind, the sibyl said, "I used to have a lovely voice. I have not spoken since my husband's burial."

"Wait," Marla said. "You're Mogrash's widow? And you shut yourself up in his *tomb*? What did you do that for?"

"I... it is my duty to protect his grave from thieves and plunderers and necromancers...."

"What about your duty to *not* live in a tomb made of sand for years upon years?" Marla said.

"Not all pulp fantasy writers were sexist, but Barrow is," Elsie said. "It's not the sibyl's fault. She's just written that way. So, we'll just be taking the axe...."

"The dark lord Barrow of Ulthar threatens the empire my husband created." The sibyl scuttled between them and the tomb, moving as fast as a spider. "This moment is a nexus of destinies. I will allow you to take the axe, and make it your own... but only if you agree to strike Barrow down."

"Always with the plot coupons." With a flick of her wrist, Elsie turned the sibyl into a pile of writhing beetles. "Who has time for all that to-ing and fro-ing?" Before Marla could react, Elsie walked to the sarcophagus and heaved the lid aside.

Marla joined her, stepping carefully so she wouldn't crush any of the beetles. "Was that really necessary?"

"If you only do what's necessary, you almost never have any fun." Elsie looked down into the coffin, where the skeletal remains of an immense man rested in ceremonial armor. A pickaxe, brutally practical-looking apart from a fat ruby embedded at the base of the handle, rested on his chest. Elsie picked up the weapon. "Ooh, this I like."

"How does that help us in our battle against the New Death?"

"Trepanner puts holes in skulls. The New Death has a skull. Assorted skulls, actually. What better weapon to hit him with?"

"I can't imagine that an axe from a fantasy novel is really going to hurt the god of death."

"Oh, it'll hurt him. Barrow *is* a god, whether you want to believe it or not, and that means this is an artifact, god-forged. I'm not positive it will actually kill the New Death, but hurt him? Most definitely. Shall we go?"

"Will you turn the sibyl back into a person?"

"She wasn't a *person*, anyway. In Barrow's world, sibyls look like humans, but the aren't, not quite. But, fine." Elsie gestured… but the beetles just kept scuttling. She scowled. "Damn it. We'd better go, Marla." Elsie took her hand… and nothing happened. "Well. Crapsicles. I think Barrow noticed us. He's exerting his view of reality pretty hard right now."

"Probably because you turned one of his antagonists into beetles. Maybe you shouldn't have done that."

"Telling someone they shouldn't have lit the fire when the house has already burned down isn't really constructive criticism, Marla. Let's go outside."

The sun no longer beat down on the island, because a fleet of flying warships, brutally spiked and bristling with cannons, had arrived to blot out the sun. Elsie sighed. "Here, hold this axe."

"What are you going to do?"

"For just this moment we have to play by Barrow's rules. That means we're stuck mostly with the powers he gave us. You're some kind of witch, I don't know what kind, but I'm familiar enough with Barrow's oeuvre to know *exactly* what he dreamed me into."

"What's that?"

She snapped one of the straps of her elaborate scaled harness. "This isn't lizardskin, it's *dragon* skin, and I'm a drake-witch." She grinned. "Funny, huh? It's not even my first time being a dragon."

"Don't remind me," Marla said.

Elsie jumped into the air, and began to transform, growing in size as she went. Marla gaped as the chaos god, in her new draconic form, attacked the warships… and then various monstrous humanoids started leaping from the ships and landing on and around the island, swimming and wading and running toward Marla, roaring as they came.

Trepanner felt good in her hands. Marla hadn't been in an honest-to-gods melee in a long time.

She lifted the axe. She roared back.

ELSIE STEPPED OVER A HEAP of tusked and snouted fallen soldiers. "Don't worry, they're not sentient. I don't think."

"I am covered in blood, and things I *wish* were blood," Marla said.

"Don't wash off in the sea. You'll attract all sorts of nasty creatures." The fleet of warships was crashed, sinking, burning. Elsie flickered, teleporting a dozen yards away, then back again. "Ah, good, we overloaded Barrow's bandwidth. I think we can leave now."

"You didn't kill Barrow?" Marla said. "Like the sibyl wanted?"

"I do not like to imagine the consequences of killing the one true god of this creation *inside* his creation. I think it might be like climbing into a hole and pulling the hole in after you. So, no, I didn't. Shall we?"

Marla looked around at the devastation, wiped not-blood from her forehead, and nodded. "Let's."

Back in the hospital room, they were wearing their old clothes again, but they were still covered in blood and soot, respectively. According to the clock on the wall, only about two minutes had elapsed in real-time. Marla commented, and Elsie nodded. "How else can Barrow play out his cast-of-thousands generational rise-and-fall-of-empires epic series before the sun explodes? Besides, he's a god there. Time is his to command." Elsie patted the old man's cheek. "Let's pop back to the suite in Las Vegas and shower this nastiness off, shall we?

The Scent of Lemons

"WHERE TO NOW?" MARLA SAID. "What's the last whistle-stop on this little godhood tour of yours?"

"We can get where we're going from anywhere, but first, let's find a grocery store. I want some fresh organic produce."

"Billions of dead souls are currently suffering, Elsie. I'm not in the mood to dawdle."

She waved her hand airily. "Oh, don't worry so much. Your boys aren't even done with their mission yet."

"How do you know?"

"I have a couple of, oh, magical sensors set up at likely locations along the course of their journey, and they haven't been tripped yet. We've got time. Anyway, this is *mission critical* fresh produce I'm talking about."

They made their way, mostly by walking but with a bit of judicious Earth-folding, to a small upscale market in the city. Walking among the aisles of fruit and vegetables, Marla shook her head. "I thought people in Vegas subsisted entirely on shrimp cocktail and breakfast buffets and martini olives."

"The health nuts and vegetarians get in *everywhere*." Elsie stopped by a display of citrus fruit and picked up a lemon nearly the size of a baseball. "This'll do."

Lemons? Oh, no. "Elsie, what are you going to do with that lemon?"

"What can I say? I have a zest for life." She drew one sharp red fingernail across the fruit's skin, releasing the essential oils with a burst of lemon scent.

Marla felt a great magical upwelling of *intention* from her fellow god, and then the store around them vanished, replaced by a white marble floor, with walls of gauzy white curtains.

"Huh, she's never let me in here before." Elsie dropped the lemon on the floor. "But I guess she saw I was with you, and decided to open the door."

"This is Genevieve's pocket dimension." Marla crossed her arms. "We do not need to be here, Elsie. I'm not stealing anything from Gen."

"Of course not. When you take a person, it's not stealing, it's kidnapping."

"What? No. We're not taking her anywhere. She's a reweaver. Reality is like clay for her. Along certain axes, she's more powerful than *we* are."

"Which is why I'm classing her as an honorary god, even if she doesn't have the conditional immortality and the spark of divinity we possess. She has the power of creation, or at least of *alteration*, so she's powerful enough for the sisterhood, I think." Elsie cupped her hands around her mouth. "Oh, Genevieve! Are you home? Of course you are, because if you weren't here the local reality would cease to exist. Care to come out? We used to be fellow inmates at the Blackwing Institute. Funny story, I wanted to recruit you for this assassination squad I put together a while back, but I didn't think you'd approve of the target!"

"Elsie, please stop shouting. That is a lot of shouting. Gen doesn't do well with noisy disruptions."

"Oh, but I'm an adorable disruption, everyone loves me. Genevieve!"

A golden cube six feet on each side appeared where Elsie had been, then shrank down to something the size of an end table. One of the curtains twitched aside and Genevieve walked in, ducking her head shyly, caramel-colored curls falling into her face. She initially wore a loose-fitting dress, but as she walked her garb changed to a blouse and skirt, and a dark scarf wound itself around her throat. "Marla. You've changed. You're *more*, now, aren't you?"

"I got an upgrade, yeah. I'm sorry to barge in on you, Genevieve. It wasn't my idea, and I wouldn't have let, uh, my loud friend bring me if I'd realized this was where we were going."

"She is *very* loud. She's still yelling in there. I can tell, even if I can't hear her." Genevieve sat on the cube and smiled. "It is good to see you, though. What's the latest disaster?"

"Ha, it's kind of a long story, but...." Marla sat on the floor and told her story, leaving almost nothing out. Genevieve wasn't quite family, but Marla was inordinately fond of her. Gen could change the nature of reality at a whim, but her powers were difficult to control, and she'd chosen to withdraw into a pocket dimension in order to avoid accidentally hurting anyone. Here, she could change things whenever she wanted, and the alterations wouldn't ripple into a reality shared by others. She wasn't entirely alone here, though. She had the company of constructs she'd conjured based on the memories of a couple of her old friends, who had independent reality and consciousness in her world, though they couldn't survive in the less compromising reality outside this dimension. Marla had always, before, kept Genevieve in the back of her mind as a potential nuclear option, a weapon of overwhelming power… but, like literal nuclear weapons, Genevieve was ultimately too dangerous to ever be deployed. Even now.

"So anyway," Marla finished, "I think Elsie wanted to bring you with us as a sort of living bomb, but I won't ask you to do that."

Genevieve stood up and looked at the golden cube. A small, square opening appeared in the top. "Did you have something to say?"

"Yes!" Elsie's voice was tinny and faraway, like she was shouting from the bottom of a well. "You can change reality in the *real* world, so imagine what you could do in the *underworld*, a place composed of primal chaos, material that only exists to be shaped! You could go with us, fight the New Death with us, and even if you accidentally turned everything down there into applesauce, that would be fine, because once Marla takes back her throne, she can put it all back together again with a twitch of her nose!"

"I… huh." Marla nodded. "That's a fair point, actually. Everyone in the underworld is already dead, so it's not like you'd accidentally kill anyone. Your gifts might translate into even greater power in that setting." She shook her head. "But I've got no right to drag you into my problems."

Genevieve shrugged. "That is arguable. You saved my life. You saved my sanity. Even though my madness threatened the city you loved, you treated me with kindness instead of simply snapping my neck, though that would have been far and away the simpler option. Even if I didn't owe you, there are people I care about in the underworld. My mentor, St. John. Our mutual friend Mr. Zealand. I do not like the idea of them suffering at the hands of this New Death. I would like to go with you, Marla. I will help in any way I can."

"Genevieve… even with your power, it's going to be dangerous there. I can't guarantee you'll survive, and if we fail, the consequences will be horrible."

"I have lived through horror before," she said calmly. "If it can be overcome, it will be; and if it cannot be overcome, it will be borne." She took Marla's hands in her own, then kissed her on both cheeks. "Call me when you're ready to depart." Genevieve walked toward a gauzy curtain, and behind it, and away.

Marla blinked and they were back in the grocery store, except Elsie was nowhere to be seen. Then the immense display of lemons began to move, fruit falling and rolling on the floor, and Elsie sat up from the middle of the heaped fruit. Other customers gaped, and an employee shouted, but Elsie ignored them. Marla offered her a hand to help her down. "I like that girl," Elsie said. "She's a firecracker. A whole bunch of firecrackers. Stuffed in a garbage can. Thrown into a pond. Full of ducks."

"That metaphor did get away from you," Marla said.

"As I said, they sometimes do. Well, my work is done. Now where are we going?"

"Not we, just me."

"Ha. Wanna bet?"

Marla sighed. "Fine, but you can only come partway, all right? The place I'm going… it's not safe, even for you. It's not safe for me, either, but I'm doing it anyway."

"Ooh, danger, spicy. Let's go."

"**FELPORT?**" Elsie frowned. "What's worth having in Felport?" They'd folded the Earth and landed on the observation deck at the top of the Whitcroft-Ivory building, with a view of the whole messy beautiful night-time city below them.

"Nothing. Just hang out here. I need to visit a friend, maybe go to the park."

"Why? What's in the park? Is it pine cones? I love pine cones." She bounced on the balls of her feet. "Tell tell tell."

"Elsie. Isn't it more *fun* when you don't know everything?"

The chaos god sighed. "Hoist by my own canard. Fine, go, have your little secret, I know how much they mean to you. I'll go, I don't know, frighten the new chief sorcerer or something. See you back in Vegas." Elsie flickered away before Marla could tell her to behave. Not that Elsie would ever listen anyway.

Marla looked down at the city that had once been her home, and now held her greatest hope for defeating the New Death… though it was also the greatest risk for getting herself killed. She would have to handle things delicately. Delicacy had never been her strong suit, but when the fate of countless souls were on the line, she'd give it a try.

Reconvened

MARLA PACED IN RONDEAU'S SUITE. Outside the windows, Las Vegas partied on while more sensible parts of the nation slept. "Why haven't they called yet?"

"They're *fine*." Elsie lolled on one of the oversized couches, with a washcloth draped over her eyes. Being trapped in Genevieve's golden cube of order had given her a headache, she said. "Your boys tripped two of my sensors, so they made it where they were going. I'm sure they're taking care of business and fighting the good fight. Would you try to get some sleep? I bet they'll be back by morning."

"I don't need to sleep."

"You don't need to, but it's pleasant. Besides, you're a goddess now, which means you get to have prophetic dreams sometimes."

"I don't believe in prophecy."

"Dreams that hint at probable futures, then, based on your psychic extrapolation from ongoing events, if you want to be unpoetically accurate. Give it a try."

Marla went into the bedroom Rondeau had set aside for her, sank back into the impossibly comfortable mattress, found it too comfortable to be endured, and dragged a blanket onto the floor instead. The carpet was so deep-pile luxurious it felt softer than actual beds she'd owned in the past, but it was firm enough that she could actually get some rest without feeling like she'd been smothered in the process.

In her dream, she rode an immense white raven through a battlefield of fluffy white clouds, leading a heavenly host, her soldiers mounted on horses with tails of flame, and old-timey pennyfarthing bikes, and Vincent White Shadow motorcycles. Far away, black storm clouds boiled, overtaking the white, and a host rushed forward to meet her own: the New Death, now with the skull of an alligator in place of a head, riding a huge, skeletal bird.

123

His army was made up of all her friends and relatives and acquaintances in full zombie form, all missing jaws and flaps of skin and teeth gaping through torn-open cheeks. When the hosts collided, lightning and thunder obliterated everything, and the clouds became a fuzzy, all-obscuring gray.

She opened her eyes. Sunlight leaked in around the edges of the curtains. "Dreams are stupid," she said aloud. But the night had passed, and she heard voices outside. She threw on clothes and stepped out.

"Marla!" Bradley said. He and Pelham and Rondeau were sitting on couches, looking travel-weary and disheveled. "Sorry we didn't call. It got late, and we didn't want to wake you. If the past day was as weird for you as it was for us, you probably needed your rest."

Elsie wandered in, wearing a red towel wrapped around her body and another wrapped around her hair. "Boys! You made it back. How did things go?"

"We got your sword." Rondeau tossed a bundled blanket onto the coffee table. "Though we had to go the *long* way to get it, and by the long way, I mean to the edge of the goddamn solar system." He pointed a finger at Elsie. "We're supposed to be your allies here, you know. I realize it's probably stupid to yell at a god, but I am pissed. What were you thinking? Can't you tone down your basic craziness a little bit, at least until we've saved the underworld?"

"You're angry?" Elsie put a hand to her chest in mock surprise. "I thought you'd be pleased!"

"*Pleased?*" Rondeau made a show of twiddling his finger in his ear. "Am I hearing you right? You thought we'd *like* taking that little trip?"

"You know, I invented a spell once." Elsie smiled sweetly. "It manifests a large cork, an oversized version of the sort of thing you'd use to plug a jug, in the subject's mouth, and no force on Earth or in heaven can remove it. I called it 'The Corkinator.' Would you like to see how it works? No? Then stop interrupting. Yes, *pleased*. You're the only humans to ever step foot on Pluto! Well, except for Dave's fellow survivalists, but they didn't survive long, ha ha, they were poorly named, so they hardly count. I've been to Pluto and back, obviously, setting up those lovely accommodations for you, but I'm not human anymore, so my walkabout doesn't detract from your glory, either. A free trip to the edge of the solar system, privy to vistas mortal eyes have previously been denied, and this is the thanks I get. See if I ever arrange for *you* to get teleported to Trans-Neptunian space again."

Marla sighed. "What did she do, exactly? I really hope I'm misunderstanding you." The resulting explanation—with competing input from Elsie, Pelham, and Rondeau—was pretty difficult to follow. (Bradley stayed silent, probably wisely.) Once Marla had it more-or-less straight in her mind, she turned to her fellow god. "Random excursions to former planets aside, why did you send them after a sword you took from Barrow's dreamworld in the first place? You could have just cut out the middleman and handed it to us directly."

Elsie shrugged. "I gave the Blade of Banishment to Dave *ages* ago. Months and months. Then we started this little venture and I realized it would be useful to take it back. Certainly, I could have gone back to Dave's charming little compound and taken the Blade of Banishment away from him myself, but you and I had other things to do. Or would it have made more sense for me to send these three squishy fleshlings into the lairs of assorted full- and demi-gods, while you and *me* went to beat up a survivalist with no social skills in the mountains of North Carolina? It's like communism, or superheroes: each according to his abilities. The Avengers send the Hulk and Thor to beat up gods, and they send the guy with a bow and arrow to help the civilians get to safety. You're the Hulk in this allegory, because of your anger issues, though you've been more Zen Doctor Banner here lately, not that I'm complaining."

"So I'm Hawkeye?" Rondeau said.

"You're the leather pants Black Widow wears, darling." Elsie reached out and pinched his cheek.

Marla sighed. "Okay. Fine. A little more information would have been helpful, but I know that's like telling black ice it should try to be less slippery. How does this stupid sword help us, anyway? The Plutonian Shore it sent them to was actual *Pluto*, not the underworld. Did you get your literal and your metaphorical mixed up again?"

Elsie threw open the blanket, revealing the sword, which was the stupidest-looking weapon Marla had ever seen, even with its palpable aura of displacing magic. The chaos goddess let the towel wrapped around her body drop so she could pick up the weapon with both hands.

The boys all shrank away from the sword, if not from Elsie's nakedness, and she chuckled. "Don't worry, I won't bop you back to outer space. It doesn't send away everyone it touches, it's not like an electric fence that zaps anyone who gets close, friend or foe. The wielder has to direct its power with intention. Anyway, the destination is adjustable, see?" She twisted the gems on the hilt, which turned and shifted and flickered into new configurations. Marla saw the aura around the sword change, too, from black and gray to something like a deep purple shadow.

Elsie squinted at the sword with one eye closed. "Looks right to me. Can't really test it, though. Once we use this thing, the New Death will notice the breach and plug the hole. This sword will only work because the New Death doesn't know it exists, because it *shouldn't* exist, because it was dreamed into existence by a feverishly prolific mind."

"So we can get stabbed into the underworld," Rondeau said. "How do we get back?"

"We win, and I send you back," Marla said. "Or we lose, and none of us go back at all anyway."

"Ah, right. Thanks for clearing that up. Just wanted to know the itinerary."

Marla turned on Elsie. "You gave that weapon to this guy Dave, or whatever his name is, and he killed four people with it. Am I understanding that right?"

"It's *amazing* the things people do with their free will!" Elsie said.

"You're an accessory to murder, at the very least," Marla said.

"Oh, many times over, certainly. But maybe this time I was serving the greater good? Maybe Dave's militia buddies were planning an act of horrible domestic terrorism and by sowing dissension in their ranks I saved hundreds of lives. Did you consider that?"

"Is that what happened?"

Elsie shrugged. "How should I know? I didn't do that much research before I gave him the sword. But it's certainly possible. Sorry, Marla. You're complaining about my nature. I'm both the ill wind and the good, and even I don't know which way I'll blow on any given day. You can accept that, and benefit from my admittedly fickle impulse to help, or you can tell me to piss off, and I'll find some *other* way to occupy my many empty hours."

Marla held up her hands. "All right. The partnership holds. What's that old Bulgarian proverb that FDR quoted at Yalta? 'It is permitted in times of grave danger to walk with the devil until you have crossed the bridge?'"

"Aw, you think I'm the devil? You flatter me!" Elsie beamed. "You do know *you're* the lord of Hell in this room, though, don't you? I'm the one holding your hand… but not because I need to cross a bridge. I can fly. I just like holding hands. Figuratively, at least." She dropped naked onto the couch. "I say we order just an *immensity* of room service breakfast. Pelham, go do that, heavy on the poached everything. While we wait, and eat, and digest, Marla can tell us a story, and after that, we'll make our preparations to invade Hell, whee."

"We have more important things to do than tell stories—" Marla said.

Elsie stomped her foot. "You owe me, Marla. Tonight we dine in Hell, and I don't want your friends here to die without hearing my captivating origin story." She smiled around at them. "It's really wonderful, a real rags-to-riches tale of triumph and personal growth."

Marla sighed. "Do I have to? It... doesn't really paint me in the best light, Elsie. Which, hearing myself say that, I realize isn't likely to dissuade you."

The chaos god batted her eyelashes. "Oh, *please*, dread queen Marla? Regale us with the story of my ascent to goddess-hood? Tell them how I *completely* outsmarted you?"

"I wouldn't say completely," she muttered. "All right. Gather round, fellas. This happened in the underworld a while back, during my last stint in Hell before we fought the Outsider, when my *real* husband was still around...."

A Serpent in the Roots of the World

THE DREAD QUEEN OF THE UNDERWORLD and her husband the god of death had no need to eat, but since she was still intermittently human, and he'd grown (or rather been adjusted) to admire much about humankind, they sometimes donned human appearances and dined together, speaking with one another as mortals do.

The morning her quest began, the queen sat on one side of an octagonal table made from a single immense piece of shaped obsidian. Made, rather than carved, because no one had actually *carved* it.

She lifted a forkful into her mouth, chewed it, and made a face. "The hollandaise is perfect."

"The food of the gods," Death said. "So why do you sound disappointed?"

"You know how I like to complain, and this is so perfect, there's nothing to complain about. My compliments to the chef. But do we even have a chef, or is this stuff just wished into existence?"

"Technically, the eggs are no more real than this table." Death thumped his ringed fingers against the stone. "Which is to say, we have willed them into reality, and in this place, our will *is* reality." He took a bite. "I've had eggs benedict in the world above, though, and it didn't taste notably different from this, except not as good."

The Bride—as her followers, the cult of the Bride of Death, called her, to her cold and considerable amusement—lifted up her poached egg with her fork and looked underneath. "This isn't Canadian bacon. It's regular bacon. So this isn't eggs benedict, it's eggs blackstone."

"As always, I appreciate your tireless efforts to educate me. Blackstone. Like the table. I like that. It wouldn't be a bad alias for me to use if I have to go to the world above and pretend to be human, sometime."

"I can see your passport now: Mr. Mortimer Blackstone. There's a Blackstone in my ancestry, a few generations back. John Henry Blackstone."

"Did he invent this egg dish?"

She snorted. "I doubt it. Someone would have probably mentioned it if he had. He was a horse thief."

"You could go downstairs and look him up. See what kind of afterlife he's conjured for himself—if it's full of demonic horses because he felt guilty, or if it's full of happy little ponies frolicking freely. You could even nudge him toward a happier eternity if he's concocted something really terrible for himself. I know you disapprove of nepotism, but what's the point of power if you don't harmlessly abuse it every once in a while?"

"I don't even look in on dead relatives I *knew*," she said. "Let alone ones who died before I was born. I think I'll pass." She put her fork down. "Are we done small-talking? Don't we have any big talk instead? Matters of life and death, or mostly death, that need our attention?"

"Mmm. There are certain situations that would benefit from our presence. There's an epidemic brewing in southeast Asia, and a chemical spill in North America. I'm giving them a bit of my attention now. I know you don't like dealing with the human side of things, though—the shepherding, and coordinating the psychopomps, and all that."

She shrugged. "I just have trouble focusing on individuals from this vantage point. It's like trying to pick out a particular grain of sand and appreciate it for its unique and winning qualities. The woman with the scythe doesn't have time to get to know every stalk of wheat she mows down personally—she's concerned about the state of the whole field. You know I'm better with larger things, like the cycles of the seasons, both terrestrial and metaphysical. I'm bad with people. Even when I'm in human form, with my perceptions curtailed, when it's easier to tell all the scuttling mortals apart—even *then* I'm bad with people. I'm practically famous for it."

Death took another bite with obvious relish. "I think you're too hard on your mortal self. *You* can be perfect, in your way, or at least perfectly suited to your role. You're a god, so whatever you do is the right thing, almost by definition. During the months when you're mortal, you're.... only human. Holding your mortal self to your divine standard is unfair."

"What's fair got to do with it? We're the gods of death. Fair's got nothing to do with death."

He held up his hands in a gesture of concession, or conciliation. "I'm happy to let you play to your strengths, darling. As it happens, there have been some troubling occurrences, down below. I sent some autonomous personality fragments to investigate it—"

"Demons." She grinned, showing pointed teeth.

He sighed. "Yes, demons, if it pleases you. They never came back. They just... vanished. Which makes me think something dangerous is happening down at the bottom of the underworld. Would you care to take a look?"

"What kind of troubling occurrences are we talking about?"

"A few of the dead have disappeared from their afterlives. It happens, occasionally—after a very long time, they lose psychological coherence, or else they grow weary of their torments or delights, and they turn to oblivion. But the rate of attrition has been more frequent lately, and the raw substance of their denatured afterlives isn't returning to the cauldron of chaos after they disappear. Instead, something is taking the substance of their afterlives and...." He shrugged.

"Stealing it? Using it? Eating it? Are we talking about metaphysical thieves, or the world's greatest necromancer, or just some kind of underworld rodents getting into the cupboards?"

"I haven't a clue," Death said. "It could simply be a malfunction in the system. A leak of some kind. An imbalance. I couldn't say."

"'The system,'" the Bride said. "That's one way to describe it." She and her husband were the absolute and undisputed rulers of the underworld, but that was a bit like being the ruler of the sea: their realm was vast, largely unknowable, full of dark places, and populated mostly by creatures with no idea they *had* a ruler, some of whom would try to eat anyone who claimed the title in their presence.

The essence of the underworld was a sea of raw potential. Any creature that could dream or fear an afterlife ended up there after death, and found themselves in a little bubble of potentiality, a formless void to be shaped by their own hopes and worries and expectations. In those pocket realities, the departed souls inhabited the Hell, Heaven, happy hunting ground, Purgatory, Sheol, or Valhalla of their own imagining: some of the afterlives were fantastically baroque, or indescribably cruel, or unspeakable beautiful. Sometimes lovers or friends or families would drift together, their bubbles overlapping into a shared space, but more often any afterlife that demanded dearly departed relatives would be filled merely with simulacrums of the same. Some people truly expected, and thus received, only oblivion, or dissolved into a cloud of ego-less bliss—but most people didn't really believe, deep down inside, that *they* would ever cease to exist, and lose continuity of identity, and so most went on, in some form or another.

And now some of them were vanishing, and their bubbles of void-to-be-infinitely-shaped disappearing with them. That was interesting.

"Have you ever heard of this sort of thing happening before?" the Bride asked.

Death took a sip of blood orange juice, which his wife was convinced he drank mostly because of the name. If there were something called "murderfruit" he would have sipped its juice instead. "There's nothing in the memory of any of my predecessors that seems entirely similar, no."

"It could be a monster," she said. "Down there, underneath the everything, there's just the raw stuff of creation, and who knows what dwells there?"

"A monster? Well, it's possible. You know how these mythic situations can be. Even if it's just a malfunction, it could *present* as a monster. If you go down, just be careful, all right?"

"I'm a god of death," she said. "What could possibly happen to me?"

"You're not the first god of death," he pointed out. "And neither am I. Some of us retired gracefully, or dried up like dew in the sun, or switched off like lights. Others of us came to bad ends. There aren't many things that can harm gods, but there are a few."

"If anything like that threatens me," the Bride said, "there's going to be one *less* of them."

BEFORE THE BRIDE began her descent, she dressed herself in divine raiment, which in her case meant loose-fitting white linen pants and a snug white sleeveless blouse, with golden slippers that provided better footing than the best work boots she'd ever had. ("Linen" and "blouse" and "golden" and "footing" were all as unnecessary as eating eggs blackstone here, but she was a corona of divine fire flickering around a core of mortal woman, and so she still enjoyed the trappings of the physical.) She took up a rod of lapis lazuli, a scepter three feet long with a pleasing weight, because there was something down below that was killing their demons, and it would be pleasant to hit it with a stick. She wore a heavy golden necklace, and, golden bracelets, and, of course, her wedding ring on the appropriate finger of the appropriate hand. The Bride was not vain, but she might encounter some of the dead, and if they looked upon their queen, they should see *some* glamour.

The Bride set out from the palace, which wasn't really a palace, except sometimes. When she stepped outside—if you could call the interior of an immense cavern "outside"—she looked back to see what shape the residence had taken today. The obsidian theme had continued, and it seemed she currently lived in a mountain of glittering black glass, with no openings at all but the arched front entrance. Wasn't there a reference in some poem or story to Lucifer living in a palace of mirrors? This was undeniably more stylish. She wondered if the shape of the place was based on a passing fancy of hers or her husband's. They could shape things consciously, but if they didn't bother, the subconscious did the job well enough.

She tilted her head back to look up at what, for want of a better word, she thought of as the sky. There were things that looked like falling stars above her, a constant meteor shower, with new streaks of light appearing at the rate of about two lights per second, though there were occasional stretches with fewer and occasional bursts of more—sometimes many more. Those lights were the souls of the newly dead, streaking down to their afterlives. Sparrows, ravens, owls, winged human figures, and even the occasional spectral dog or horse occasionally flew or ran alongside a particular falling speck, but not many people believed in the necessity of psychopomps to escort their souls to the afterlife anymore, so such creatures were rare, and in any case evaporated in the atmosphere. Not many people paid the ferryman's toll to cross by water anymore, as far as that went. Most of the falling dead were just unaccompanied lights streaking through the dark.

The Bride walked along a path of stones the color of yellowed skulls until she reached a river, which ran swift and black and straight, twenty yards wide. Far away from here the famed River Styx ran, a useful barrier for keeping out mortals who managed to wander in through some forgotten portal or dread spell. (There was a train tunnel running under the river for those in the know, though. Progress marches relentlessly onward, Death said, even in the underworld.) *This* river, though, was almost as famous as the Styx: the Lethe, a river whose waters granted forgetfulness. Lethe water was highly sought-after by mortal sorcerers, since it could be used to wipe whole minds clean, or selectively edit specific memories. Under the regimes of previous gods of death, necromancers had been able to induce spirits and demons to bring small quantities of the stuff to the world above, and the Bride and her husband tolerated the practice under her reign, too.

Mostly because, as the mortal Marla Mason, the Bride had taken Lethe water twice herself. The second time, she'd used it to remove the memory of sex with a lovetalker, since those who were touched once by such supernaturally gifted lovers could never thereafter be satisfied by the touch of an ordinary human, and she'd hoped to have enjoyable sex again sometime.

The *first* time she drank Lethe water, though she'd used a lot more, and erased great swaths of memory—including the memory of drinking the water in the first place. But no corner of her own mind was closed to her god-self, and while she dwelt in the underworld in the fullness of her power, the Bride could look over the course of her entire life, just as she could look over any other mortal timeline. The reason for her first taste of Lethe water was just one of the *many* secrets the Bride knew, that her mortal self did not, and never would.

The Bride thought about that boy she walked along the riverbank. His name was—had been—Daniel. He'd been Marla Mason's first love. Her fellow apprentice, under the tutelage of the sorcerer Artie Mann, learning alongside Marla and their friend Jenny Click. All three of them were dead, now. Artie murdered by a serial killer on a mission given to him by things that called themselves angels. Jenny self-immolated in the extremity of her grief. And Daniel.... Daniel had died at Marla's hands, when a terrible compulsion forced him to dark acts, and made him raise his hand against her.

The guilt and loss over Daniel's death had so consumed her that taking Lethe water to erase all memory of her love, to erase the fact that she'd ever loved *anyone*, had seemed the only way forward. The Bride wondered how her mortal life would have been different, if she'd held on to that memory of young love. The sense of loss was a distant and unimportant thing, in her current form, when all mortal concerns seemed basically trivial. Thinking of Daniel's death while she was a god was like looking at a distant star. Thinking of it during her mortal life had been like being plunged into the *heart* of that star.

The detachment of being a god was almost as good as Lethe water, anyway.

She walked along the river, and whenever the course of the water began to meander, she straightened it out, because she had places to go. The presence of rivers in Hell was well attested to in the literature, so their existence was no surprise, but what people seldom stopped to think about was that rivers, by and large, ran down to the *sea*. And what kind of sea would you find in Hell?

The Bride stopped at the mouth of the river, where it emptied into a vast subterranean ocean that extended far beyond the limits of even her considerable vision. The sea shimmered in the light of the falling souls above, all of which struck the water in their turn, and vanished. There didn't need to be an ocean, or a river, or a shore (the sand was black, and under a microscope, would doubtless turn out to be composed of millions of tiny grinning skulls, or something similarly macabre). All this was just metaphor. But as her husband said, everything had to look like *something*: it would be boring and confusing to deal with pure abstractions all the time.

She walked along the stony shore, picking up the pebbles that made up the beach, and filling her pockets—she had pockets, now that she needed them—with smooth clicking stones. Once she felt sufficiently weighted, she took a last look at the flickering sky, and then walked into the sea.

The sea wasn't really a sea, of course, but a vast reservoir of chaos, the raw stuff of reality, in a form capable of being shaped by the minds of the dead. Occasionally, in the world above, there arose powerful psychics called reweavers, who could force the shape of reality itself to change according to their whims or their unconscious desires. In the afterlife, everyone was a reweaver, creating their own vividly realized worlds, from nightmares to paradises to everything in between.

But they were creating those worlds in the Bride's realm, and unlike most of the dead souls in this sea, she knew how to consciously manipulate the primordial chaos. Besides, this was *her* world. As such, she had the power to influence the afterlives of the dead, or even entirely override them, if she saw fit. She seldom bothered to do so, though occasionally she indulged the impulses for justice or revenge that bubbled up from the core of her mortal self. She'd look in on people she'd loved or admired in life, and if she thought they were being too hard on themselves, tweak the parameters to make their afterlives a bit more pleasant. Or she'd look in on old enemies and villains, and if their lack of guilt or remorse had led them to create afterlives that were too pleasant, she'd inject a bit of tribulation into their eternities.

Now she sank beneath the waves, through murky waters, and exhaled a cascade of bubbles that flew up and obscured her vision… and when the vision cleared, she floated in a vast black space occupied by billions of bubbles as small as apples and as large as suns, colored in shades ranging from pale gold to dark violet. The stones in her pockets evaporated, as she no longer needed them to pull her down. She was weightless, here.

The Bride drifted close to one sphere, a lurid magenta in color, and peered inside, seeing a plain of cracked black earth, dotted by ivory towers with a disturbingly organic quality. A human form raced along the ground, pursued by monsters that shifted through forms as she watched, but that mostly involved toothy jaws and waving pseudopods. The nightmare world of someone not terribly creative, with symbols even Freud would have found a bit too crude and obvious.

The Bride willed herself downward, past other spheroid afterlives, pausing at one that shimmered, prismatic. She looked into that one, and saw the final panel of Bosch's "Garden of Earthly Delights," down to every last detail, including the curiously affectless demons and surreal monsters tormenting equally blank-faced humans... except for one woman, who howled as the devil on the night-chair consumed her.

People talked about the "screams of the dying" but in her experience they weren't half as disturbing as the screams of the dead.

The Bride wrinkled her nose and checked the manifest that fluttered inside her mind. No, this wasn't Hieronymous Bosch's personal Hell, but one that belonged to a professor of art history who carried a lot of guilt for her dalliance with a fetching blonde undergrad. The Bride waved her hand and the edges of the Boschian hellscape shimmered into the blurry peace of a watercolor by Monet, which began to spread inward. The Bosch would reassert itself, eventually—you couldn't save someone from *herself*—but the Bride wanted to be able to tell her husband, "See, I'm capable of acts of pointless generosity, just like *you*."

She drifted downward again, pausing by a mottled gray sphere with an almost fungal aspect. Ah, yes, this world was familiar. Her mortal core had a particular antipathy for the soul who lived in *this* afterlife—he'd died long before her birth, but a necromancer had returned him to life some years back, and he'd caused Marla personal difficulties during his time above. The Bride decided to do her other self a favor and make the man's unpleasant eternity even worse. She didn't just peer into this bubble, but stepped inside, letting the locality drape her in appropriate attire, in this case a modest, dark gray dress and a hat that she could only think to describe as "stupid."

She stood on a rainy street—had it really been raining that day?—before Ford's Theater. She went inside, clucking her tongue at the sketchy quality of the setting. The employees and theater-goers in the lobby were faceless automatons, the carpet so threadbare in places you could see the pure chaos peeking through underneath. The theater itself was full of twittering shadows, but up in balcony, things clarified: there sat president Abraham Lincoln, beside his wife Mary Todd, though her face was blurry. The Bride stood on her tiptoes, and then kept rising, drifting toward the ceiling, so she could get a good view of the action.

Assassin, actor, and former revivified mummy John Wilkes Booth stepped into the box, a pistol in his hand, and said "Sic Semper Tyrannis!" as he pointed it at Lincoln's head.

The Bride *almost* smiled as she waved her hand, and the pistol flew from Booth's hand, unfired. He gaped and stumbled backward. Well, why not? He'd experienced this—assassination, flight, days on the run, death in a fire—thousands and thousands of times, without anything other than minor variations in the ordeal. Booth was a sufficiently arrogant and vile man that his afterlife hadn't been unpleasant at all, until Death stepped in and made it nastier on Marla's behalf, trapping him in a loop reliving his crime and downfall.

Another wiggle of her fingers, and Lincoln rose up, enraged, holding a bare cavalry saber in his hand. People thought of Lincoln as a dignified man in a beard and stovepipe hat, but he'd been a rail-splitter, and had attended at least one duel armed with a sword—though his opponent had seen reason and called things off before steel clashed with steel.

Lincoln opened his mouth and *roared*, swinging the sword in an arc over his wife's head. (She paid no mind at all, her eyes fixed on the stage, where shadowy actors milled around to no effect, doubtless saying the Civil War-era-actor's equivalent of "rhubarb, rhubarb, rhubarb" and "peas and carrots" at one another.) Booth leapt back in terror, then returned to his usual script by jumping from the balcony and landing on the stage below. He'd done that in real life, too, and made his escape from there.

This time Lincoln jumped after him, and when the president landed on the stage, the whole *theater* shook, and the president howled again, racing backstage after Booth, sword upraised.

The Bride sank down to the floor, then on through the floor, then out the bottom of Booth's festering bubble of misery and back into the blackness of the primordial sea. She accelerated her descent, the bubbles flickering past her so quickly now that she seemed to move through a sort of liquid rainbow. Despite the speed, she recognized a few of the bubbles as they went past. The afterlives of enemies her mortal self had contended with—the mad priest Mutex, the cannibal witch Bethany, and even a recent arrival, the cult leader and devourer of lives called the Eater. (She peeked into his afterlife, and saw he'd exactly recreated the small town where he'd ruled when he was alive. The banality of the place, she decided, was punishment enough.)

The orbs of dead friends caught her attention, too. A sphere of glittering chrome where Ernesto the junkyard mage dwelt among contraptions of infinite intricacy. The burning sphere where Jenny Click scourged all her personal demons with fire. A verdant green sphere where Lao Tsung, the man who'd taught her to fight, ruled as a philosopher king in a vast city of step pyramids. And a bubble the color of wet pavement, where Marla's first love Daniel suffered in eternal misery. Marla had never asked Death to make Daniel's afterlife more pleasant, because she didn't *remember* Daniel. As far as Marla Mason was concerned, she'd never loved anyone before the god of Death.

She glanced into the bubble as she went by. Daniel didn't even look human—he'd died after a fall from the top of a high building, and he looked as he had after the impact... except he was awake, aware, and mewling.

The Bride decided she'd indulged enough sentimentality today, and left the bubble behind, sinking toward the depths. She had a mystery to solve, and, if she was lucky, a monster to slay. What mattered the suffering of one mortal among billions?

After a long time, the bubbles thinned out, and the darkness thickened. She'd reached the bottom of the sea, where there was *another* sea, this one a shadowy, roiling black cloud illuminated by flickers of something that superficially resembled lightning.

She hovered, looking down into the primordial chaos from which her entire realm was built, the seemingly infinite supply of raw material that could be shaped by the unconscious minds of the dead, or by the whim of the gods of death. As she watched, new bubbles rose from the clouded chaos and drifted up to join the galaxies of spheres above, as the recently dead began their fresh new afterlives.

Suddenly, not far from her, a bubble the *exact* color of a dragonfly's wings... popped, and its iridescent substance rained down into the chaos, the droplets vanishing into the dark. *That* wasn't supposed to happen. She gestured, and drew up a few filaments of chaos, shaping them loosely with her mind and giving them just enough independent spin that she wouldn't have to do *all* the work of controlling the subsequent creation's actions.

The resulting demon was roughly the size of a six-year-old child, and had the head of a goat. Almost all her demons had goat heads, unless she consciously willed them to look otherwise—she had no idea why.

Something lodged in her mortal core's subconscious mind, probably. The ungulates *were* associated with the devil in some cultures, and she'd always found the horizontal slit pupils disconcerting. This demon had the body of a monkey, more or less, though its knees were on backwards, and it was covered in reddish fur. The demon knuckled its forehead, right between the stubby horns, and said, "Mistress?"

She reached out and plucked a hair from its head, holding it in her clenched fist. "Be a darling and descend into the cloud down there, then come back and tell me if you see anything unusual."

The demon cocked its head. "So... anything that's not primordial nothingness, then?"

"You understand me perfectly."

The demon shrugged and dove into the black clouds with the form of a high-diver, which was unnecessarily theatrical, but that was demons for you. She waited a while, the hair in her fist inert, and soon the demon leapt up out of the cloud and floated before her. "It's *very* odd, mistress. There's a sort of... carved-out space down there? As if someone dug a hole in the chaos and kept digging until they'd excavated a chamber."

The Bride frowned. "What kind of shovel would you use to dig up chaos? And how do you keep the chaos from rushing *in* again?"

"It's magic beyond my understanding, mistress, but I was only born a few minutes ago. Perhaps it would make more sense to you. There's a hole in the ceiling of the chamber, and I clambered inside. There's not much to see, really. Just an empty space. Except... there's a hole in the floor, and stairs leading down, and then a set of doors. I didn't try to open them. I thought I'd best report back."

"Go back down and see what's beyond the doors. Just *look*, mind you. Come back and tell me."

The demon sighed the sigh of put-upon underlings everywhere and dove back into the darkness.

After a few minutes, the hair the Bride clutched in her hand unraveled back into pure chaos again. Something had killed the demon. "Killed" wasn't quite the right word for such constructs, but it conveyed the essential idea.

"Hmm." The Bride tapped her rod of lapis lazuli against her palm. She was uneasy—an unfamiliar sensation, and not one she enjoyed. There shouldn't be anything down there that could destroy something *she'd* created. In point of fact, there shouldn't be anything down there but more *nothing*.

Nobody discorporated her demons but *her*. Whatever was down there, it was going to get hit.

As the Bride descended, she swept chaos out of her way, but it was like baling a boat with a colander, and the clouds kept oozing back. Soon she gave up and just fell through the murk. The chaos caressed her, velvety one moment, cold and damp as fog the next. She descended until she felt something solid under her feet, where there should have been nothing substantial at all. She took a double handful of chaos and shaped it into a torch, flaming end blazing as she swept it around, clearing away the clouds long enough to make out that she was standing on top of an immense dome of red-veined black marble. She walked along, her golden slippers giving her sure footing, until she reached the hole the demon had mentioned, about the size of a manhole, at the apex of the dome. Without hesitation she stepped into the hole, drifting down as slowly as a leaf, for what seemed to be a hundred yards or so. She landed on a floor made of the same stone, in a circular room. Frowning, she lengthened the lapis lazuli rod in her hand into a staff six feet long, and brought it down sharply on the floor.

The stone zigzagged and cracked, and the walls around her and the dome above her puffed into undifferentiated chaos again. As she walked across the floor, she let it crumble into nothing behind her, until she reached the stairs leading down. She'd expected something suitable for descent into a crypt or a dungeon, but the broad stairs were just dirty black, with walls of dingy brown tile on either side. The steps resembled nothing so much as the entry to a subway station, and there was a row of four closed gray metal doors at the bottom. She went down the steps, letting each riser dissolve after her foot left it, and when she reached the doors, she smashed two of them open with her lapis lazuli staff. The metal shrieked and tore as the doors flew inward, puffing into nothingness before the shards could land.

The Bride strode through the opening, into a small anteroom, this time with a floor of red marble with black veins. There was a counter on one side of the room, and behind it sat a bored-looking old woman with iron-gray hair, dressed like a waiter in an old-fashioned bistro, with a vest and bow tie. A single door of dark wood, beveled in a vaguely art deco design, stood closed in the far wall.

"Welcome to the roots of the world." The woman's voice was that of a thousand-pack-a-year smoker, with a lot of years piled up behind her. "Before you enter, you'll need to check your personal items."

The Bride looked at the woman, and saw no soul inside her, and no history of life. She was a construct, like the demons, whether she knew it herself or not. The Bride gestured with her rod—but the woman didn't disappear, or even seem aware that a god had just tried to dissolve her.

The Bride almost smiled for the second time in one day, a nearly unprecedented occurrence. She'd been afraid this would be easy. Instead, it grew more interesting. "Did you eat my demon?" she asked.

The coat-check woman shook her head. "That goat-headed thing? It ignored me and tried to go through the door. But unreal things can't go through the door at *all*. They just go back to being unreal again. Are you real? You seem like you might be real, under all that." Her hand-flapping gesture took in the Bride's clothes, her slippers, her lapis lazuli rod, her jewelry.

"I am a god of death, sometimes called the Bride of Death, and this is my realm."

The woman shook her head. "No, ma'am. Out there, it might be your realm. But not here. This was nobody's realm, *nothing's* realm, but now it belongs to someone else."

"Who?"

"*My* god," she said. "Some people have crises of faith, or so I hear. I don't. I have total faith. I know who made me, and what she made me for. My mistress told me herself."

"Listen, you talking mannequin." The Bride leveled her staff at the woman's face. "Your mistress may be able to turn my demons back into primordial nothing, but I'm not made of chaos. I'm the *mistress* of chaos."

The woman's eyes widened, and she covered her mouth, and then, to the Bride's surprise—and something like horror—she began to laugh. "Oh!" she said. "Oh, that's funny, that's *so* funny. Just you wait and see. You'll think it's funny too. If you go to meet her, anyway. But first, like I said: you have to leave your personal items."

"You want me to give up my rod? My jewelry?"

"And your garments. Everything." She gestured to the empty cubbyholes and clothes hangers in the space behind her. "You must go into the presence of my mistress stripped of all your fineries."

"You're seriously trying to pull the Descent of Inanna trick on *me*?" Inanna's descent was an ancient Sumerian myth, one of the oldest stories humans remembered. Inanna, the goddess of fertility and war, wanted to go to the realm of the dead to attend the funeral of a god. Before she was allowed to enter that dread domain, she was stripped of her fine garments and jewelry and her *own* lapis lazuli rod—symbolically giving up her divine power. She went naked into the presence of the god of death, who was her sister. There was a definite component of sibling rivalry involved.

Things didn't work out well for Inanna in the underworld, when she gave up her godhood, though she came back to life eventually.

"Inanna?" the coat-check woman said. "Never heard of her."

"No one's educated in the classics anymore—except I think your mistress must be. Who is she?" The Bride reached out with her additional senses, but could tell nothing at all about what waited beyond the door. She sensed not even chaos: just a blank space, unknowable, impenetrable.

"She is the serpent who gnaws at the roots of the world. I don't know who she *used* to be."

The Bride turned to the door and banged her lapis lazuli rod against the wood.

The rod shattered, breaking into seven fragments that fell to the floor, and when the Bride tried to will them back together, nothing happened: they just glittered, blue and shining and ruined.

The woman sniffed. "You can break your things and rend your garments instead, if you like. But if you leave your belongings with me, you can have them when you come back. *If* you come back."

The Bride kicked the door, and wrenched on the handle, but it wouldn't budge, even when she put the full force of her power behind it. She might as well have been an ant assailing a mountain. Someone with a *very* strong will, or a very deep understanding of the primordial magic of creation, was behind that door, imposing her own vision of reality so firmly that the Bride couldn't break it. Was it another god? Maybe an *old* god? There had been other gods of death—the Bride had even met one who, for want of a better term, could be considered her husband's father. Those old gods had died, because even death dies eventually, but did *they* have an afterlife, too, somewhere deep in the primordial sea? Had one of them rested uneasily and decided to carve out a little fiefdom in the lightning-filled shadows?

The coat-check woman sighed. "Look, lady, you can strip and walk through the door, or you can turn around and go back wherever you came from. I don't *care*. Just stop loitering. I was going to go on break in a minute. I need a cigarette."

The Bride had two choices: retreat, or go forward. The first was antithetical to her nature. She wasn't thrilled about the conditions attached to going forward, but who cared about her jewels and her clothing, anyway? She'd conjured almost all of it from airy nothing this morning, and would return it to airy nothing when she tired of them. Giving them up was no loss.

So she removed her necklace, and her bracelets, and her blouse, and her pants, and her slippers, and piled them all on the counter. The coat-check woman folded them neatly and put them all away, not commenting on the Bride's pale body or her many carefully chosen scars. She just clucked her tongue. "*Everything*," she said.

The Bride twisted the wedding ring from her finger, and put it gently on the counter. The ring *was* real—so real her mortal counterpart wore it on a necklace in the world above during the months she spent pretending she was still part of mundane reality. The ring was only a symbol, though. She'd been married to Death before he ever gave her that bit of gold, no matter how wrapped up the ring was in magics both protective and predictive. She didn't feel at *all* different when she took it off. She told herself that firmly.

The coat check girl put the ring in a cubby, too. "Okay. Go on in. You're expected."

The Bride frowned. "How am I possibly *expected*?"

"Maybe not you, in particular," the woman conceded. "But my mistress said someone would come down eventually."

"Enjoy your break. You're going to cease to exist shortly."

The Bride got only a fatalistic shrug in return. "Easy come, easy go." The woman gestured, and the brown door swung open. The Bride ground her teeth and stepped through the door.

The space beyond was a cave. There was no mistaking it for anything else: the walls were rough stone, there were stalactites above and stalagmites below, and the distant *plink plink plink* of the dripping water that had carved out this space over millennia, or would have, if this cave had existed in a place with actual geology. There were roots dangling from the ceiling, immense dangling things as thick as the trunks of thousand-year oaks, but pale as parsnips. An immense pile of red earth lay in the center of the cavern—

The heap moved, lifting its head, and suddenly its shape resolved in the Bride's vision. Not a pile of dirt, or a pile of anything at all, but a *dragon*, with scales in shades of red clay, Martian sand, and old rust. The beast was the size of an ocean liner.

Monster, the Bride thought.

The dragon lifted its immense head, looked at the Bride, and said: "Marla? Is that *you*?"

Then the wooden door slammed shut behind her, and the Bride of Death ceased to exist.

MARLA MASON OPENED her eyes, but that didn't help much. After a moment, she realized she was staring at dark stone. The reason being, she was face *down* on damp stone. She rolled over on her back and looked up at more dark stone, far overhead. She was in a cave. The stone was cold on her body, and equally cold on every *part* of her body, which meant she was *naked* in a cave.

That part was actually fine. She was used to it. She'd done it a few times before. Her life followed a particular pattern. She spent a month doing whatever it was she did as co-god of the underworld—maybe opening chthonic shopping malls, or plucking coins off the eyes of corpses and putting them in a goat-shaped piggy bank, or walking a three-headed dog and picking up its infernal poop, or making sure the seasons happened on time, or fending off assaults from other more evil gods, or holding the structure of reality together—and then she got to spend a month as a *real* person, on Earth, doing real person things, like eating sandwiches and punching morons. She never remembered what happened during her month in Hell, and for her, the passing of the time in between her mortal months felt like a single night of dreamless sleep. When it was time to bounce back onto the mortal coil, she *always* woke up naked, in a cave.

But she usually woke up submerged in dirt, because her husband (or her god-self) thought it was amusing to make her sit up in her own shallow grave when she came back to life. She also usually woke up in a cave in Death Valley, which looked *nothing* like this cave. The rocks were all wrong. So where was she? Had someone changed her supernatural travel itinerary without informing her? Gods could be inconsiderate that way.

"Oh, Marla, are you all right? I think you fainted." The voice was *immense*, but not like it was amplified electronically: like it came by that boom honestly.

Marla sprang to her feet, wishing very much for a knife or, at least, some pants.

"Of course, having your divinity stripped from you probably *is* something of a shock."

The voice seemed to emerge from a big… red… mountain? Was it a mountain? You didn't often get mountains in caverns, but what else could that thing under those dangling roots *be*?

"You gave up your divinity willingly, too! Although you didn't realize it at the time. Hilarious. You always were arrogant. I mean, I am *too*, I can relate, but still. I bet you thought to yourself, 'Oh, the ring and the scepter and all that, they're just *symbols*.' But we're in a place of pure formless void, to be shaped by whoever has the strongest will—*everything* here is a symbol, and when you stepped into my parlor, I decided those symbols of your divinity were as real as anything."

The big red thing lifted its head and Marla realized it was a dragon. That was alarming. But not as alarming as something else. A memory had appeared in her head, quite prominently, just lodged there, taking up great acres of mental space, and it was a memory that she *remembered entirely forgetting*. "Holy shit," she said. "When I was a teenager I had a *boyfriend*?"

The dragon rested its immense chin on the stone ledge where Marla stood and regarded her with eyes the diameter of carousels. "You know, Marla, not *many* things surprise me, but you? You really consistently do."

"His name was Daniel." Marla tasted his name in her mouth. "Oh, damn. I *killed* him."

"Huh. Well, sure. That's how most of my relationships end, too."

A wave of shame, dismay, and grief rolled over Marla, and she lowered herself to the ground, settling onto her back and staring upward. Tears trickled from her eyes and ran down her face and got into her ears. That first memory of Daniel's face led to other memories: Driving along a coast road with Daniel beside her, laughing. Skimming over the ocean in a boat with their mentor Artie Mann and their fellow apprentice Jenny Click. The first time she and Daniel had fucked—no, damn it, the ridiculous phrase "made love" was more accurate—in Daniel's room. The day he'd bought her the cursed purple-and-white cloak that had so defined her early magical career, and given her a silver stag beetle-shaped pin to hold it closed. Their missions, breaking into the mansions of rival sorcerers together. Daniel's disappearance on a mission with Jenny, and Jenny's subsequent self-immolation.

She'd remembered all of those *events* before, but the existence of Daniel had been neatly edited out of all of them. Now he was back, a core figure of her formative years. Gods. How badly had she screwed herself up, stunted herself emotionally, by magically forgetting the one time she'd actually really truly been in *love*?

But then she remembered Daniel's return, years after his disappearance, driven mad by seven years spent trapped on the bottom of the sea, subsisting by draining the life force of creatures down there with him. She recalled her joy at his return, and how it had transformed into horror when he insisted he had to bring their dead mentor back to life, and tried to drain *her* life force when she attempted to stop him. She'd been forced to kill Daniel to save herself. She shivered, all over, and not just because the stone beneath her was cold. She took in a deep, shuddering breath, and gasped, and sucked in another, and realized she was sobbing.

Yes. She could see why she'd cut Daniel out of her mind. How could you go *on* with grief like this?

"I can see you're going through some stuff," the dragon said. "I hate to interrupt, but I sort of had this idea that I was going to reveal my identity right about now—"

Marla sat up, wiping her tears away, marshaling years of iron-willed self-control and pushing her feelings down. "I know who you are, Elsie. It's not like your voice is any different."

Elsie Jarrow was a legendary figure in the magical world, the most powerful chaos witch in history, so potent that just being in her presence tended to give people cancer, as random mutations cascaded through their cells. Elsie had led a group of sorcerers on a mission to assassinate Marla a while back, and Marla had defeated her. Not *killed* her—killing Elsie Jarrow had been beyond her abilities back then—but she'd cast Elsie's mind out of her body and dissolved the witch's essence into the sea, spreading the particles of her being far and wide, with the hope that she'd lose all intellectual coherence in the process.

Apparently it hadn't worked, or anyway, not permanently. But Marla had more resources now.

"Do you like my new body?" Elsie said. She stretched her vast neck and took a bite out of one of the dangling roots, chewing it and swallowing.

"You haven't lost your flair for the dramatic. Wasn't there a dragon in Norse mythology that gnawed on the roots of the great world tree?"

"Very good! The dragon Nidhogg. Well, its name was a bit different in Old Norse, but that's as good a transliteration as any. That's what I'm doing down here, Marla: gnawing at the roots of the world. Have you figured out where we are yet?"

Marla looked around carefully. She licked her fingertip and held it up to the wind. She knelt and thumped the stone with her first. She pressed her ear against the cold stone. She picked up a loose stone and tossed it off the ledge, where it fell down into the cavern that Elsie's draconic body more-or-less filled, and nodded to herself when she heard it hit bottom.

"Looks like we're in some kind of big stupid cave, Elsie," she said.

Elsie laughed, and the cavern trembled. "You don't even *smell* afraid. How is that possible?"

Marla shrugged. "Last time I faced you, I was still mortal. I've had an upgrade since then. I can't die anymore, which makes me a lot less inclined to worry. I'm immortal, by marriage."

"Oh, *really*? If I eat you, digest you, and turn you into dragon shit, you won't be dead?"

"I doubt I'd enjoy the experience, but no—I'd be whole and healthy again pretty soon. There's a good chance I'd come back to life inside your stomach, actually, and you know what I'd do *then*?" Marla grinned up into a face as broad as a football stadium. "I'd kick my way *out*. So, no, you don't scare me. What do you want?"

Elsie rested her chin on the ledge again and gave a happy sigh that felt like a gale-force wind to Marla. At least it was warm. "You know, I've missed you, Marla. I always liked talking to you."

"You tried to kill me."

The dragon rolled her eyes. "Oh, well, that was just, you know. A thing. Besides, didn't we go so deep into being enemies that we practically came out the other side as friends?"

Marla frowned. "I must have missed that particular transition."

Elsie ignored her. "And now that you're a god, we can basically converse as equals!"

Marla snorted. "Good to know your opinion of yourself hasn't suffered. I defeated you just fine when I was your inferior, you know."

Another warm sigh. "That's not really something to be proud of. A prion, which is a thing that isn't even *alive*, can get into a person's brain and reproduce itself until the gray matter looks like a sponge, reducing the greatest mind in the multiverse to lumpy porridge. The inferior can *often* defeat the superior. That's what makes life so deliciously unpredictable." Elsie flickered out her tongue, and Marla leapt aside to avoid being struck by the forked muscle, which was as big as an ocean pier. "Normally, Marla, I enjoy the confusion of my enemies *and* my friends *and* also strangers, but since you seem to be constitutionally immune to suffering uncertainty, I'm going to tell you a few things. First of all: we aren't on Earth."

Marla nodded. "The presence of the giant tree roots sort of tipped me off. This is one of those mythic sorts of things, I figure."

"You're righter than you know. Where we are, Marla, is in the land of the *dead*. You know, your home away from home?"

A little trickle of worry flowed down Marla's spine. She'd been to the underworld as a mortal, more than once, but she wasn't supposed to do that anymore. She spent half her *life* in the underworld—but when she was here, she wasn't just Marla Mason. She was the Bride of Death, co-regent of the land of the dead, and her conscious mortal mind was dormant or expanded or incorporated into her god-self, which was vaster, more merciless, and even bitchier than Marla herself at her worst. She definitely wasn't feeling particularly god-like right now. When she was the Bride, she knew, the travails and torments of individual humans didn't matter to her, any more than one broken stalk of wheat would matter to a farmer striding into a field with a scythe. The Bride certainly wouldn't cry about *Daniel*, or anyone else.

"You brought me to Hell?" Marla said.

"Oh, sweetie. You were already *here*. This isn't your month of mortality. You're only partway through your month of being divine. Death and his Bride must have noticed me down here at the bottom of the sea of chaos, eating up the souls of the dead for sustenance, building my own little kingdom. You—the Bride—came down to investigate, and I tricked her—tricking people is one of my favorite things—into giving up her divine power before she could face me."

Marla made a face. "The descent of Inanna trick."

"You're repeating yourself, Marla. But, yes. When you strip the *goddess* away from the Bride of Death, what's left... is you."

Marla thought about that for a moment. "Death is going to notice, Elsie. He's awfully fond of me, in both my forms. And since you're a soul in his domain, under his control—"

"Ah, that's where you're wrong. I'm not dead. I came to this place alive, Marla. I was just a million loose particles of incoherence spread throughout the sea, driving the occasional squid insane just in passing, but then a little bit of me collected around a... vent, sort of. A hole. A portal. There was magic, there, and something in me responded to it, like iron filings drawn to a magnet."

Marla nodded. There were a few places where you could reach the underworld from the world above—the heart of the odd volcano, the deepest chasm of the occasional sea. There was a long tradition of giving humans a chance to enter the underworld and win back their loved ones, but Death said there was no reason to make it *too* easy.

"Bits of me collected there," Elsie said, "until enough of me came together that I could *think* again, and then, because I'm a curious sort, I went exploring, and I found this place. The land of the dead, billions of sentient souls, all in their own little bubbles of existence, creating their own afterlives."

"So you're alive. Do you think that *helps* you?" Marla shook her head. "This is Death's domain. He can boot you out. He can kill you for real. You'd better clear out, Elsie."

"Do you realize what the underworld is made of, Marla? It's made of chaos. The formless nothing of pure potential. The basic state from which all order arises. The dividing line between order and disorder, and the shift between the two, that's where I live! The first thing I did when I came down here was turn myself into a dragon, just to see if I could. That's not all I can do. I can be a god here. I can create anything I want, and unlike those poor dumb dead souls up there, I can do it *consciously.*"

Marla nodded. "Okay. So... do that, then. I think we have enough chaos to go around. You can be the big bad monster lurking at the bottom of the primordial sea. Create your own perfect paradise. I don't mind. Death might get territorial about it, but I'll talk him down. How about it? We'll be benevolently negligent landlords."

Another sigh, this one like a summer breeze. "You know, I tried that. I made a mansion on the moon and filled it with harem boys and girls and others. I conjured armies of monsters clashing on fields of flame. I made skyscrapers fall into each other like dominos. I bred contagious lunacies. But none of it *satisfied* me, because there's one way the dead people in this place have it better than me: they think their worlds are real. But, me, I know better. I know I made it all up. It's impossible for me to be *surprised.*"

"It's a pretty sweet situation, though, still. Lots of people would love to live in a fantasy world of their own creation."

"I am not most people, Marla. This play-pretend world simply isn't as good as real life. It's like punching a pillow instead of a face. It's like eating *carob.* I need real people to mess around with."

"Okay," Marla said. "So, what, you want me to show you the door? I can probably do that, and get you back to the world above."

"Unfortunately, I don't have a *body* to go back to. You know that. Out there in the world, I grew *too* powerful, became too much the embodiment of chaos, and even if I stole someone else's body, it would just rot around me. Besides, the inside of other people's heads always smell terrible."

"I'm at a loss, then, Elsie. What's your plan here? I know you *like* having plans, the more elaborate the better, because that way you can gain power when they inevitably go wrong. For you, every lose-lose situation is a win-win."

"I've given this a lot of thought, Marla, and to be honest, it was *your* example that gave me the idea. I think it's pretty clear that I've transcended what it conventionally means to be 'human.' There are people who've called me a demi-god, even—an avatar of disorder. But since I don't believe in doing things halfway... I've decided I'd like to become a god. For real. For really real."

"Huh. How do you intend to go about doing that? I only managed it by marriage, and sorry, Death's not polyamorous."

"I thought maybe if I ate some souls, that would help, so I've been doing that—snacking on the immortal sparks of any afterlife-bubble that drifts too close to me. They were delicious, very refreshing, and frankly some of them make pretty decent hallucinogenic drugs, but if eating them has made me more like a god, I haven't noticed. Still, the devouring served a dual purpose: to get the *attention* of a god."

"Ah. So the plan is, eat me, then?"

"The *plan* was to strip you of your divinity and cloak myself in that raiment instead. Except most of the things you stripped off just returned to nothingness when I touched them. The only things that stayed real were some broken bits of stone, and this ring." A huge claw rose up, and there was her wedding band, pinched between two enormous claws that narrowed to the sharpness of needles. "I tried putting it on, but— nothing."

"Well, sure. The ring's an artifact, but it's not like whatever wears the ring is married to Death. That would be a really stupid way to arrange things. Can I have it back?"

Elsie shrugged—Marla could now cross "see a dragon shrug" off her life list—and flicked the ring through the air. Marla snatched it as it fell. She'd had some vague hope that it would flood her with divine power, but no dice, not even when she put it on her finger. Oh well. It had never given her any godlike powers when she wore it in the mortal world, either. She felt good having it back, though.

"I think there is power in some of these objects," Elsie said, "but the power is specific to *you*. I can't use it. It's like a dress that won't fit. Or maybe like an transplanted organ I rejected."

"So, not to keep harping on this, but—what now?"

"Oh, I figure I'll keep you here until Death starts wondering where you went, and then I'll hold you for ransom and make him *give* me his divine power—"

Marla bent down, picked up a stone, and flung it as hard as she could right at the center of one of Elsie's immense eyes. The dragon roared and reared back, but by then Marla was already running for the door. If the door didn't open, she'd have a problem, but it swung open under her hand. Typical. A rational person would have made the cave inescapable, but Elsie wasn't a fan of locked rooms. She liked leaving the possibility of things going wrong.

Marla stepped out into a marble foyer, like the lobby of a fancy hotel, and an old woman behind a coat-check counter looked at her in alarm. Marla ignored her and started running, and her foot struck something as she ran—a shard of bluish stone about the size of her hand. There were half a dozen other shards of the same stuff. A snatch of a poem by Yeats fluttered through her mind—something about lapis lazuli—and she remembered that Inanna had carried a lapis lazuli measuring rod with her when she descended into the underworld.

Marla bent and picked up the hunk of stone, and felt a *jolt*, like a flicker of lightning passing through her body, and suddenly her senses expanded, and she could *feel* the vastness just beyond the opening on the far side of the room. The stone melted away, dissolving into her hand, but the power it imparted remained.

Ha. She'd snatched up a piece of her surrendered divinity. Not enough to turn her back into the Bride, to get full access to the whole suite of divine powers, but maybe enough to get her out of here. She rushed through the hole where some doors had clearly once been—

—and into a cloudy black nothing, where lightning flashed. Shit shit shit. She gestured instinctively, and a set of rickety wooden stairs assembled themselves from raw chaos, heading upward. Right. The stuff around her was formless void, but it could be shaped by someone with power and will. Marla was a *tiny* bit short of power, but she sure as hell had will.

Fuck the stairs, then. Marla lifted her chin, looked upward, and *flew*.

SHE DRIFTED AMONG BUBBLES in assorted colors, some beautiful, some just gross. She'd created some clothes for herself from shreds of chaos, briefly considering dragon-slaying armor before settling on her customary garb, loose shirt and pants and big stomping boots. Freedom of movement and the power of kicking: what more did a woman need? After a moment's thought she made a dagger, too, then decided to go bigger, and turned it into a double-edged sword. She'd wielded a sword forged in Hell in the past, and if this one wasn't so much *forged* as imagined, well, she still felt better having it. She sheathed the blade on her back and pondered her next move.

Something needed to be done about Elsie. The smart thing would be to keep flying upward until she found Death, fill him in on what had happened, and let him bring his divine wrath down on Elsie. The idea didn't sit right with her, though. She'd descended into this primordial sea to set things right, and even if she didn't remember taking on that mission, she didn't like the idea of admitting defeat. She was no match for Elsie, though, in her current state.

Marla didn't even know if she was still indestructible. Her mortal body couldn't die on Earth, but this wasn't Earth, and she had no idea if this was even her real body. She had some bit of the Bride's power, and access to buried memories that weren't available on Earth, so what the hell *was* she? Some kind of Bride-Marla hybrid? A demi-god?

One of the lessons she'd learned in recent years was that she couldn't do *everything* herself. Sometimes, you had to ask for help. Crawling back to her husband and asking him to save her was an intolerable idea, though. What alternative did she have?

She looked at one of the passing bubbles, the color of mud, and her mind said: That's Carl Offenson's afterlife, and it's mostly a bar situated by a slow-moving river full of trout, where his tab never comes due and the jukebox always plays his favorite Eagles songs. She propelled herself through space—not thinking about *how* she did it, the same way a millipede shouldn't think about how it moves its individual legs—and looked at more bubbles. A milky-white one full of infinite ice, where a man snowboarded forever. Another was a smoky hell of warehouses and piers. One was just a swimming pool the size of an aircraft carrier, filled with topless mermaids. Another was an entire galaxy, with a spaceship the size of a small planet drifting through the void, piloted by a steely-eyed war hero who'd been an avid computer gamer in his mortal life. Yet another was an endless field of delicious mastodon who lifted their heads and welcomed the spear.

She knew the names of everyone in every bubble around her, and what their afterlives contained. She thought, *Daniel?*

A grayish sphere rushed through the void and hovered before her. The interior was heartbreaking.

She stepped into it, and found herself on a rainy street in the city of Felport, where she'd lived, and where Daniel had died. He'd been a formidable sorcerer, with a power she'd never encountered in exactly that form since: the ability to manipulate the life forces of everything around him. He could animate unliving things, and he could drain life from those around him. He liked a good meal, but he didn't need to eat, since he could subsist on tiny bits of life force drawn from flowers, trees, animals, anything around him, taking quantities small enough that they were never missed, but that, combined, sustained him. That's how he'd lived in the aftermath of that terrible mission with Jenny Click, lost on the bottom of the sea, in a sort of coma, leeching just enough energy to survive from the life around him. When their mentor Artie Mann had died, a geas laid on Daniel had spurred him to return to the world. Artie had wanted Daniel to bring him back to life, but by the time Daniel made it to Felport, their teacher had been dead for a long time, and if that rotting corpse had been animated, it would have come back as a horror. Something with Artie's memories, maybe, but souls weren't meant to be snatched out of hell and restored to their bodies, and he would have come back *wrong*.

Marla had tried to explain the dangers, but Daniel hadn't been able to see reason, and he'd attacked her... and she'd fought back.

She found him now, a mewling wreck of a broken body, and knelt, putting her hand on what had once been his back. She closed her eyes, sought the little spark of divinity within her, and exerted her will.

When she opened her eyes, Daniel was whole again, heartbreakingly beautiful, long lashes and baffled eyes. "Marla?" he said. "What—what happened?"

"You had a terrible accident, baby." She touched his face.

"I—you—you got older."

She snorted. "Just what a woman wants to hear. I can't help it. You died young, and I was stuck living on without you."

He looked around at the shadowy, half-formed cityscape. "Oh. This... Isn't really Felport." His hand reached out, as if of its own volition, and took hers.

She squeezed his fingers in her own. Oh, Daniel. Her Daniel. "It's the underworld, hon. Your very own bit of the afterlife. You didn't make a very pleasant eternity for yourself, but I can see why. You had a rough life, there at the end."

"I don't... really remember."

"That's probably for the best." She considered how much to tell him, and decided to err on the side of simplicity. "I had to come down here because there's a bad thing rising in the depths. It's a woman that looks like a dragon and wants to be a god. I have to stop her. I was wondering—do you want to help?"

"I—what? How can I help? I'm dead."

"In the underworld, that's not necessarily a disadvantage. You're a soul: pure intention, unencumbered by biology. Lucky bastard. Here, you can shape reality. Give it a try."

He frowned, and the rain clouds above them parted, sunlight streaming down. "Huh," he said. "That's… wow."

"Nicely done," she said. "You can make whatever kind of world here you *want*. The afterlife isn't something imposed on you, and it's not punishment. It's what you make it." She laughed, only a little harshly. "It's sort of like *actual* life, that way. I want you to know you have that power, that you can make existence here sweet, if you like. If you want to stay and play around with your new mastery of reality, that's fine. But if you'd like to come on one last mission with me first, and help me slay a dragon…."

"I'm already dead, right? So… I can't die?"

"I'll be honest with you. The dragon has been eating the souls of the dead. I think when she does that, what happens to them is just… oblivion. So there's some danger here."

Daniel scratched his chin. "Not much point in playing a game if there are no stakes, huh?" He suddenly grabbed her, pulled her close, and kissed her, and the sweetness took her breath away.

I'm a married woman, she thought. Oh well. This hardly seemed the time to bring that up. Death would understand. Probably. Or maybe he wouldn't. He didn't exactly have any old girlfriends, after all.

"You've aged well," he said after he pulled away.

"You could stand to work on your flattery skills." He was too young for her anyway, now. She wasn't the woman who'd loved him, even if he was still exactly the man she'd loved. "So you're game?"

"I've been suffering, splattered on a sidewalk, for I don't know how long. Going out and fighting something sounds *great*." He rose. "So where's Jenny?"

Marla opened her mouth to say "She died" but then realized *that* was hardly a problem. "Let's go get her," she said instead.

JENNY'S WORLD WAS ALL FIRE, but Daniel had the hang of altering reality down already. He'd always been a fast learner, and naturally gifted, unlike Marla, who'd had to claw and struggle her way toward a mastery of magic. They floated in the upper atmosphere of the burning world, and Daniel kept them safe in a bubble of air. They flew through the smokeless flames, flickering in every shade of orange, yellow, and red, until a figure rose up and hovered before them. Marla recognized her old friend Jenny, but she was something more, here: a goddess of flame, with hair made of fire, and a dress made of fire, and really everything made of fire. She smiled, and her teeth were burning coals. "*Marla?*" she said. "And *Daniel?*"

"Hey, J," Daniel said. "How'd you like to try your flames against a dragon?"

Jenny laughed, and a column of fire burst from her throat, spraying droplets of plasma. "I think I'd like that."

"NO FUCKING WAY." Artie Mann spat on the grass, then shifted his position on the wrought-iron park bench and let out a ripsaw fart. "I've got a cushy situation here. Why should I risk getting eaten up by *Elsie Fucking Jarrow*? I was scared of her when I was alive, and back then, I had nothing to lose but my *life*."

Jenny was a flying bird of flame, zipping around the baroque towers of Artie's London, and Daniel was making every plant and tree underneath the glass panels of the Crystal Palace grow and swell and flourish with life. Leaving Marla to negotiate.

"Are you sure?" she said. "The old team, back together, it doesn't appeal to you at all?"

"Hey, fuck you, Marla Mason," Artie said. "You were supposed to avenge me when I died, and instead you let the murderer live, and used some magical bullshit to escape the compulsion!"

"He died *eventually*," she said. "And his life wasn't so great in the meantime."

"Whatever. Daniel was supposed to bring me back to life, and he failed, too. What's even the *point* of laying a magical compulsion on your apprentices if they can just slither out of it?" Artie gnawed an unlit cigar and scowled. Death hadn't made him any less fat, dumpy, or generally objectionable.

"Daniel didn't so much slither out of anything as get killed." She sighed. "I figured you'd take it like this, but I wanted to try."

"Yeah, yeah." Artie waved a hand. "I'm not as mad I should be. I twigged pretty early on that I must be dead, but this is a pretty good heaven, you know? Like that little pocket reality I made back on Earth, but so much *bigger*."

"You know, all this shit got real popular after you died." She gestured toward the cyborg governesses walking through the park, and the genetically-engineered gorilla wearing a tuxedo, and the zeppelins drifting overhead. "People dress up in top hats with gears on them and wear brass monocles and shit. There are about a million novels and comic books about it, Victorian England with weird tech. They call it 'steampunk.' You were ahead of your time."

"Fucking K.W. Jeter called it steampunk in the '80s. Fucking *Infernal Devices*. Goddamn Moorcock's *Warlord of the Air*. That was the real shit. You say steampunk got trendy? Glad I died before I saw *that*."

"Death hasn't changed you, Artie. You're sure you don't want to pilot an armored zeppelin and drop bombs on a dragon?"

"Fuck. You. In. The. Ear."

Marla kissed his cheek. He still smelled like cigars and body odor. Good old Artie.

DANIEL, JENNY, AND MARLA descended to the lowest reaches of the primordial chaos. Jenny kept sending fireballs spiraling through the darkness, but it didn't seem to hurt anything. Jenny was an uncomplicated creature, but when it came to pure gleeful destructive ability, she was hard to beat. Daniel was a subtler thinker, but just as powerful. With them, Marla thought she had a shot at taking Elsie down, or at least hurting her badly enough to make her flee the underworld. She could have gathered more dead allies, and it had crossed her mind—Lao Tsung, Mr. Zealand, Ernesto—but somehow going in with her oldest friends felt right. There were also limits on how long she could stand spend to-ing and fro-ing. Elsie was doubtless plotting her plots, and eventually, Death *would* come down here looking for her. She wanted to settle all this before that happened.

They reached the rickety wooden stairs she'd created, and Jenny made them explode into splinters. They floated down to the metal doors, which were still broken, something that heartened Marla. They strode into the anteroom, and the coat-check woman said, "Here, now, you aren't welcome—"

Jenny gestured, and the woman burst into flame, white-hot, and in moments, only vapor remained. "Oh," she said. "Was I supposed to do that?"

"Doesn't bother me. She was just a chaos robot anyway." Marla knelt by the broken bits of lapis lazuli, and gathered them in her hands, where they melted into her body. Her vision doubled, then somehow re-doubled, and she felt more power suffuse her. Deep in her mind something vast *turned over*, like a giant disturbed in its slumber. The Bride was still there, the spark of divinity burning more brightly now, but Marla wasn't ready to let her wake up fully yet.

"Jenny, open up that door," Marla said.

The burning girl pointed, and the wooden door glowed with heat, then dimmed, but still stood, unbroken and unharmed.

"That much heat would have melted the *moon*," Jenny said.

Marla sighed, walked up, and rapped on the door sharply with her knuckles. "Elsie! Open the door. You're in a closed system in there, very stable, it's not good for you. Come on. Add a few variables. Who *knows* what might happen?"

From beyond the door, there came a chuckle, and the door unlocked itself with a quiet *click*.

The three of them rushed in, and did battle.

AFTER ABOUT HALF AN HOUR, Marla lay gasping on her back, Jenny crouched beside her, burning like a bonfire. Daniel had his hands up, moving them around like a puppeteer manipulating invisible marionettes. "She's... getting... loose," he said, gritting his teeth with effort.

Marla groaned and sat up. The dragon Elsie Jarrow was suspended upside down, wrapped up in the roots of the world tree—or whatever the hell kind of tree Elsie had conjured, if there even *was* a tree up there, and not just roots for the look of the thing. Daniel had caused the roots to grow and slither and bind their enemy, but Elsie was gamely gnawing on them.

The dragon and Jenny had traded fire for a while, but they might as well have been throwing buckets of confetti back and forth, for all the damage it did either of them. Daniel had tried to suck out all of Elsie's life force, but she was somehow tapped into the raw stuff of chaos, and replenished her power endlessly. He set up a nice feedback loop, though, linking all their life forces so Elsie couldn't harm him *or* Marla without inflicting even more damage on herself, which had cut down on the direct attacks.

"This is stupid." Marla stood up and brushed soot off her knees. "Elsie! Don't you think? This is stupid?"

The dragon stopped chewing on the roots and let her head flop backward, looking at Marla upside-down. "It was fun at first," she admitted. "But, yes. Now it's stupid. We're fighting a real battle in an imaginary place. We're all good at hurling bits of the impossible at each other, but we're not really *getting* anywhere. I figure, we'll just keep battling until your month of divinity is up, Marla, and the law of the universe will drag you back to the mortal world. Without your divine spark lending these two strength and providing them with a day pass out of their respective afterlives, I'll be able to eat them. It's going to be slow, and *boring*, and I hate it more than I hate brussels sprouts, but that seems to be what we're doing. Oh well."

"Huh," Marla said. "Did you want to take a break and drink some tea or something?"

THEY CONJURED A LITTLE TABLE and a pot of tea and a few cups. Jenny boiled the water, then went flying around in the cavern, throwing fireballs at stalactites. She'd never been much of one for sitting down. Elsie stopped being a dragon, and took on a human form. Marla had never seen the woman in her original body, and wondered if this was a facsimile. She was petite, with a mouth that was a bit too wide to be pretty, and bright red lipstick that matched her hair.

"Why didn't you just change into a smaller form to escape the roots when I made them grab you?" Daniel said.

"Oh, I could have, but you were trying so hard. I didn't want to disappoint you."

Elsie, Daniel, and Marla sat sipping green tea and staring at each other. Finally, Daniel raised a tentative hand. "So, I have a question. Is there some reason Elsie *shouldn't* become a god?"

"Only logistical ones," the chaos witch said.

"And ethical ones," Marla said. "She's a murderer."

"Says the god of *Death*," Elsie retorted. "How many did you kill, even before that was your job?"

"Also, she's insane," Marla said. "The phrase 'insane god' is not a comfortable one."

"I was insane, yes. But only because I didn't have a body, and being a human mind without a body is confusing and very stressful. Also, everywhere I went, people died all the time, even if I didn't want them to. That sort of thing will put some cracks in your composure, Marla. If I were a god, I wouldn't need a body, or I could *make* a body, and I'd only be toxic if I *wanted* to be." She leaned forward, smiling at Marla, eyes twinkling . "Come on. I'd be a *wonderful* trickster god. The world would be a much more interesting place with me in it. It's not like I'm evil. I'm just... vivacious."

"Even if I thought you'd make a non-terrible god, it's not like it's up to me." Marla scowled. "I don't have a magic wand I can wave and say—'Poof, you're a god.'"

"I do," Daniel said. "Well, not a wand. But magic? Sure."

Elsie looked at him. "You are very handsome and smart. I can see why Marla likes you."

"What are you talking about?" Marla said.

Daniel reached out and touched Marla with his fingertip, right between her breasts. "There's a spark of divinity in you. I can see it, glowing, so much brighter than your ordinary life force. You know my power: I move energy around. I could take a bit of your spark and move it over to Elsie. It's no harder than draining life from one person and using it to strengthen another."

"Sure, but that would *diminish* me," Marla said.

Jenny landed beside them. "It's a spark, you said? It's a fire?" She shrugged, flames shimmering around her shoulders. "So... it's easy to make a fire bigger. You just feed it."

"Feed it *what*?" Marla said.

"Feed it primordial chaos." Elsie slapped the table. "That's where gods came from in the first place, anyway. This stuff, swirling all around us... it's basically the stem cells of creation, right? It can be whatever we *need*. Even divinity."

"I do not like this idea." Marla crossed her arms.

"Oh, that's just because you're locked into this win/lose paradigm, Marla sweetie." Elsie reached over and patted her hand. "But this way, you win by letting *me* win."

"That first part, about me winning, that's okay. It's that *other* part...." Marla drummed her fingers on the table. Her eyes caught the tattoo on her wrist: the words "Do Better," inscribed on her flesh by her god-self as an admonition, an encouragement... and mission. *Was* Marla just being stubborn and vindictive? Think about it. So Elsie became a god. What was the harm? Oh, sure, it could go terribly wrong, but really, before the woman had gone insane, she hadn't been famed as a slavering monster. She'd been known in the sorcerous community for her sometimes terrifying whimsy, her twisted sense of justice (which overlapped with her twisted sense of humor), and, yes, for being *fun*, in a certain wild bacchanalian sort of way. Unpredictable, dangerous, afflicting the comfortable, but no, never what you'd call evil, not until her power destroyed her body and she lost her mind.

"If you become a god, are you going to just murder a bunch of people?"

Elsie shook her head. "Dead people are boring, anyway. No offense, Daniel and Jenny. Alive people can *do* things. I like it when people do things."

"No causing plane crashes for kicks, either, understood?" Marla said. "Or ferry disasters, bus crashes, earthquakes… that kind of stuff is my purview. I realize I can't tell you not to *mess* with people, but don't mess with *lots* of people all at once."

"I can work with that. The personal touch is more my style anyway."

"Hmm. No doing damage to the structure of reality, either. You can't turn cities into, I don't know, giant mushrooms, or anything."

"I wouldn't dream of it. And if I do, I won't act on it." Elsie bounced up and down a little in her chair. "I get to be a god? Really truly a god? I've always *wanted* to be a god."

"If you're sure you won't be an *evil* god."

"Hmm, well, evil depends a lot on your viewpoint, but I don't have the patience to be an effective sadist, so I wouldn't worry about it."

Marla put her face in her hands. Do Better. "I can't believe I'm even *considering* this," she said.

"Should I do it?" Daniel said.

"I… Yeah. Okay. But listen. After you move some of my divine spark into her, I want you to fan the flames of *my* godhood first. Give me back the fullness of my power, and then do Elsie. I don't want her to be the only full-blown god in the room, not even for a second."

"Very prudent," Elsie said. "I can't be trusted. Which is why I'll be such a good trickster god. I wonder if Coyote is real. Or Hermes. Ooh, or Kokopelli. They're going to love me."

Marla leaned across to Daniel, and kissed him on the lips rather more chastely than she wanted to. "When you, ah, turn my divinity back up to full power, I might… change."

Daniel nodded. "I understand. Getting to see you at all, to fight with you again… that's more than I ever expected anyway."

Marla turned to Jenny. "Did you have fun?"

"I thought of lots of interesting new things I can set on fire when I get back home," she said.

"I'm, uh, sorry. That you died," Marla said.

"I was pretty bad at being alive," Jenny said. "This is better, for me."

Marla took a breath, exhaled, and nodded. "Okay then. Let's do a god transfusion."

Daniel took Elsie's hand, and then Marla's, and closed his eyes. Marla felt something inside her shift and then bleed away, passing through Daniel. Elsie's eyes widened, and she gasped, then trembled in entirely too erotic a fashion.

Daniel squeezed Marla's hand, and suddenly *torrents* of power flooded into her, the fire at the center of her going from spark to fire to bonfire to inferno to sun—

Marla closed her eyes.

The Bride opened them. She looked around, and what she saw displeased her, but an agreement had been made, and when gods made promises, those promises were kept, even if a stupid mortal part of the god had done the promising.

She released the hand of the dead boy beside her, wiping her palm on her pants. The red-haired woman—no, the red-haired *god*, now—stood and stretched, great prismatic wings unfurling from her back. She leapt into the air.

The Bride grabbed her foot and pulled her back down. "No you don't. We agreed to terms in principle, but we're going to hammer out some details now."

Elsie laughed. "We're both gods, you can't hold me here. I have a whole world to play in! A whole universe!"

"You fool," the Bride said. "We are both gods, but you are in my realm, and while there are many ways to enter the land of the dead, no one leaves this place without my permission. If you want to go play in that world of yours, we need to have a talk first."

Elsie sighed. "You're no fun." She fluttered back down to the ground.

"Marla?" the dead boy said, and the Bride waved a hand, banishing him and the burning girl back to their respective afterlives, and also from her mind.

"Your sharp teeth are so *pretty*," Elsie said cheerfully.

"So she's a trickster god now." Death sipped a brandy with cocaine dissolved in it—he'd read about the drink in some book, apparently. "Do you think *that* was a good idea?"

The Bride sighed. "I told Elsie if she got up to anything too destructive, we'd come down on her hard. There are two of us: we're twice the god she is. She says she's going to wander around being a fairy godmother, and occasionally a *reverse* fairy godmother. Giving people epiphanies, and ripping away the veil, and other nonsense. She might spawn some new religions, but I can't imagine any of them will last long. I don't think she's interested in conquering the world or anything. She just wants to make the world more interesting, and now she won't give people cancer just by walking past them, so what do I care? I escorted her to a passage back to the world above, and barred her from entering here again."

Death nodded. "Still. I'm surprised you didn't fight her to the bitter end instead, even if it *would* have required asking me for help. Defeating your enemy by giving her what she wants—that's an unusual approach for you."

The Bride bared her sharpened teeth. "I don't like it. Don't blame *me*. It was my mortal self's idea. True, I wanted Marla to change, to become a better person, to be less selfish, less rash, less short-sighted and pig-headed, but I didn't expect her to develop all this pointless *mercy*. The one thing she always did that I approved of was implacably fighting her enemies."

"Mmm. Are you going to let your mortal self keep the memories of this experience?"

The Bride shuddered. "Of course not. If I let her know it's possible to keep her own mind, with a measure of my powers, in *this* place? You know she'd try to find a way to keep her continuity of personality during the monthly transition, and remain entirely herself during her time in the underworld. That would be a disaster. She'd lose all objectivity, and would meddle in all sorts of trivial personal matters, here *and* on Earth. Just look at what she did this time, recruiting her dead friends to help her face Elsie, instead of turning to you for help! Stubborn, but at the same time sentimental. No, she doesn't have the right mindset to be a god. She takes things too personally. The… distance, the objectivity… I have in this form is what makes it possible for me to do my *work*. She can't have those memories. It's too dangerous."

"Not even her memories of Daniel?"

"Especially not of Daniel. Gods, who knows what she'd do if she remembered him? She might try to bring him back to life, and with her current abilities, she could probably do it—which would be ironic, since she killed him partly because he wanted to bring Artie Mann back to life. She's better off forgetting the boy." She sniffed. "You're enough one true love for anyone, anyway."

"I like to think so. Hmm. Seems a shame Marla went through all that, though, and won't retain any of the experience. It's the sort of thing that could change a person."

"Oh, well. I might leave a *little* thought in her mind." The Bride smiled. "A strong antipathy toward being overly merciful to her enemies, perhaps. Defeating someone by letting them win? It sets a terrible precedent, and I'd rather not have her repeat it."

"I'm sure you know best," Death said, with husbandly tact. "You have to go back to Earth soon. Your month here is almost over, and you need to deal with that thing that escaped from the caverns below Death Valley."

"Oh, right. The vermin from Elsewhere. How tedious. I can't believe the trivial things Marla chooses to spend her time on."

"Oh, I don't know. Creatures like that disturb me greatly. It's not from this universe, and so it's beyond our powers of life and death." He shuddered.

The Bride laughed. "You've never been mortal. When you're alive, *most* things are beyond your powers of life and death. Mortals gets used to it." She leaned over and kissed his cheek. "I will miss you while I'm gone. Perhaps we can spend some time together when I return? The workings of the world won't suffer much if we spend an afternoon crafting our *own* little paradise, will it?"

"I can't wait," he said, and kissed her back.

The Dead Boyfriends Club

ELSIE CLAPPED HER HANDS. "Bravo. What a romantic and, in retrospect, sad ending, though really you should have lingered more on my moment of triumph and elevation. Oh well. I'll write up some editorial notes, you can tell it better next time."

"Huh." Rondeau gazed thoughtfully at the ceiling. They were surrounded by the remnants of pancakes, sausage, eggs, toast, and the other detritus of a pricy breakfast. "All this time you had a dead boyfriend. Tragic love. Kind of puts your whole... you-ness... in a new light."

Marla sipped a glass of orange juice, her throat dry from all that talking. "I didn't *remember* he was dead, so I doubt it had much of an impact on my life choices, Rondeau."

He held up his hands in a warding-off gesture. "I know, I know, but that stuff has to get at you on some level, subconsciously or whatever... or maybe not, what do I know."

"You can join me in the tragic dead boyfriends club," Bradley said. "You be treasurer, I'll be president."

"Why can't I be president?" Marla demanded. "I literally killed my boyfriend."

"Well, me too. I got Henry into using. He wouldn't have overdosed if I hadn't handed him the needle."

Marla shook her head. "Thpt. He could've said no. I hurled my boyfriend off a roof."

"Yeah, but it was a self-defense thing. It was you or him. Nope. You're treasurer. *Maybe* secretary, but only if I see some tears on the anniversary of his death."

"I could have a dead boyfriend," Rondeau said. "I probably *do*. I mean, depending on how you define boyfriend. I have definitely slept

165

with some guys in Vegas who don't make the kind of choices that lead to a healthy lifespan."

"I have *loads* of dead boyfriends," Elsie said. "I definitely probably almost certainly killed at least a couple of them. I call vice-president!" She paused. "But wait, there was some other point to that story Marla told." She snapped her fingers. "Yes! You recruited your friends from their afterlives to help fight me. It was a terrible plan, of course, because you were up against me, so you had no chance, but it's not necessarily a terrible plan in *general*. I imagine the souls of the dead are probably eager to leave their little bubbles and cause trouble now that they're being boiled in molten feces, or whatever it is the New Death has come up with in terms of eternal torment. I was thinking: how about we stage a huge jailbreak? Flood Hell with the dead—I think given the circumstances we can technically call them the 'damned'—and give Skully something to think about."

"He would probably take vengeance on any souls who escape," Marla said. She held up her hand. "But they're already suffering unspeakable torments, etc., right, I get it. But... no. You just want massive disruption, Elsie. Any souls we come across, we'll try to restore to their former afterlives, and free from suffering, but it's not fair to ask them to fight."

"Fun is over *here*, and you are way over *there*," Elsie said.

"Tell you what. I might recruit some souls to help us, on a case-by-case basis. But nothing too indiscriminate." She looked around. "Last chance to quit, guys. No hard feelings if you choose to bow out now. Going into Hell in your physical body means you can *die* in Hell in your physical body, and your soul won't have to transmigrate very far. If we fail, you're in for an eternity of suffering, probably with some distressingly personal touches."

"I'm good," Bradley said. "Yes, eternal suffering, not fun, but we're in for that anyway, if Skully stays in charge."

"Except probably not for a while," Rondeau said. "Accelerating the timetable of eternal torment seems like a pretty bad idea." He shrugged. "But what do I care? I'm a psychic parasite inhabiting the body of a murder victim. I don't even know if I *can* die, and if I do, there's no reason to think I'd end up in your dumb human afterlife anyway. What've I got to lose?"

"There has never been any doubt that I would accompany you to the gates of Hell, Mrs. Mason, and on beyond them," Pelham said.

"Do we put all our hands together and shout 'Go team Marla' now?" Elsie said brightly. "Or can I start stabbing all of you and sending you to Hell?"

"Hold up!" Rondeau said.

"Yes." Pelham carefully looked at a point about a foot to Elsie's right. "You should put on some clothing first."

"The Greeks went naked into battle," Elsie said.

"That is true," Pelham said. "Though perhaps not relevant."

Rondeau raised his hand. "That's not what I meant. Since when do I object to naked anybody? What's I'm saying is, can you give us a couple of hours to settle our affairs, at least? By which I mean, go out and get laid one last time? You've been leaning on this 'certain death' thing pretty hard, so...."

Marla nodded. "Okay. We'll reconvene here at, say, six tonight? And then... into the pit."

"I'd better call Cole, and make sure Marzi still has a teacher after I get eaten by Cerberus or whatever."

"I should return my library books," Pelham said. "Lest they be out of circulation forever."

"I'm going to Paris so I can shop for an invasion-of-Hell outfit." Elsie vanished, presumably appearing naked in a French dress shop a moment later.

Rondeau looked at Marla. "What are you going to do?"

"I'm just going to take a walk." She closed her eyes, and folded the Earth, and when she opened her eyes again, she was in a dark office in the city of Felport, standing before a huge block of ice.

"Hi, Nicolette." She sat in a dusty chair and looked at the iceberg, which was also dusty. The room, indeed the whole building, had been magically sealed off; she could feel the wards pulsing from here, but she'd cocooned herself in obfuscating magics. "So it turns out freezing you into a block of ice was sort of hasty. A part of me I couldn't consciously access decided it was *done*, that I wasn't going to let my enemies win ever again, even if they weren't exactly enemies anymore, and even if them winning actually made the world a better place. It was a cold, nasty, vengeful personality quirk... and the truth is, I still have it. I still feel it. I'm not quite the Bride of Death right now, but I'm not quite plain old Marla Mason, either. I'm something in between, and it's less an amalgam and more oil and water, mixing and churning without ever quite blending. One goes up, the other goes down. You were a pretty terrible person, Nicolette, but if I'm honest, I've done some terrible things myself. You found your place, and you were doing good... and I threw a petulant fit, took the hard line, and stole all that away from you, deciding what you'd done was unforgivable... and that I was the person in charge of making sure *no one* ever forgave it."

She rubbed the place on her wrist where, in recent incarnations, the words "Do Better" had been tattooed. A message from her higher self, urging her to rise above petty and selfish actions, to take a wider and more inclusive view. She hadn't done a very good job of that.

Marla considered melting the ice and setting Nicolette free, but there wasn't time now to explain herself, or help undo the damage she'd done. Setting Nicolette loose now without guidance or assistance would just lead to a magical war between her and Perren River and the other sorcerers of Felport, fighting for supremacy, and sowing that kind of chaos and just walking away was more Elsie's style than Marla's. If Marla managed to survive the next day in Hell, she could see about redressing this particular wrong… and taking care of a few other things, too, before she succumbed to the inevitable consequences of her plan.

She turned the Earth, and found a nice mountaintop to sit on, and thought about all the things she'd done… and the remaining things she had to do.

Last Meal

BRADLEY TRIED TO COME BACK to the suite early, but the sound of Rondeau and some friend and/or paid companion making the most of his remaining time on Earth in one of the bedrooms led him to flee to the kitschy old-fashioned diner in the casino.

B had settled things as best he could, made sure Marzi would continue her education if he never made it back, and said goodbye to her without making it sound like he was actually saying goodbye, because it would be just like her to insist on tagging along to the underworld.

Now his mottled reflection in the chromed napkin holder on the table turned its face toward him. "Hey. Psst. Little B."

"Hey, Big B." He took a sip of his vanilla milkshake and tried to decide how crazy he looked talking to himself. Probably not that crazy; it was Vegas, after all. "Are you here to convince me to get reabsorbed into the collective instead of throwing my life away?"

"Nah, I tried that in a couple of adjacent branches of the multiverse, and you're the same all over. It's cool you want to help Marla."

"Any glimpses of likelihoods for me? Are we totally fucked or just regular fucked?"

"Some of your counterparts didn't bother with this whole one-last-afternoon-off thing, and bounced straight down to Hell.... because Elsie just started thwacking you all with the sword without asking first, mostly. I peeked in on a branch or two of the multiverse, but none of you have come back yet, which either means you failed or you're still in the process of winning."

"That's not comforting, but it's not *not* comforting. So what did you want, anyway?"

"To be totally honest? You seemed kind of lonely."

169

Little B laughed, and then went quiet, and said, "I've been thinking about Henry."

Big B nodded. "Sure."

"He's dead in this reality. Which means he's in that underworld. Which means he's suffering."

"I hear you."

"So we *have* to win. I know I'm punching out of my weight class, here. That I'm sidekick material at best in the company of gods. But I'll do anything I have to in order to put Marla back on the throne."

Big B nodded. "Yeah. Believe me, I'm rooting for you, even if... well. It's too bad about Marla, but that's how it has to go."

Bradley frowned. "What do you mean?"

"Well, if she wins, I mean.... Oh, you hadn't put it together. Or maybe you don't have the pieces you need *to* put it together. If you ever worked on a puzzle with Marla, she'd probably hide the edges and corners, just to make it more challenging."

"Are you going to clarify what you're talking about?"

"I... don't think so? Because it might be too much like trying to influence the outcome of events in your branch of reality? I say that because the wall beside me here at my house in the center of the multiverse just bloomed a big patch of black mold, which means I'm starting to overstep my bounds again. So, uh, never mind? Fight the good fight and do your best and believe in yourself and... don't do drugs? I guess you've got that last one covered."

"The only thing worse than worrying about something is knowing there's something you *should* be worried about but not knowing what it *is*."

"Nah," Big B said. "There are at least a *million* things worse than that. Good luck avoiding an eternity of suffering, Little B."

The reflection was just a reflection after that. Bradley considered fretting, and then he considered extrapolating and deducing, and then he ordered another milkshake instead.

AT SIX, EVERYONE ARRIVED. Rondeau had a spread waiting for them, including all their favorite foods: crème brulee for himself, crab cakes for Pelham, black-and-blue steak for Bradley, chicken-fried steak and mashed potatoes for Marla, and a big messy sausage-and-vegetable egg scramble for Elsie; he'd guessed about the latter and gone for something mixed-up and chaotic. He even got lemon pudding for Genevieve, on the off chance, though she didn't appear. He presented the dishes with a flourish and a bow. "Elsie said some crap about us dining in Hell tonight, and I thought, fuck that, let's dine in *Vegas*. Who goes to Hell hungry?"

"Just don't get overly full," Elsie said. She was wearing a dramatic white dress, the sort of thing an evil fashion magazine editor would wear in a movie. "The toilets in the underworld are simply not to be spoken of."

"Like in that Bosch thing, the Garden of Earthly Delights," Bradley said. "The beaked devil in the night chair, eating a guy and pooping out another guy."

"We might literally see that. I peeked into the afterlife of a very guilty art historian not long ago and saw exactly that tableau." Marla picked at her chicken fried steak, prepared almost exactly the way her favorite diner in Felport used to make it. Rondeau's gesture was thoughtful, but she couldn't help but think of condemned people on death row getting the last meal of their choice. "Skully said something about Bosch as an inspiration before he kicked me out, too. Expect to see an environment drawing heavily on the classics."

"But you need fear no devilish beak!" Elsie produced a pillowcase from somewhere and began pulling out helmets and passing them out. "Marla stole these from a god's workshop. They're the hoity-toitiest of haute couture in the area of godly, uh… millinery. Put them on and the New Death won't be able to eat your brains quite as easily."

Pelham put on his helmet, of a modified Spartan design (the actual Spartans wouldn't have included so many ornamental curlicues) without hesitation, and Bradley and Rondeau made noises of surprise when it shimmered and vanished. Rondeau reached out and thumped Pelham on the head with his knuckles. "Do you feel that?"

"Regrettably," Pelham said.

Elsie gave a heavy sigh. "These helmets protect against *mental* attacks. And attacks on your perception of reality."

Rondeau put on his bucketlike knight's helm, and Bradley his golden ornamental helmet, feeling their own scalps after the helmets vanished. "Weird."

"Do I get one?" Genevieve emerged shyly from one of the suites, one foot pointed behind her, like she might retreat at any moment.

"Certainly." Marla took the last helmet, an ivory one that looked like something a comic book supervillain would wear, and took it to her old friend. The helmet flickered in Genevieve's hands, giving way to the imposition of her own reality, changing into a fedora and back. She looked at it for a long time. "Hmm. It shields me from the outside, but doesn't inhibit my insides turning into outsides. That's good." She put the helmet on, and it faded to translucence before vanishing. "I am garbed for war. Do we go soon? I don't like being in the world like this for too long. I get distracted and things start to turn into birds when I don't mean them to."

"Birds are okay," Elsie said. "You should try beetles. God loves them. Darwin said so."

"One time Genevieve turned my TV into a lemon," Rondeau said.

"*That* was deliberate," Genevieve said. "You contacted me for a frivolous reason."

Rondeau held up his hands. "It's mea culpas all the way down, ma'am. Happy to have you on the team, by the way."

"If everyone's done eating, we should go," Marla said.

"If it were done when 'tis done, then 'twere well it were done quickly," Pelham murmured.

"That's the benefit of a classical education, right there," Bradley said. "A quote for every occasion."

"My thing about beetles was classic." Elsie's remark was generally ignored.

Marla turned to face her cohort. "Since we're getting all Shakespearean, this is probably the part where I should do my St. Crispin's Day speech. You know I've always been long on action and short on eloquence, and it turns out, getting a spark of the divine hasn't made me any more articulate. But I'll do my best. We're going to attempt something that might be impossible, but if anyone can do it, *we* can. I've known some of you longer than others, but I've known you all for a while, and I know all of you well."

She tried not to think *last words*, but it was hard. Maybe best to proceed like they were, though. There was no telling what awaited them in Hell. "Rondeau, you like to play at being the world's laziest fuck-up, but you've got more heart than a dozen decks of cards, and even when I've been furious at you, you've always been my best friend. You'd die for me and I'd kill for you, and maybe even vice versa."

"How can you not be attached to the girl who ripped off your jaw when you were a kid?" Rondeau said.

Marla turned her head. "Pelly, you came to me as an employee, but it didn't take long for you to prove yourself the bravest man I've ever known, willing to lay down your life and your sanity for the things you believe in, and now I'm proud to call you a friend."

"It is an honor to serve alongside you, Mrs. Mason," Pelham said.

"Bradley, you were my first, last, and only apprentice, and I was a terrible teacher, but you were an amazing student—and more than that, you became a better brother to me than my actual brother could ever be."

"Maybe that's why Jason doesn't like me," Bradley said. "Metaphysical sibling rivalry."

Marla looked at Genevieve, who ducked her head. "Gen, when I first met you, I thought you were my enemy, but then I realized you had more generosity of spirit, more basic human kindness, than anyone I'd ever met. You made me want to be a better person. I don't have a sister, but I wish I did, and I wish she was you."

"We can say so, and it can be so," Genevieve replied.

Marla faced Elsie, who looked at her coolly, and with a sort of detached curiosity. "Elsie Jarrow. First you were a sick person I had to keep locked away for the safety of the world. Then you were an assassin, doing your best to kill me, and an enemy I defeated at a greater cost than I realized at the time. Then you became a dragon, gnawing at the roots of my world, yet another monster for me to slay. Except, instead, I gave you a part of myself, and it's possible—just possible—that we both became better for it." She paused. "You're also dangerous and terrifying and I'm afraid you're going to stab me in the kidneys when we get down to Hell, just for the lulz."

"I won't *now*, not when I know you'll be expecting it." Elsie smiled. "You're somewhere between my midwife and my mother, Marla, but we both know I have all the loyalty of a spider to its ten thousand children, which is to say, not a whit. I still say the world is more interesting with you in it, and there's no higher compliment I can give." She brandished Night's Plutonian Sword. "Before the stabbings commence, do you have an actual plan?"

"Something like one," Marla said. "We're off to overthrow the god of Death. Weirdly enough, this isn't the first time I've tried to do that... but it's going to be a lot harder this time. Our goal is to cause enough trouble to get Skully himself to come for me. Then Genevieve will try to trap him, Elsie will hit him with a pickaxe, and I'll... work my magic. The rest of you are support staff. I don't know what the New Death will throw at us, but Rondeau and Bradley have the psychic sphere covered, and Pelham is pretty much panic-proof, so just keep any demons or Boschian weirdo-monsters off us. There's no point in making a more detailed plan than that, because the terrain could literally change around us. If we fail, billions of souls will suffer for eternity. So. No failing. Are we good?"

"Fate of the world shit," Rondeau said. "Always it's fate of the world shit with you."

"I wouldn't show up for anything less, darling." Elsie brandished the blade in a more-than-usually terrifying way. "Can I stab now?"

"Stab away." Marla picked up her battered leather bag, with its precious cargo, and slipped the strap over her shoulder. "Start with me."

"Yay!" Elsie shouted, and plunged the blade into Pelham's heart. His eyes widened an instant before he disappeared.

"Uh," Bradley said. "A little warning would be—"

She stabbed him next, then spun and slashed the blade through Rondeau.

"Elsie!" Marla grabbed her elbow. "I said start with me!"

"Sorry, sorry, I got linear time all *backwards* again." Elsie stabbed Marla, and winked when she did it.

Hell Is Some Other People

THE TRANSITION WAS INSTANTANEOUS, and not at all painful. One moment Marla was in Rondeau's suite, and the next, she was in a grove of twisted black trees, under a sky where, instead of stars, burning embers glowed. The trunks of the trees enclosed the bodies of damned souls, faces twisted in anguish, and the branches shook and rattled. Marla was conversant enough with her Dante to know this was his Wood of Suicides, with the souls of those who'd killed themselves entombed in bleeding trees where vile harpies roosted, and shat, and pecked. Skully really had embraced the classics.

She looked down at her clothing, frowned, and changed into the raiment she'd worn when she went down to battle Elsie. Only her leather bag remained unchanged, and she slung it comfortably across her back. A rod of lapis lazuli appeared in her hand: not necessary to channel her power, but a useful prop, and it was enjoyable to point it at things and make them explode. Then she looked around for her friends.

Rondeau was nearby, talking to a tree that appeared to hold a pretty young woman. She gazed farther afield, and there was Genevieve, approaching from the outskirts of the wood, gazing up at the sky with a look of concern and concentration.

There was no sign of Elsie, Pelham, or Bradley. Had they been separated already? "Fall in, troops," she called.

Rondeau turned toward her, and the moment his back turned, something dropped from the branches toward him: winged, with an avian body and claws, but the head of a woman, with long, scraggly hair, and a mouth that was somehow both beaked *and* fanged. The harpy squawked, and Rondeau spun, raising up his hands to ward off the attack—

A lemon fell at his feet. He stared at it for a moment, then looked up. "Guys. Guys, I just saw a harpy turn into a lemon. That just happened. This is going to be a pretty fucked up day, isn't it?"

"You and your lemons." Marla smiled at Genevieve. She'd never felt affection for anyone but Death when she was in the underworld before, apart from that interval when Elsie had stripped her divinity away. Bradley's memory-restoration had integrated her mind, mingling her mortal sensibilities and her godlike perspective. She could feel the arctic cold of the Bride's aloofness under the surface of her mind—assessing her friends only as potential tools to be used for her goals, to be sacrificed as necessary—but there still *was* a surface, and the capacity for human fondness. She'd been a little worried the Bride's aloofness would take over when she returned here.

"I don't know why it's always lemons." Genevieve shook her head. "I just like the smell, really." She gestured, and the grove of suicides transformed, black trunks turning brown, black leaves turning green, and countless bird-women shrieking and howling, briefly, before they turned into lemons, too. A thoroughly convincing sun bloomed in the sky, banishing the blackness and embers, and clouds scudded past. They could have been standing in an Italian lemon orchard. Marla took a deep breath. The air smelled... heavenly.

"So where are the others?" Rondeau said.

Marla shook her head. "I don't have my full awareness of the underworld, not with all Skully's interference, so I can't sense them. I saw Elsie poof Bradley and Pelham, though, so they're down here somewhere, unless Elsie's sword malfunctioned and sent them back to Pluto."

"Or she *made* it malfunction," Rondeau said. "Because she thought it would be funny."

"I landed in a graveyard full of burning tombs," Genevieve said. "I didn't like it there, so I turned it into a carnival I liked as a child. Then I crossed a boiling river of blood before I found you here in the wood. The others might have simply landed farther afield."

"With luck, we'll find them. I can't believe I'm saying this, but I hope Elsie's with them. I'd feel better if they had a god on their side, too."

"I'm glad I ended up on your team, Marla," Rondeau said. "Though I do wish I had a tommy gun or something."

Gen started to gesture, but Marla touched her wrist. "Wish *harder*, Rondeau. You should get the hang of manipulating things here."

Rondeau nodded, squinched up his face, and a moment later, a long-barreled black gun with a round drum attached appeared in his hands.

"All *right*." He looked the weapon over, then frowned. "Hey, this is just, like, a block of wood and metal. There's not even a hole in the barrel, or any place to load the ammo, and the trigger doesn't move...."

Genevieve clucked her tongue. "You either have to imagine *very thoroughly*, or you have to use your psychic powers to reach into the minds of those nearby who have a complete understanding of whatever you wish to create, and let their knowledge fill in the conceptual gaps. Here, when we are near so many of the dead, there is surely someone who knows the workings of such a mechanism intimately...." She held out her hand, and a tommy gun appeared there. Her garb shifted, too: stockings, a tight skirt, a blouse under a gray suit jacket, and a fedora. Her hair went black, and a beauty mark appeared on her cheek.

"Gun moll Genevieve. I like it." Rondeau gritted his teeth, and his own outfit shifted to a suit a forties mobster might have worn, with a fedora of his own. His gun subtly changed, too, into something functional instead of merely decorative.

"I'm not sure I like the outlaw theme," Marla said, "but it's good practice." She looked around. "What happened to the souls trapped in the trees?"

"Oh, they're over there. I think I shrank them?" Genevieve pointed, and Marla noticed a rising cascade of colored bubbles in the center of the orchard, floating from the ground into the sky. She went closer, and recognized the tiny self-contained worlds of the dead. Peering into a few, she saw some scenes of torment, but also scenes of pleasure, delight, and soft-focus tranquility. For the moment, Genevieve had freed these souls from the pains imposed upon them by the New Death.

That would piss him off.

"Where to?" Rondeau said.

"Oh, I think we should pick up a couple of assistants." She watched the rising bubbles carefully until she saw one roiling with flame, then took it in her hands, set it down in the grass, and whispered to it.

The bubble burst, and Jenny Click stood before her, dressed in flames, hair a whirl of fire. Jenny hugged her, hard, and it didn't burn. "Marla! You're back! I was a *tree*, it was terrible, birds pooped on me and I couldn't set them on fire, why was I a tree?"

Marla pulled back and smiled at her old friend, who'd immolated herself so many years ago in the extremity of her grief. "The underworld's under new management. The new boss has some strange ideas about rehabilitation. We're here to overthrow him. Want to help?"

"Ooh. Maybe. I had fun last time you brought me along for a conquering." She looked Rondeau up and down. "Who's your friend?"

"Rondeau. Uh. He's gay."

Jenny grinned. "So? That's okay. I'm *flaming*." She turned on Genevieve. "Whoa. What are *you* a goddess of?"

"It varies," Genevieve said.

Jenny rubbed her hands together. Smoke rose from her palms. "Are we going to go get Daniel now?"

Marla started to say no, they needed to press on and find their friends and assault the palace, but then she paused. Daniel's ability to affect life force, including the spark of divinity, might be useful... plus, it would be nice to see her dead boyfriend again. "I'd like to, but I'm not sure where he is...."

"What's he guilty of?" Rondeau said. "We're in, what, the seventh circle of Hell in this living Dante fanfic here? Jenny committed suicide, and she was right where you'd expect her to be. So what was Daniel's defining sin?"

"Nothing, he was a sweetheart, he always tried to do the right thing, he even *died* trying to do the right thing." But to the New Death, everyone was guilty of something, so what would he consider the core of Daniel's guilt? For some people it was easy to figure out: the old pornomancer Artie Mann, for example, would be in the second circle with the other lustful dead—

Ah. "Oathbreaking," Marla said. "Daniel was trying to fulfill a vow, to bring our mentor Artie Mann back from the dead, when he died. He didn't fulfill his promise, so I bet Skully considers him an oathbreaker."

"That's, what, lake of ice?" Rondeau said. "Circle nine?"

"I had no idea you read Dante," she said.

"I figured since my best friend was queen of Hell I should study up," he said. "So I read a graphic novel, and played a video game. There was this cool photo set online, too, some guy recreated all nine circles of the Inferno with Legos. I got the general outlines."

"I'll conjure us a ride." Marla concentrated, and the first monstrous steed that appeared was a reasonable facsimile of the flying monster Geryon, which had ferried Dante and Virgil across the eighth circle of Hell in *The Inferno*... but that was playing a bit too much into Skully's iconography, even if it was amusing to hear Rondeau squeak in alarm at Geryon's monstrous, multiform appearance. Instead she recreated a chimera she'd flown on, once, when Genevieve's exothermic nightmares were transforming her city: a large creature with the body of a bull and the wings and head of a seagull. Once it had precipitated fully into existence, the chimera turned its black-eyed head to her, then settled down on its forelimbs. Marla remembered her dream. If you squinted, it looked a *little* like a white raven. She climbed on, patting its neck, then looked to the others. "Coming?"

"I'll fly," Jenny said, rising up in a hazy nimbus of flame.

"Mmm. Me too." Genevieve stood on her tiptoes, then levitated further, hovering a few feet off the ground, still holding her tommy gun.

"That looks like advanced class." Rondeau slung his gun onto his back—it grew a strap, conveniently—and then clambered onto the back of the chimera. "Yip yip," he said, and the chimera took flight.

The sunlit lemon grove vanished rapidly behind them, and the sky went black again. They passed over a burning desert populated by roving packs of monstrous dogs pursuing the damned; Genevieve turned the desert into a sunny beach and the dogs into a pack of gamboling puppies playing in the surf.

Soon they passed an imperceptible border, and approached stony ditches spanned by rough-hewn rock bridges, the chasms below full of wailing, miserable souls. Immense centipedes—they seemed somehow more in keeping with Skull Island from *King Kong* than anything from Dante to Marla's eye—scuttled out of the ditches and rose up as if to attack them. Jenny whooped and blasted the creatures with torrents of fire.

Rondeau shouted, "I'm not going straight or anything, but Jenny's pretty hot."

"Puns are forbidden in Hell." Marla guided the chimera with her thoughts, sending it zooming around a skyscraper-sized centipede with mandibles to match. Genevieve floated along behind them, and in her wake the sky turned blue and flowers bloomed in the ditches. Bubbles ranging in size from ping-pong balls to houses floated up from the ditches as she set the dead free from the constraints of the New Death's grim worldview.

Soon they left the circle of the fraudulent behind, and landed on the edge of a frozen sea. Marla dismounted and walked to the ice, frowning. There were people trapped beneath the ice, their faces contorted in terror, their eyes moving and alive. Was Daniel here? He'd spent years trapped at the bottom of an *actual* sea after a disastrous magical mission, unable to escape, and he only survived by stealing the life force of passing sea life. He would have remained under the sea forever, barely subsisting, if a geas hadn't driven him to return to try and raise Artie Mann from the dead. Would being trapped under water again be peaceful for Daniel, or a nightmare?

She gestured with her rod, and the ice began to melt. First there were small cracks, then vast ones, and Jenny joined in, burning away ice with delicate streams of fire, almost laser-like, careful not to cause the dead harm. Genevieve took a more direct approach, causing the ice to turn directly into bubbles, freeing the trapped souls. She could overcome the New Death's vision of reality here with such apparent ease, and while that wasn't exactly surprising given how easily she could alter even physical reality, it was still damned impressive.

Rondeau just helped drag people out of the ice when they got sufficiently thawed out, but Marla was sure the people he assisted appreciated it. Each according to his abilities... There was no sign of Daniel, though, even when all the ice was gone and nothing was left but marshy earth drying under Genevieve's latest sun, and none of the bubbles belonged to him. Marla reached out with her godly senses, trying to find him, but there were whole sections of Hell blocked off to her vision: territory still firmly held by the New Death's worldview. Daniel must be in one of those areas. She hoped he wasn't a midnight snack for the devil in the night chair.

"Aw, poop." Jenny set a random patch of earth on fire. "No Danny-boy."

"It's a big underworld," Marla said. "He must be around here somewhere."

Rondeau scratched his nose and gazed around thoughtfully. "You know, Marla, Genevieve has thoroughly disrupted four-ninths of the circles of Hell, and the innermost four, at that. Shouldn't Skully be attacking us with his hellishly host by now?"

"I did figure he'd take more notice of our arrival," Marla said. "Maybe he's lying in wait. Setting an ambush."

"Or the others are keeping him busy," Genevieve said. "I suspect Elsie can be very... distracting."

"I wouldn't wish Elsie Jarrow on my worst enemy," Rondeau said. "But on Marla's worse enemy? Yeah. Okay. He deserves her."

Marla watched the bubbles of afterlives stream into the sky. "If Skully won't come to us, we'll find him. Let's go to my palace."

Unearthly Delights

BRADLEY *BLIPPED* OUT OF THE SUITE and found himself standing, understandably a bit disoriented, on a bridge made of flame-blackened stones, with the vague shape of buildings—mills? factories?—off in the distance, either belching out pollution or simply on fire themselves. A tattered flag bearing no sigil flapped in the brutally hot wind, and the creek flowing beneath the bridge wasn't water at all, but a feculent mixture of animal waste and blood. The stench was ghastly.

He looked to the left, and saw indistinct figures howling, waving weapons, and charging toward the bridge. Bradley opted to run to the right, and once he was off the bridge, decide to run *away* from the smoking, blackened buildings. If they were factories, they were factories generating misery. He looked over his shoulder and saw the eccentrically armored host leading an assault on one of the mills, and knew he'd made the right choice.

The earth beneath his feet was reddish-brown, like the soil was made of scabs, and when he crested a hill, he looked down on a dizzyingly surreal vista. There were ambulatory, gargantuan body parts—a set of ears the size of monster truck tires with a blade protruding between them, a heart bristling with javelin-sized spines, and skulls the size of buildings, the latter seemingly remnants of malformed giant cattle or horses. There were musical instruments, too, but of ridiculous size, and transformed into instruments of torture: harps with screaming people tangled in their strings, an immense lute with writhing figures bound to its neck, people impaled on flutes sticking up from the ground. There were more human figures than he could count, naked and terrified, some running from spotted catlike beasts, some trying to climb over one another in an effort to escape smoldering pits. He tried not to think of them as *people*, because if he did, the magnitude of their suffering made him too dizzy to function.

Some of the bizarre elements, at least, he recognized. He didn't remember the bridge or the Satanic mills, but maybe they were in the background of the image, overshadowed by the more bizarre foreground. The rest of these horrors were drawn from the right-hand panel of Bosch's triptych "Garden of Earthly Delights," depicting twisted symbolic torments of the damn. Far off the distance, he could even make out the figure of a beaked monstrosity perched on a high seat: the devil in the night chair.

"I had to go and mention Bosch," he muttered. Though he didn't think this landscape was his fault. Marla said this place could be shaped according to thoughts, but his vague memory of the painting surely hadn't been powerful enough to bring about all *this*. The New Death was just leaning on the old classics, as promised.

"The strange thing is, Hieronymous Bosch is doubtless *in* this underworld somewhere." Pelham emerged from beneath a huge, dusty skull, wiping dust from his suit. "Do you think he's here, now, horrified by his prescience?"

"If he is, he's probably screaming, 'But it's an *allegory*,'" Bradley said. "It's good to see you. I was afraid I was here all alone."

"As was I. I do not know what has become of the others."

Bradley looked around, and Elsie was *right there*, not even ten feet away, with a pickaxe slung across her back on a strap, and a trident with overcomplicated barbs on its tines in her hand. "Gentlemen!" she called. "The unpredictable nature of the terrain in the underworld seems to have separated us from Marla. But, you're in luck, you're still in the company of a god, so you *might* not die immediately." She sighed. "No offense, but I wish I'd stumbled across the reweaver instead of the actor and the butler. She can probably paint over this old artwork with something all bright and shiny with a wave of her hand, but we'll have to settle for my personal forte, creative disruption."

Elsie gestured with the trident, and a wave of changes rippled across the field. Some of the humans grew to immense size, and some of the lumbering giant monstrosities shrank. The newly empowered humans struck back at their tormentors, or began to tear apart the engines of their agonies. The devil on the night chair unfurled wings and tried to fly away, but a giant woman swatted it out of the sky, and began to stomp on its body. The scene was no more *pleasant* than before, and if anything it was more chaotic, but at least now the tormented had a chance to take revenge.

"Mmm, lovely, lovely," Elsie said. "Let's go look for the big bastard boss in charge and step on his neck, what do you say?"

"Sure." Bradley frowned. "But which way do we *go*?"

"Call up an oracle and see, silly! We're in *Hell*, there should be a spirit or two you can summon."

"Uh...." Bradley reached out with his senses, and yes, there was a *clamor* of supernatural forces, all eager to be brought into immanence. He'd never encountered such a crowded field before, but it made sense. He drew on residual supernatural energies, and this place was *all* supernatural energy. He chose a spirit that seemed small and manageable, and called it up.

The air thickened and became a goat-headed demon the size of a small child, with the malformed body of a monkey. It looked around. "Huh. I didn't think I'd ever exist again."

Elsie frowned. "Didn't I eat you?"

The demon looked up at her, picking its nose unselfconsciously. "Did you used to be a dragon? You *bit* me, and dissolved me back into chaos, yeah."

"Lovely to see you again," she said. "Where's the new lord of Hell?"

"I'll tell you, but he needs to make me a promise first." He jabbed his thumb in Bradley's direction.

Bradley nodded. "There's always a price. What do you want?"

"Tell my dread queen that I served her faithfully, and deserve to be given permanent existence."

He shook his head. "I can pass on the message, but I can't make Marla do anything."

The demon shrugged. "I just want you to put a word in."

"That I can do."

The creature frowned. "You agreed too easily. I should've asked for more. I want a name, too, my own name, like *you* get."

Bradley nodded seriously. "What name?"

The demon considered. "Muscles," it said at last. "I'm Muscles Malone."

Bradley maintained his solemn expression. "Okay, Muscles. I'll pass it on."

Muscles looked around, then leapt into the air, hovering about four feet up. "Mmm. I smell the new boss that way." He pointed. "Want me to guide you?"

Elsie chuckled. "Sniveling little conniver, trying to trick us into giving you more time in a coherent form."

"She sounds so *approving* when she says that." At some point Pelham had picked up a length of bone half as tall as himself, like a stretched-out femur, the color of ancient ivory. He held it like a walking stick, which, in his hands, was the same as saying he held it like a lethal weapon.

"It's fine," Bradley said. "Lead on, Muscles."

The goatish thing bobbed along like a balloon before them, setting a pace somewhere between a fast walk and a slow run. They left the garden of unearthly torments behind, moving into a wasteland of gravel… except, on closer examination, the gravel was actually millions of human teeth, some trailing bloody roots. "I don't like this place," Bradley said.

Elsie kicked up a shower of teeth. "Oh, I don't know. The New Death has a ridiculous aesthetic, but he really commits to the vision. He—"

"Incoming!" the demon shouted, and floated into the air to a height of about twenty feet. The teeth half a dozen yards away began to shift, move, and scatter, as something began to rise up from the depths: a hulking bear-sized demon with wrinkled elephantine skin, arms as big as telephone poles, and no facial features beyond a maw that gaped like a manhole, its bloody gums studded with hundreds of mismatched teeth, from the needle fangs of snakes to the triangular incisors of sharks to the jagged bladelike teeth of komodo dragons. The thing roared and rushed toward them, and Pelham darted forward, beating it about the head with his walking stick, surprising it with the ferocity of his assault. It tried to grab Pelham, but the monster was slow, and Pelham was quick—but after several sorties, the treacherous, slippery ground turned under Pelham's foot, and he stumbled.

Bradley tried to lash out with his psychic powers, but the thing had no mind at all, not even the rudimentary consciousness of a dog, nothing he could send to sleep or daze into confusion.

As the beast hunched over Pelham, opening its mouth impossibly wider, Elsie calmly dropped her trident, took her pickaxe in hand, and drove the point into the back of what, for lack of a better word, Bradley supposed was the monster's head.

The toothsome demon slouched, and then *kept* slouching, melting into itself like a mound of filthy snow dissolving in the rain. Pelham rolled out of the way and got to his feet, moving away from the spreading puddle of gray ooze. "Thank you for assisting me." His tone was stiff, formal, and scrupulously polite. Bradley knew that Elsie Jarrow was pretty much an affront to everything Pelham believed in—order, manners, civilization—but he was nothing if not gracious.

Elsie grabbed him in a headlock and gave him a noogie, then released him. "Can't let anybody hurt old Pelly. Marla would never forgive me, and that girl can hold a *grudge*." She stowed her pickaxe, but left the trident on the ground. After a moment, Bradley bent and picked it up. He was a thinker, not a fighter, but maybe it was a good time to try being both.

"Get down here, goat!" Elsie hollered.

Muscles drifted down to a height of eight feet or so. "All right, all right. This way." They set off again, and the toothy plain gave way to a valley of ragged, bloody fingernails, and then a plain of—and this was the worst—great matted wads of human hair in every conceivable color and texture, some cut, some apparently ripped from scalps.

"What vision of Hell did he get *this* from?" Elsie complained.

"Perhaps he decided to draw on images from nightmare," Pelham said.

"Or maybe we just haven't read every book or seen every piece of art about the underworld." Bradley stepped over a particularly bloody patch of blonde hair. "This is like the most horrible barbershop floor in the world."

"We're nearly to the palace," the goat-demon said.

"I do so love palaces." Elsie gave a little shiver of anticipation. "They make such interesting sounds when they implode."

The sky, which had hardly been bright before, darkened further, and the wads of hair gradually thinned out, revealing gray stone underneath. In the distance, jagged mountains loomed, but a tall mount stood much closer, all alone, a cave mouth the size of an airplane hangar door yawning in its side. Reddish light flickered from the interior. "That's the palace." The goat demon drifted higher, as if edging toward an escape.

"That is a *cave*." Elsie shook her head. "The New Death lives in a *cave*?"

"Marla said he was kind of… austere," Bradley said.

"It does seem a poor habitation for a god, however," Pelham said.

"The first gods lived in caves." The voice seemed to whisper intimately into Bradley's ear, and from the way Pelham jerked and stared around, he'd heard it the same way. "Because the first humans capable of *believing* in gods sheltered in those caves, and the gods lived among the people, then. Gods have often dwelt on mountain tops, and in high lonely places, and in dark caverns beneath the Earth."

Elsie clucked her tongue. "I prefer to dwell in places with swim-up bars. What's the point of being immortal if you don't *live* a little?"

A figure appeared in the cave opening, the silhouette of a stocky, broad-shouldered man, with a misshapen head. Bradley fought off an urge to avert his eyes, or to fall prostrate. The New Death radiated power, and Bradley could feel him *pushing*, trying to do… something. Overpower Bradley's mind, or change his body, or transform his surroundings. His scalp began to tingle. Maybe Elsie's invisible helmets really did something after all.

The landscape blurred, and suddenly the three of them were no longer a hundred yards away from the mountain, but directly in front of it, standing mere feet away from the New Death. He had the skull of some horned creature that wasn't quite a bull; maybe an aurochs. "How dare you invade my domain, newborn god?"

Elsie laughed her outsized laugh. "You call *me* newborn? I'm older than you by months, at least. Respect your elders, sonny, and your betters, too. Either way, respect *me*."

"I am of an ancient lineage, and pure." Skully clenched and unclenched his fists. "*You* are tainted by humanity, and of an upstart line."

Elsie drew herself up, and for the first time, Bradley felt something like awe in *her* presence, too: she was turning up her god-wattage, and it shone. "I may not be from a line as old as Death, but *nearly*, because as soon as people realized there was such a thing as death, they started figuring out ways to *cheat* death. I'm a god of hairsbreadth escapes and sudden reversals. You're the stone wall, and I'm the dynamite. You're the coyote, and I'm the roadrunner." She paused. "I know traditionally coyotes are seen as tricksters, but there's this classic cartoon, you've probably never seen it because you're literally an infant, where this coyote chases a roadrunner, and never catches it, and in some ways it's a reversal of the traditional iconography—"

"Cease your prattle!" Skully lashed out with one hand, clearly intending to slap Elsie across the face

But Pelham moved in a flash, and smacked the New Death's hand aside with his bone walking stick. The god turned, roaring, and Bradley thought *oh fuck oh fuck of fuckity fuck* and tried to stab Skully with his trident. The spikes bent like wire on impact, the skin of the New Death's abdomen not even dented. Skully tore the trident away anyway, hurling it into the cave behind him, then snatched the walking stick from Pelly's grasp, snapping it in two as easily as Bradley would break a twig.

Then the New Death groaned and fell to his knees. Elsie stood behind him, both hands wrapped around the haft of her pickaxe Trepanner. The point of the axe was buried right in the top of Skully's head. The god coughed, and burning embers floated from his bony mouth. His hands clenched and twitched and spasmed.

"Good work distracting him there, boys." Elsie beamed at them. "Who even *needs* Marla, right? Maybe I should seize the throne myself, huh? I'd be a great dread queen. The dreadliest."

Skully slowly lifted his hands. He didn't reach for Bradley or Pelham, or try to wrench out the pickaxe. Instead, he lifted his aurochs's skull from his shoulders, axe and all, twisting the skull with a sound of tearing cartilage and flesh. He tossed the skull and axe aside and rose to his feet, stumbling, headless, into the cave.

Elsie stood, apparently dumbfounded. She picked up the axe, the aurochs skull still stuck on the end. She lifted the axe high, staring at it blankly, then began to giggle. "It's like a candy apple on a stick, isn't it?" She pointed the axe downward, put her foot on the skull, and stomped, knocking the skull loose, leaving a neat star-shaped hole in the bone. "I bet I could sell one gently-used death god skull on the supernatural black market for *crazy* money. It's a shame I've transcended any need for material wealth, huh? That's always the way it goes."

"The New Death is wounded," Pelham said. "How shall we proceed?"

Elsie swung the pickaxe in a casual arc. "We *could* charge in there and try to kill him again. But I'm starting to think the whole 'murder Death itself' thing might suffer from certain logistical difficulties. Like, maybe we're trying to burn the sun or freeze ice or drown water or something, you see what I'm saying?"

Bradley let out a low whistle. "You think we can't kill him?"

"I thought the chances were fifty-fifty with Trepanner here. Looks like we got the wrong fifty though. So, at this point, we can go all suicide-mission, with the consequences for suicide being eternal torment with a *personal* touch for you two, and I don't even *know* what kind of horror for me. What do gods do to other gods who try and fail to kill them? I mean, I can imagine what *I* would do, and I don't want to be on the receiving end of anything in that conceptual vicinity."

"Mrs. Mason suggested that she had plans beyond a simple brute force attack," Pelham said.

Elsie nodded. "Yeah. I know her endgame, I think, because I know *her*, and how she thinks, but I'm not sure how she expects to get to that point."

"We could ask her," Muscles called. "My queen approaches!"

"Always fashionably late," Elsie said.

The Palace of Death

THREE FIGURES STOOD BEFORE THE MOUNTAIN the New Death had in lieu of a palace, and Marla's heart rose. Bradley and Pelham were okay. Also Elsie was there, which didn't make her happy, exactly, but by and large it was better to have the chaos god where you could see her.

"Marla!" Elsie said. "And your merry band of miscreants, plus that friend of yours who tried to set me on fire last time we met. Welcome, welcome. We confronted your enemy and I axed him in the head. I was *majestic.*" She gestured grandly. "The boys helped. Oh, and a sort of goat-demon thing, too, named Muscles Malone, that wants you to make it a real boy. I think it flew away, or maybe it just quit existing for a minute. It's so hard to find good—"

"Wait, you killed Death?" Marla stared at the skull on the ground at Elsie's feet. She hadn't sensed when the old Death died, so the New Death could certainly die without her sensing it, she supposed... but if so, it was oddly anticlimactic. The good part was that she could throw the thing in her shoulder bag into a deep pit instead of using it.

But Bradley shook his head. "The New Death just, uh, tore his skull off and stumbled into the cave. He's hurt, maybe? But I don't know how badly."

"He's got a whole interchangeable head thing going," Marla said. "I thought it was purely cosmetic, but I guess it's got its practical side too." She climbed off the chimera and patted its flank, then let if fly away, though it wouldn't last long without her attention. She tilted her head back and looked up at the mountain. "This is *all* wrong."

"Would you like me to redecorate?" Genevieve said.

Marla shook her head. "No, I can feel my power waxing. We've broken the New Death's absolute control of this realm, and the balance is shifting." She cocked her head, and the mountain transformed into a

189

palace of white marble, akin to an elaborate tomb but scaled up to make a suitable habitation for giants. "There. Much better." Her clothing changed, too, the armor of bones and ice and metal appearing when she willed it.

"Whoa. Full Valkyrie."

"Thanks, Rondeau. But I'm more like the one who employs the Valkyries." She tried to summon Death's terrible sword to her hand—possessing that blade was crucial to her ultimate success—but it wouldn't come. The New Death must be wielding it, then.

That was okay. She'd just need to take it away from him. "Is everyone ready? Same plan as before: help me clear a path to Skully."

Pelham stretched out his hand, and a walking stick with a brass ball on one end appeared in his hand. Rondeau hefted his gun, and Elsie spun Trepanner around in her hands with a grin. Bradley and Genevieve were empty-handed, but they had other resources.

Marla led the way, the rod of lapis lazuli in her hand. The entrance was big enough to accommodate a zeppelin, and the foyer was a vast ballroom of marble, with candles floating unsupported in the heights. At the edges of her vision, the marble flickered, transforming into rough stone walls and back, but wherever she focused her attention, her version of local reality held sway.

Elsie really *had* hurt Skully, at least enough to loosen his control. Or maybe Marla was just better able to use her powers now that her mortal mind and her godly perception were fully integrated. The whole bargain she'd made, separating her mortal life form her divine one, had been a profound miscalculation. She'd been so desperate to hold on to her humanity, to keep her mortal self separate, that she'd essentially given herself dissociative identity disorder. She'd made the Bride of Death into a separate personality, practically a separate person, and an antagonistic one, at that. Now, for the first time since her ascension to godhood, she was fully herself, just one thing, truly whole, and in the place where she belonged.

Scores of human-sized doorways opened in all directions, some at floor level, some placed at random heights on the walls, but Marla recognized a trivial delaying tactic when she saw one. She gestured, and all the doors vanished, except the one that actually *led* somewhere: straight ahead. "He's through there." She sensed a ripple in the chaos, a gathering of power, a reallocation of energy and matter. "Um. Expect resistance."

A horde poured out of the doorway, bellowing in rage. Marla had expected cartoon devils, three-dimensional renderings of demons from old illustrations, or predictable, recycled pop-cultural nightmares. Instead, Skully had conjured monsters drawn from the pasts and minds of his enemies.

Among the dozens of monsters were versions of Bradley with shards of mirror for teeth, a writhing golem made of flesh-stripping beetles, a shambling corpse with its flesh sprouting deathcap mushrooms, disheveled men crackling with electricity, pale dogs, and a passable imitation of the Beast of Felport. They were all just conjurations, though, little wads of chaos given shape and limited autonomy, and she waved her lapis lazuli rod and turned them into puffs of cloud and nothing before they got within twenty feet.

"Aww," Rondeau said. "You could've left a few for me to shoot."

"Trepanner hungers for brainmeats, Marla," Elsie agreed.

"Skully is trying to delay us, and that means he wants time to *do* something, even if it's just finding a new head. I'm not inclined to give him an extra second." She started forward, but more figures emerged from the door… and these had a heft of independent reality the others hadn't.

"Oh, hell," Genevieve said. "Pun intended. And I thought *I* assembled a pretty good Marla Mason Revenge Squad."

The first time Marla had come to Hell, she'd been forced to confront the spirits of everyone she'd killed. Skully's recruitment was a bit more broad, though: this seemed to be just about every dead person who'd ever borne her a grudge.

"Hello, Marla." Regina Queen, dressed in floor-length white fur coat, offered an icicle smile. "You asked for my help, and repaid me with assassination." Her son, the pale subterranean sorcerer Viscarro, skittered forward in his mother's wake, dressed in ragged monk's robes. He looked worse actually dead than he had when he was undead.

Marla shrugged. "Well, Regina, you're a murderous psychopath. That's just how it had to go. Hey, Vicky. Wasn't your whole goal in life cheating death? How'd that work out?"

The two of them were joined by Marla's old rival Susan Wellstone, who still bore the bloodstain over her heart from when Marla's dark doppelganger the Mason had killed her.

"It's bad enough your arrogance led to my death," Susan said. "To be forced to spend eternity under your rule is intolerable. You weren't even fit to rule a city, let alone the entire afterlife."

"Good to see you again too, Sue. Did you bring along Gregor? Ah, there he is." The conniving dark-haired sorcerer smirked at her, hiding behind more formidable shades. Susan and Gregor had been a real pain in her ass, once upon a time, and apparently they were getting the band back together.

The mad priest Mutex was there, too, face impassive, an obsidian knife in each hand. The cannibal witch Bethany as well, sprouting wings of scrap metal, her teeth filed to points. The anti-mancer Christian Decomain—well, he was probably here for Elsie; she was the one who'd turned him into frogs and then stomped on a bunch of them. The shapeshifter Finch, transforming into a grizzly bear as he approached.

Marla scowled. "Finch? What do you have against me? I killed the guy who killed *you*! He's standing right there! Or are you still pissed I interrupted your stupid swingers party?"

The bear just growled. Others filed in. Somerset, the old chief sorcerer of Felport, trailing a cloud of pigeons. The shimmering, indistinct blur that was doubtless Gustavus Lupo. That haole sorcerer who'd styled himself king of the Hawaiian wizards, the one she'd called Greaseface, still wearing his absurd feathered cloak. Jason's thuggish friend Danny Two-Saints, holding a straight razor. The half-burned, ambulatory form of John Wilkes Booth, carrying a pistol. And more, and more, and more, all dead by her hand or at least in her vicinity—

"Marla, don't let yourself get sidetracked." Rondeau put his hand on her shoulder and gave her a little shake. "Like you said, Skully is just trying to buy time, you can't settle old business with all these... oh, shit, is that Campbell Campion? Cam-Cam? Aw, man I'm so sorry, I didn't know Jason was planning to kill you—"

Pelham slammed his walking stick down hard on the floor, three times, *crack crack crack*. "We must not be delayed! These poor souls have all died. Their lives are finished, and that old business is done. We must move forward."

"We aren't here to delay you." Regina seemed to be taking charge, which wasn't too shocking. She'd always gravitated naturally to authority, fueled by her endless fount of arrogance. "We're here to kill you. Being dead is terrible, Marla. You're going to hate it."

"I'm the *good* queen here, you idiots," Marla said. "Most of you are straight-up villains, and the New Death believes you've earned an eternity of nightmarish torment. Believe me, you'd *much* rather have me in charge, with my laissez-faire policies. You should be helping me defeat him."

"He's promised us paradise if we slay your friends and bring you to him," Regina said. "Paradises *beyond* our own capabilities to imagine."

"We're happy with our decision," Susan said. She never could stand to let anyone else be in charge. "Kill them!" she shouted.

Marla tried to banish the dead back to their afterlives, but they were *locked*, impossible for her to budge: Skully was pouring a considerable percentage of his attention into keeping them solid and present.

Mutex came at her first, knives weaving, and though she cracked him across the face with her lapis lazuli staff, he didn't even flinch away. "Fight them!" Marla shouted. "Take them apart, they don't feel pain!"

The next few minutes were confusion. Elsie cackled gleefully, laying about with Trepanner, making a special point of driving the axe into the head of Christian, which was good; his magic-suppressing skills still worked here, but anti-mancy was no protection against a heavy metal object bashing in your skull. He fell—and then vanished. Marla gasped. She could sense that Christian's soul was *gone*. He'd been cast out, into oblivion, and had ceased entirely to exist. A magical pickaxe that could wound gods could erase the souls of the dead, too, it seemed.

Marla's other friends fought less definitively, but their attacks were effective, too. The bodies of their enemies were constructs made of primordial chaos, and being dead already meant they couldn't be killed, but they *could* be disabled. Rondeau kept falling back, blasting away with his tommy gun, managing to cut Lupo nearly in half with gunfire. There was no blood, of course, and the skinchanger flickered through assorted identities while sprawled on the ground. Pelham seemed to be dancing with Viscarro, his walking stick cracking hard against the subterranean sorcerer's long, nearly skeletal limbs. Jenny Click poured fire into Regina, who poured ice right back: at least their elemental antagonism seemed evenly matched. Bradley was fighting with Gregor, who dodged and spun with grim intensity. For her part, Marla had to fight off Susan Wellstone, who was now riding around on Finch in his bear form, one hurling magics, the other swiping with claws. Bethany was trying to flank her, and Booth was taking potshots with his pistol, though she was one tyrant he wouldn't be able to assassinate; her armor was more than sufficient to turn bullets, at least.

Where the hell was *Genevieve*? She was the trump card, and she should have been able to end all this easily: dropping this rogues gallery into a pit, weaving cages around them, manipulating the environment in ways even Marla couldn't. Marla kicked Bethany in the chest, dodged around the bear, and scanned the corners of the palace.

Gen was separated from the others, on the ground, scuttling away from an advancing attacker, someone Marla didn't recognize, a bald white guy in a dirty peacoat. Genevieve could alter *reality*. Why was she afraid of some random—

"Oh, shit. When did he die?" The man coming for Genevieve was objectively the least formidable person in this group by several orders of magnitude. He was stupid and brutish, with no magic and no impulse control, just a common street thug. But back when he was alive, he'd brutally attacked Genevieve, sending her already-fragile psyche over the edge. Genevieve had later faced him, and realized he wasn't a monster of mythic proportions, but just some asshole, and it had seemed to help her psychologically... but apparently seeing him here, now, coming at her again, was too much of a shock, and she'd forgotten her own progress, and her own powers. He was her PTSD personified. Marla had to—

Something drove Marla to her knees, a terrific weight and force slamming into her back, and she smelled fur and sweat and the stink of bear-breath.

"Elsie! Jenny!" She flung out one arm, pointing with her lapis lazuli rod at Genevieve's personal boogeyman. "Get rid of him!"

Jenny broke off attacking Regina and flew across the room, and Elsie pirouetted and giggled her way in that direction, too. The thug—what was his name, Terry?—looked around, eyes wide in totally justified terror.

Jenny made him burst into flame, and Elsie started beating him with her axe like he was a vein of gold she was trying to mine.

Marla heaved upward with godlike strength, flinging the grizzly from her back, and ran toward her frightened friend. "Gen! Genevieve, you're okay, he's down, but we need help!"

Genevieve looked at her, eyes wet and blank, then shook her head and got unsteadily to her feet. "I—I'm sorry, seeing him was just such a shock, I didn't even know he was dead...." Her eyes widened as she took in the scene, a decent cross-section of Marla's personal murderers' row doing their best to kill her friends.

"No!" Genevieve shouted. She brought her hands together, and there was a sound like a thunderclap, flinging all the antagonistic souls flying in every direction, slamming them hard against the marble walls. The wind she'd conjured didn't touch Marla's friends, only her adversaries, even the fallen ones. Tentacles and arms of white marble emerged from the walls, grabbing onto the dazed souls, and pulling them all—some screaming in fear, some shouting curses, some rendered incapable of sound by the battle previously—into the walls, where they disappeared as cleanly as pebbles dropped into a pond.

The sudden silence was resounding. Marla looked around. "Is everyone okay?"

"No." Bradley's voice wavered. "No, not everyone."

She turned, and her heart became a falling stone. Bradley knelt beside a spreading pool of blood, and at the center, there was Pelham, an obsidian knife still protruding from his chest, his eyes open and empty.

"Pelly!" Rondeau dropped his gun and raced to his friend's side, sliding on his knees in the blood. He tore the knife out of Pelham's heart and threw it aside. "Marla, Genevieve, somebody, you have to heal him, come on, it's just a little hole!"

Marla lowered her eyes. "I can't... Rondeau, he's gone." Pelham's body was an empty shell, his soul already departed. She closed her eyes, trying to sense his immortal self, and there he was, a falling star among many others in the heavens over Hell, streaking toward the great sea of primal chaos where he would make his afterlife.

Marla had known the chances of everyone getting through this unscathed were pretty much zero, but *Pelly*... he'd barely even had a life. He'd been raised on an estate, trained to serve aristocratic magicians, and had only been given a brief time to make his own way in the world. She'd never had a more loyal friend, and she couldn't think of anyone she'd known who was a better man.

Rondeau sat in the blood, put his head in his hands, and sobbed. Bradley embraced him, pressing his face into Rondeau's shoulder, but from the way his shoulders shook, he was crying too.

"He was a sweet little guy," Elsie said. "But we don't have time to mourn so much just now. We've got to save the underworld."

"Shit." Rondeau's voice was muffled by emotion and, probably, snot. "Pelly was my best friend, Marla. You used to be, and probably if somebody had asked me yesterday I still would've said it was you, but you haven't been around so much lately, and he... he was *there*. He was better than me, Marla. Made me try to be better, too, on my best days. Ah, fuck."

"The afterlife isn't so bad." Tiny flames still flickered around Jenny's head, but she looked more human and less elemental now, her face shadowed by grief. She hadn't known Pelham before today... but seeing his loss had probably reminded her of her own fallen friends. "At least, when the New Death isn't *making* it bad."

"Yeah, but I don't get to enjoy the afterlife." Rondeau shook off Bradley and got to his feet. "I'm stuck with plain old *life*. Mutex didn't kill Pelham.

He didn't even *know* Pelham. Mutex was just the weapon the New Death used. Let's go, Marla. Let's fucking tear that skull-faced shitlord to pieces."

"Mmm, vengeance is my *favorite* motivation," Elsie said.

Bradley rose, too. "For Pelham."

Marla nodded. "For Pelham."

"Would you… I could clean you up." Genevieve's voice was shy.

Rondeau shook his head. "Not me. I'll wash Pelham's blood off when Skully is dead."

"Okay then," Marla said. She looked at Pelham's body, and the scene flickered. A marble bier appeared, his body resting on the stone, the spreading pool of blood gone. His suit was impeccable again, and his wounds invisible. He'd always hated to be messy. "We'll see to a proper burial, a memorial, and everything… after all this."

She turned toward the doorway. No more monsters appeared. Whatever the New Death had been buying time for, he must have finished it. There was no telling what they were walking into.

"Remember what I told you, Genevieve?" she said.

"Yes, I do."

"Good. Be ready."

"Ooh, is there a secret plan?" Elsie clapped her hands together. "I hope *I'm* a crucial part of it!"

"Yeah, you've got a role to play." She walked toward the doorway. "Let's end this. Let's take back Hell for the good guys."

The New Death and the Old

THE OTHERS ALL FOLLOWED MARLA into the corridor… except Jenny. She hit an invisible wall that Marla couldn't knock down. Where they were going, apparently, the dead couldn't go… or, at least, not any of the dead on Marla's side.

"I'll stay here and watch over Pelham." She embraced Marla, and kissed her cheek. "Thanks for letting me out of the bubble. Go in there and win, okay?"

Marla returned to the others, and they were a solemn and serious crew, even Elsie—though the solemnity looked false on her face. The corridor twisted and doglegged and finally led to a dank cavern lit by smoky torches on the wall. The surroundings stubbornly refused to give in to Marla's will. The rest of the underworld was open to her alterations, now, she could sense. The New Death had consolidated his attention and power in this particular place, and so focused, it was more than she could overcome.

Her husband stood in the back of the cave, arms crossed over his chest. He'd acquired a new head, the oversized skull of a viper, with curving fangs as long as knives.

"A venomous snake?" she said. "You really have no imagination at all, do you?"

"Did you enjoy meeting your old friends?" he said. "Would you like to see a few more?" He gestured, and suddenly figures appeared before him, kneeling in a row, arms bound behind them, heads bowed.

Marla hissed in a breath. Daniel was there, front and center. That's why she hadn't been able to find him. Skully was using him… and others. She recognized all the captives but one, a young woman on the end. At least Pelham wasn't among the captives. She'd made a point of lending

197

some of her attention to his soul, to keep him out of the New Death's grasp, but she hadn't possessed the foresight or energy to protect *everyone*.

"Oh, no," Bradley whispered. "Henry." His dead boyfriend was kneeling beside Daniel.

"Is that... St. John?" Genevieve took a step forward, then a step back, and whimpered. Her old mentor was there, too.

"Hey. Juliana?" Rondeau frowned at Skully. "Dude, that was the best you could do? My old bartender? I mean, we were friends, she left me her club after she died, but really?"

"Rondeau?" Juliana looked up, her eyes still heavily shadowed, as they had been in life, when she was subject to strange and debilitating addictions. "What happened to my club?"

"Oh. Well, I mean... I ran it for a while, but then I had to leave the city, and I sold it to Hamil, he's taking good care of it though."

"You ass," she said.

"Silence!" the New Death shouted. His terrible sword appeared in his hand, its hilt made of bone, its blade made of shadows and starlight. "Do you recognize this sword, woman?"

"I've held it more often than you have, so yeah."

Death swung the sword in a flat arc over the heads of his kneeling captives, close enough to ruffle Daniel's hair. "Then you know it can destroy almost anything. It can certainly consign these souls to oblivion. They have died once. Would you have them die *forever*?" The skull couldn't smirk, of course, but his voice managed it just fine.

"Okay." He could send Daniel and the others to oblivion as easily as Elsie had dispatched Christian, but she refused to let her nervousness show. "What's your offer?"

"I want you to do as you're *told*!" he bellowed. "Leave this place to me, and return to Earth. The fact that you care for these pitiful shades proves you're unfit to rule here. Your mortality is a weakness."

"If I leave, you'll subject them all to an eternity of horrible torment anyway, bonehead. Oblivion is a better deal for them than endless agony."

"I am... not unwilling to negotiate. These few could be given more pleasant afterlives. Left to their own devices, to do what they will with eternity."

"If you're willing to go that far, why not make more concessions? Like doing away with *all* the eternal torments?"

"I could be persuaded to create a system that is more... merit based. To torture only those who committed torture, to give pain to those who caused pain. Lesser offenses could receive lesser punishments. A sliding scale of misery."

Marla thought about it. The idea of negotiating with Skully was repulsive to her… but was that just a vestige of her old pig-headed stubbornness, her unwillingness to give an inch?

No. The New Death was holding the souls of her friends hostage, and he was a sadist. Gods were bound by the bargains they made, yes, but they were also adept at finding loopholes and edges and places where they could wriggle out of them. Any agreement they made would still end with billions of people suffering needlessly, and for eternity. "You're only willing to negotiate with me because you know you might lose," Marla said.

"Of course." He swung the sword again. "But you can't beat me without suffering considerable losses of your *own*."

"Holy shit, is that my *kid*?" Elsie said abruptly. "Ha, I was thinking, 'Why don't *I* get emotionally blackmailed, I hate being left out,' but there she is!"

The kneeling girl, the one Marla hadn't recognized, flinched at Elsie's voice.

"What did I name you, anyway? Vanessa?"

"Clarissa," the girl whispered.

"Hmm, if you say so. What even happened to you? I mean, what's a nice girl like you doing in an afterlife like this?"

"Cuh… car accident. In college."

"How about that. I always meant to look you up and see how you were doing." Elsie lunged forward, swinging Trepanner in an overhand arc, and slammed the point into her daughter's head. The girl vanished.

Even Skully was taken aback by the sudden attack, his attention wavering, his sword dropping, and Marla *pushed* as hard as she could, taking advantage of her husband's distraction to send the other hostages into the primal sea of chaos.

Skully howled and lifted his sword when his hostages vanished, apparently willing to find out what would happen if he killed her after all.

"Gen, now!" Marla shouted.

Bradley and Rondeau vanished, transported by Genevieve's will to a safer location, back to the foyer of the palace. Elsie's godhood made her impossible for Gen to banish, but a human-sized cage of golden bars appeared around her, trapping her, still holding the weapon she'd used to consign her own daughter to oblivion. A horrific act, morally indefensible… but utterly unexpected, which was just what Marla had come to expect from Elsie.

The cavern disappeared, Genevieve and Marla's wills combined to create a hall of mirrors. She'd gotten the idea from Bradley and Pelham's tale of traversing the mirror world. Her plan depended on Skully being frustrated, impatient, hasty, and confused, and what better milieu for that than a hall of mirrors?

Marla stood alone in a hallway, listening hard, and was rewarded with a howl of outrage and the sound of breaking glass off on one side.

"Come and get me!" She raced down a mirrored corridor, then another, taking turns at random, vanishing deeper into the maze.

"Woman!" Skully bellowed. He wasn't following passageways: he was smashing the mirrors, moving in a straight line.

She opened her shoulder bag and removed an artifact of her own design. It was a clay pot, bulbous and hand-made, covered in sinuous scribbles. An order mage named Mr. Beadle had helped her make it— very reluctantly—when she took her solo trip to Felport. The pot was a scale model of its much larger counterpart, buried beneath Fludd Park. The original was the sort of pot used to capture genies, though wrapped in more formidable magics than anything Solomon had ever mastered.

They'd used that pot months earlier to capture and imprison the Outsider, a being from another universe. A being capable of devouring gods.

Marla set her miniature pot on the ground and stared at it for a long moment. It swelled, and grew, and altered, taking on the form of a woman, first shaped of clay, and then gradually developing skin tone, hair, facial features, and armor. Marla breathed onto the figure, and the clay imitation of herself blinked its eyes, cocked its head, and looked at its outstretched hands. Just as she could conjure demons from chaos, she'd cloaked the pot in a body made of the same raw stuff of creation. If Skully really *looked* at it, with his full attention, he'd realize it was a simulacrum, but if he was angry enough, blinded by his rage….

A mirror crashed, very close by.

Marla turned, stepped toward an intact mirror in the hallway, and then stepped *into* it, sliding behind the glass, disguising herself as an illusion: she looked like a reflection of the clay Marla she'd just made.

Skully stepped into the corridor and faced the doppelganger, sword in hand. "*You,*" he said. "I don't know what will happen if I kill you. Perhaps such a transgression will lead to my own oblivion, but I would gladly pay that price to spare this realm from your human sentimentality."

Get on with it, Marla thought. Her clay double wasn't really capable of snappy repartee.

Fortunately, Skully wasn't the type to wait and see what a woman had to say. He roared and swung his sword, a blow meant to cut Marla in half at the waist.

When the blade struck her double, the false Marla shattered, and transformed into fragments of a clay pot. Skully stared down at the wreckage dumbly... and then screamed when a sucking black spiral of void opened on the floor amid the shards, pulling him toward it with a terrible, inescapable gravity.

Marla stepped out of the mirror and slapped the sword out of the New Death's hands, because she didn't want to lose *that*—and if he had it with him, he might even manage to survive where he was going, and escape.

Skully stared at her with his streaming-ember eyes, and tried to grab her, but his body was already elongating, being drawn into the black spiral, and she avoided him easily.

"I couldn't kill you." She bent and picked up the sword. "Just like you said: who knows what the consequences would be?"

"You think you can trap me? *Contain* me?" His lower body had almost entirely disappeared into the darkness, but he was still scrabbling at the floor, trying to drag himself out. "Put me in a bottle like one of those spirits of fire from the desert? I am a *god*."

"Oh, I don't know. I might be able to hold you. That pot you broke was magically linked to a much bigger version of itself, a prison made to hold a being of incredible power, and that's where you're going. Except... you aren't the being of incredible power I'm talking about. This isn't a jar to hold you, Skully. This prison is already occupied. Now it's a killing jar."

The New Death howled, fingernails clawing deep scratches into the floor. Marla stood at a respectful distance. The trap should only work to pull in the one who'd broken the jar—which was why Marla had padded it *very* carefully—but better safe than eaten by an extradimensional nightmare beast.

Her husband lost his grip, and vanished into the dark maelstrom, screaming defiance as he went. The void stopped swirling, then, and Marla moved a little closer, looking into the black circle, no bigger than a manhole. Skully was way down there, stomping around, peering into the darkness on all sides... and then tendrils of shadow grew toward him.

The Outsider had given up its semblance of a human form and reverted to its truer shape, a kind of hungering, ambulatory darkness. Skully thrashed as the dark tendrils wrapped around his limbs, his waist, his chest, and Marla closed her eyes and stepped away, waving a hand to close the opening of the trap. The Outsider had eaten a god before. She had no doubt it would consume Skully with the same ease. Mr. Beadle had assured her the prison was strong enough to hold the Outsider even if it devoured half a dozen gods and took on their power, and when it came to knowing tolerances, she trusted the order mage implicitly.

The new Death was dead. Long live the old.

Cutting Out the Core

MARLA LET THE HALL OF MIRRORS VANISH and returned to her lost throne room, with the walls of obsidian and the jeweled thrones. Genevieve was sitting on the floor, humming to herself, making a cat's cradle with a piece of purple string. She looked up. "Everything okay?"

"I'm now a deicide. Again. And also a mariticide. But since I didn't *technically* kill my husband, just put him in a room with a monster, I think I get to dodge any mythic blowback."

"Oh, good." Genevieve stood, the string vanishing from her hands. "Can I go home? I... seeing my attacker, and then St. John again, it was hard on me. I can feel myself starting to fray."

"I'm so sorry I brought you into this, Genevieve."

"Don't be. I'm glad I could help. I don't often feel *useful*. Mostly I have to be happy with the fact that I'm not making the world worse, so it's nice to be able to say, this time, that I made it better."

"Can I hug you?"

Genevieve consented, and Marla kissed her cheek, too, before sending her back to Earth. Genevieve could make her own way to her personal bubble universe from there.

Marla sat on the throne of emerald and put her chin in her hands. Now that the immediate threat had been dealt with, she had a moment to brood a little about the future. Maybe she was being childish... but if so, it was nice to be able to *be* childish, sometimes, and soon she would have to put away all those childish things.

"Ahem. Ahem ahem *ahem*."

Sighing, Marla waved a hand, and the golden cage that held Elsie disappeared.

Elsie came out dancing. "You slurped the New Death into the same pot where you kept the Outsider, didn't you?"

203

Marla nodded. "It seemed like the best way to get rid of him without bloodying my own hands."

A pirouette, on point. "I thought that's what you were doing when you insisted on spending time alone in Felport. You could have told me. I might have helped."

"Sure, if the coin flip showed heads. If it showed tails, you might have warned the New Death, or shoved me into the evil genie's bottle instead."

Elsie stopped twirling and said, "Ahhhhh. Is that why you had Genevieve lock me up in a cage?"

Marla shrugged. "I thought there was a good chance that at the moment of victory you'd hit me in the head with your pickaxe, yes. You know, pull off a last-minute betrayal. That's the sort of thing you'd do. We both know it."

Elsie started to sit on the sapphire throne, then clearly thought better of it, and conjured herself a three-legged stool made of diamonds to perch on instead. "Yes, but the idea of me betraying you is so obvious that it's not actually unpredictable. In fact, it's the opposite of predictable, it's practically *inevitable*, so of course, I couldn't do it." She sniffed. "Still, it's good to see you still have the sort of mind that plans for contingencies. I don't like being put in a cage, though. It's possible I'll hold a grudge, assuming I remember to." She shifted a little on the stool. "Congratulations, your majesty. You're the one and only reigning monarch of the underworld now."

"Hurray for me."

"Of course, you're still just the second fiddle. Or banana. Banana fiddle. In another week or two or three, the primordial womb will barf up another principal god of death."

"Wombs don't barf. You should've said stomach. Or birthed. Either one."

"I do so love your literary critiques, Mrs. Mason. But my point stands."

"Except it doesn't stand. You know that. You figured out what I had in mind ages ago."

"I *am* very astute. But I wasn't sure you'd have the guts, or, forgive me, the heart, to go through with it. Who knows, maybe the next god of death will be a benevolent philosopher king."

"I've met three death gods. They were megalomaniacal, smugly superior, and sadistic. I made the second one into a better man, but I don't have much confidence in the natural, or supernatural, processes doing the same. I could perch on the edge of chaos with my terrible sword and try to carve out the bad parts of the next god who emerges, but it's a risk. They come out pretty powerful, it seems."

"You don't have to talk me into your plan," Elsie said, "and I assume you've already talked yourself into it. So. Are you going to follow this to its logical conclusion now?"

"I don't have much choice." Marla rose from the throne. She held the terrible sword of death—her sword, now—aloft. The weapon twisted, shrank, and became a dagger: her old dagger of office, from the days when she'd been in charge of Felport.

The alteration was entirely superficial, though. The blade remained the sharpest thing in any possible universe, capable of cutting astral tethers, carving up time, sending souls to oblivion, killing dreams, and performing metaphysical surgery.

"Do you want me to do it?" Elsie said. "I've got a steady hand."

"No. I need to do this myself. Also, I don't trust you."

"You gods are so wise."

Marla closed her eyes, turned the knife in her hands, and plunged it into her own mortal heart.

The Dread Queen
on Her Throne

BRADLEY AND RONDEAU SAT ALONE on the floor beside Pelham's bier. Jenny Click had flown off a while ago, saying something about having worlds to burn.

"We haven't been beheaded and sentenced to spend eternity in a Goya painting or something yet," Bradley said. "So maybe things are going okay?"

"Why did Marla kick us out?" Rondeau said. "We came with her this far. Then she ditches us?"

"I'm guessing, after losing Pelham, she wasn't willing to risk losing us, too. Her and the New Death and Elsie and Genevieve are probably lobbing some major bombs at each other, anyway." He glanced around the marble hall. "This place is still intact, though. Seriously, I'm hopeful."

"Good for you. You know who else was always hopeful? Pelly. He was such an optimist he made *me* feel like a cynic. Look where that got him."

Elsie Jarrow strolled out of a door in the wall that hadn't been there a moment before. "Boys! Good news. Mr. Bones is no more. Marla opened a portal to the Outsider's prison and dropped her husband into it, just like you'd feed a newborn mouse to a pet snake."

"Wow." Bradley got to his feet. "That's… well, she always comes up with something, doesn't she? Where is she?" He narrowed his eyes. "Wait, you didn't *turn* on her, did you?"

"Ugh, no, why does everyone think that, it would be so *boring*. Her one-time assassin trying to kill her again? Where's the twist? No, I was true blue until the end." She wiggled her fingers. "Surprise!"

"So why are you here instead of Marla?" Rondeau demanded.

"She's got a whole underworld to run, not to mention, I don't know, seasons and things, cycles of rebirth to oversee, she's *busy*. She's also currently slicing out her own heart. Want to see?"

Before they could answer, Elsie spun around, her skirts twirling, and then the whole *room* twirled, and when it settled down again, they were in a black-walled room before two jeweled thrones... and Marla was sitting on the floor, dressed only in a white shift, surrounded by blood. Her chest was a bloody ruin, and she held a pulsing red *thing* in her hands.

Rondeau launched himself at Elsie, howling, but she froze him in the air with a gesture. "Bad boy. *I* didn't do this. Marla's wounds are self-inflicted."

Marla seemed entirely unaware of them, gazing at the twitching thing in her hands.

Bradley reached out for her, but stopped himself. "What... why did she do this? I don't understand."

"Of course you don't, Little B. You're only human." Elsie knelt and looked at the heart in Marla's hand. B noticed it was still faintly beating. "Marla is cutting out her own mortality. Slicing out her mortal core. She has to give up her humanity entirely, and become wholly divine. Otherwise, the primal god-womb will sense the absence of such a spirit, and produce another death god to fill the vacuum. We can't have that."

"Wait, so... what does this mean? What's going to happen to her?"

Elsie shrugged. "It means Marla has to give up her own immortal soul, for one thing. She loses her ticket to the human afterlife, and she's stuck with... whatever it is gods get. There's a lot of debate about that. Some of the gods think they get a whole afterlife of their own, *way* better than the one you mortals get, but I doubt it. The pure gods emerge from primal chaos, shaped by who knows what forces—human belief, human need, some metaphysical vacuum that nature abhors, I don't know. But I suspect that, when they die, they return to that undifferentiated state, like a metal sculpture that gets melted down into raw materials again. One-hundred-percent recycled gods. That's why you won't see me give up *my* mortality. If I ever get tricked into losing my status as a trickster god, I'll at least get my own afterlife down here to play in." She shook her head. "That Marla. Selfless to the end, huh?"

"You can let me go now." Rondeau spoke through gritted teeth, barely able to move his mouth. Elsie chuckled and waved at him.

He stumbled, then caught himself, and glared at the chaos god. "So, what... Marla's going to go full-dread-queen now? All skulls and black tongue and no pity and laying waste?"

"Hard to say! Guess we'll find out, won't we?" Elsie peered at Marla, then whistled. "No, wait, I take that back. It looks like she did a little *more* surgery on herself, now that I'm looking more closely. She cut off some her god-self's nastier attributes. Let's see, what's on the cutting room floor… looks like she got rid of the total indifference to individual human lives, and the sense of detachment that in a human would be termed psychopathic, and the vengeful streak. Well, well, well. Marla's committed some acts of radical self-improvement. I guess she figured out a way to do better, after all."

Still seemingly unaware of them, Marla squeezed her hands together, crushing her own heart between her palms, squeezing hard. Tears leaked form her eyes, sparkling in the light that shone from the cracks in her fingers. When she opened her hands, a single diamond rested on her palm.

After a moment, the diamond crumbled into dust, and Marla lifted her eyes to them.

"Hey, guys." Marla cleared her throat. The blood around her vanished, and her disheveled shift was replaced by a loose white silk shirt and matching pants. She stood up, absently wiping her tears away with the back of her hand. "So. Uh. I'm afraid I have to regretfully announce my… imminent retirement from public life."

"What are you talking about?" Rondeau said.

"No more month-on, month-off deal. I'm the one and only deity down here now. I can't do the part-time god thing anymore." She sighed. "I used to talk about duty, you know? I was so upset when I was ousted from Felport, because protecting that city was my responsibility, my life's work. But when I was offered the opportunity to take on a much *bigger* duty, I didn't want it. I felt this job was being forced on me, and, well… I've always had a contrary streak."

"I notice you didn't cut out *that* part of yourself," Elsie observed.

Marla ignored her. "I was selfish, and I fought against accepting my new role. I was happy to take the advantages of being a god, while shirking the responsibilities. I can't afford to do that, not any more."

"Oh, well, I'll miss seeing you around upstairs," Elsie said. "I—"

"Elsie, I thank you sincerely, and I owe you a favor I'm sure you'll call in one day, but for now—please fuck off." The queen of the dead waved her hand, and Elsie vanished. "Gods, I was sick of her."

Bradley couldn't help but laugh. "Yeah, us too. So… that's it? You're withdrawing from mortal life? Doing the god thing full time?"

Marla nodded.

"Why can't you still hang out in our world sometimes?" Rondeau said. "Reva wanders around up there, you know? Elsie does too."

"Elsie does whatever she wants, and Reva's people are the living, Rondeau. My people are the dead. I might make the occasional appearance on Earth, I'm not going full isolationist like Skully did, but... gods shouldn't dwell too long among mortals. We distort things. Alter causality. Make people join cults, or commit murders, or burn things down. We have a spiritual gravity—even during my months on Earth as a mortal, I drew trouble to myself, and summoned cultists, and...." She shook her head. "It's just time for me to move on, and step up."

"I played Dungeons and Dragons in high school," Bradley said. "Our characters were eventually so badass they became demi-gods. After that, the dungeon master wouldn't let us play them anymore. They were too powerful, so they got transformed into non-player characters: handing out quests instead of going on them."

Rondeau and Marla looked at B for a moment. "Nerd," they said, in unison.

Rondeau smiled at Marla, then frowned. "Seriously, though? First Pelham, then you? I have to lose *both* my best friends today? I hope you're ready to level up, B, because I've got vacancies in my innermost social circle. I'm not playing Tunnels and Trolls or whatever with you though."

Marla snapped her fingers, and Pelham emerged from behind her throne. He looked just as he had in life... except, if anything, he seemed happier.

Rondeau hooted with joy, ran to Pelham, picked him up, and spun him around. Then he put him down and frowned. "Crap, you're still dead, aren't you?"

Pelham nodded. "I am, regretfully, no longer among the living, though I am coming to terms with my new circumstances. I will be very sorry to see you less often, my friend."

"Yeah, yeah. It wouldn't bother me so much if I thought *I* was going to end up here someday, but I don't know what happens when I die. Who knows if the band will ever get back together?"

Bradley put a hand on Rondeau's shoulder. "We'll do some research, man. Maybe we can figure something out."

Pelham turned toward his queen. "Mrs. Mason. You look well. Pure divinity suits you."

"Yeah. I'm pretty sure I won't get pimples or split ends anymore. I'm sorry I couldn't keep you safe, Pelham."

He waved a hand, like his death was a matter of no importance. "To die in your service is a privilege."

"I'm glad you feel that way... because I'm wondering if you'd be willing to do a little *more* service for me. I know you're owed an eternity in an afterlife of your own choosing, so it's entirely okay if you say no."

"If I created my perfect afterlife, it would likely involve me working with a simulacrum of you, Mrs. Mason, so I am pleased to help the real you, instead. How may I be of assistance?"

Marla smiled. Good old Pelly. "I need a steward to help me rule here. I'll take a few weeks to show you the ropes, and set everything the New Death screwed up back to rights. Once I make sure it's all ticking along smoothly, I'll put day-to-day operations into your hands, but only temporarily. I won't be gone long. A month, at most, I think."

"Where are you going?" Bradley said.

"Well..." She leaned back in her throne. "You and Rondeau haven't quite seen the last of me. Before I settle in here permanently—or however long I last—I have a few pieces of unfinished business to take care of on Earth. I'd really love it if the two of you would help me. Call it one last hurrah."

"Like the party you throw for your buddy, right before he has to start a prison sentence," Rondeau said. He sounded glum, but then he perked up. "I *do* like parties."

"So that's the party bit taken care of," Bradley said. "What's the business part?"

"First of all, I need to unfreeze Nicolette, and try to set that whole mess right." She sighed. "That's not a conversation I'm looking forward to. Nicolette's not gracious at the best of times, and she's got legitimate grievances this time. I have some other wrongs I need to set right, too. Plus some people I need closure with, some farewells I need to say, some hash to settle, that kind of thing."

Bradley cocked his head and stared at her.

"What? Why are you looking at me like that?"

"I'm being perceptive at you, Marla. What aren't you telling us? What *else* do you have to do?"

She tilted her head back and looked at the ceiling. "Look. It's just. Here's the thing. I'm the main god of Death, now. There's a way things are done here. It's halfway between tradition and natural law. Basically, if I'm going to rule down here... I need to find a mortal consort to rule beside me."

There was a moment of silence, and then Rondeau began to cackle. "Oh, man. This is the greatest thing ever. You have *got* to let me write your online dating profiles."

"I can set you up with some guys I know," Bradley said. "Or girls maybe too? Or neither, I've got some genderfluid friends who'd make good gods, I bet. Just let me know your parameters. I never got a real handle on your sexual orientation, to be totally honest."

"There are some eligible descendants of royalty," Pelham said thoughtfully. "It is important to think strategically when considering a marriage. After all, you aren't *just* Marla Mason any more, you are also a regent. We should wait a respectable interval after the death of your first husband before we plan the wedding, of course...."

"A wedding!" Rondeau howled. "Yes! We have to throw a *big* wedding! I know just the right chapel of love in Vegas, the officiant dresses up like an elf from *The Lord of the Rings* movies, it'll be great."

"You can all go straight to Hell," the queen said.

Acknowledgments

THANKS FIRST AND ALWAYS TO MY WIFE HEATHER SHAW and our son River, who love and support me, and who both in their own ways give me the help I need to keep doing this strange book-writing things. Thanks to my tireless agent Ginger Clark, to my inventive artist Zack Stella, to my splendiforous cover designer Jenn Reese, my patient copyeditor Elektra Hammond, and to the indomitable John Teehan of Merry Blacksmith Press. My occasional writing buddies Effie Seiberg and Erin Cashier make this less of a lonely business. Finally, and most importantly, my great thanks to the more than 300 people who supported this project on Kickstarter. (The future is a wonderful place.) Say their names: @RhiReading; Aaron McConnell; Adam Caldwell; Aitor; Al Clay; Alexa Gulliford; Amy Kim; Andreas Gustafsson; Andrew and Kate Barton; Andrew Felle; Andrew Hatchell; Andrew J Clark IV; Andrew Lin; Angela Perry; Ann Lemay; Anne Roberti; Anton Nath; Arlene Parker; As Shadow; Audra Johnson; Ava Jarvis; becca; Ben Esacove; Ben Meginnis; Besha Grey, Queen of Bourbon; Beth Bernobich; Beth Rheaume; Beth Wodzinski; Bill Jennings; Brian Jackel; Brittany; Bryan Sims; Bryant Durrell; C.C. Finlay; Caity Zimmerman; Caleb Wilson; Carol J. Guess; Cat Rambo; Cathy Mullican; CE Murphy; Chad Bowden; Chad Lowe; Chad Price; Chelle Parker; Chris Connelly; Chris McLaren; Christian Decomain; Christian Lane; Christian Stegmann; Christin Steinbruch; Christine Chen; Christine Maia-Fleres; Christopher Todd Kjergaard; Christy Corp-Minamiji; Chuck Lawson; Cinnamon Davis; Claire Connelly; Claudius Reich; Cliff Winnig; Colette Reap; Colleen L; Colon Anderson; corey; Corey Klinzing; Craig Hackl; Craig Marquis; Cynthia Anne Cofer; Dan Percival; Dan Walma; Dana Cate; Dani; Dani Danooli Daly; Daniel Ethan Winter; Danielle Benson; Danika Hadgraft; Dave Lawson; Dave Thompson; David Bell; David Bennett; David

Burkett; David Green; David Harrison; David Martinez; David Rains; Dean M. Roddick; Deanna Stanley; Deb "Seattlejo" Schumacher; Dena Heilik; Denise Murray; Don, Beth & Meghan Ferris; Donald Mayne; Duck Dodgers; Duncan McNiff; Ed Matuskey; Eduardo; Edward Smola; ejhuff; Elias F. Combarro; Ellen Sandberg; Elliotte Bowerman; Elsa; Emrya; Enrica P; Ergo Ojasoo; Evan Vigil-McClanahan; Evangeline Z; EY; Ferran Selles; Feyrie Southeast; Fred Kiesche; Gann and Constance Bierner; Garret Reece; Gary Singer; Gavran; Glenn Seiler; Glennis LeBlanc; Glyph; Greg Levick; Grumpysteen; Guillaume Actif; Gunnar Hogberg; Haddayr Copley-Woods; Harvey King; Hathway; Heather Pritchett; Heidi Berthiaume; Hugh Berkson; Hynek Schlawack; Ian Mond; Isaac "Will It Work" Dansicker; J Leee; J Quincy; J.R. Murdock; Jacob "Ryoku" Walker; Jade; Jake Mandel; James Burbidge; James H. Murphy Jr.; James M. Yager; Jamie Grove; Jared wynn; Jason Rogers; Jay Garpetti; Jay Turpin; Jaym Gates; Jeff; Jeff Gregory; Jeff Huse; Jeffrey Reed; Jen Sparenberg; Jen Woods; Jenn Snively; Jennifer Berk; Jennifer T; Jeremy Carter; Jeremy Rosehary; Jessi Harding; Jim Crose; Joanna Fuller; Joe McTee; Joe Rosenblum; John Blankenship; John Curley; John Dees; John Devenny; Jon Eichten; Jon Hansen; Jon Lundy; Jonathan Duhrkoop; Jonathan Lupa; Jonathan Pruett; Jordy Jensky; Josh Mathews; Josh S.; Joshua Clark; Julia Shaw; Juliana Rew; Julie Gammad; Justin Morton; Justine Baker; Kaitlin Thorsen; Karen Brigitta Goetz; Kate Dollarhyde; Kathleen T Hanrahan; Keith Teklits; Keith Weinzerl; Kelly Angelina Hong; KendallPB; Kenn Luby; Kerim; Kerry Liu; Kevin Hogan; Khalil L; Konstantin Gorelyy; Kristin Bodreau; Kristin Evenson Hirst; Laura; Laura A. Burns; Lee DeBoer; Lila Taylor; Liran Lotker; Lisa Mia Moore; Lori Gildersleeve; Lori Lum; M. A. Klee; M. Murakami; Marcel van Os; Marius Gedminas; Mark Rowe; Max; Max Kaehn; Maxime G.; Maynard Garrett; Melissa Tabon; Michael "Maikeruu" Pierno; Michael Bernardi; Michael Bowman; Michael D. Blanchard; Michelle Matel; Michelle Ossiander; Mikael Vikström; Mike Bavister; Mike Dawson; Mike Wilson; Mirandia Berthold; MK Carroll; Monster Alice; Mur Lafferty; Myk Pilgrim; Natalie Luhrs; Nathan Bremmer; Nathan Turner; Neil Campbell; Nicole Dutton; Niels Erik Knudsen; none; Patrick Darden; Patti Short; Paul Bulmer; Paul Echeverri; Paul Rubin; Pete Milan; Peter Heller; Phil Adler; Phil Dawson; Phillip Jones; Q Fortier; Raghu T; Ragi Gonçalves; Randall Wald; Reed Lindner; Renee LeBeau; Rhel; Richard Leaver; Richard Naxton; Rick Cambere; Rick F; RKBookman; Rob Hobart; Rob Steinberger; Robert Adam II; Robin Mayer; Rodelle Ladia Jr.; Rodrigo Martin; Roger Silverstein; Roman Pauer; Ron Jarrell; Ron Pearson; Russ Matthews; Russ

Wilcox; Ryan Rapp; Ryan Spicher; S. aucuparia; S. K. Suchak; S. Rune Emerson; Sam Conway; Sam Courtney; Samuel Montgomery-Blinn; Sarah Heitz; Scott Drummond; Scott Serafin; Sean; Sean Elliott; Shanna Germain; Sharon Wood; Shef Reynolds; Shelley Cass; Sheryl R. Hayes; SPL; Sraedi Scatterbug; Stephen Ballentine; Stephen Boucher; Steve Feldon; Steven "Sammo" Simmons; Steven Saus; summervillain; Susan Marie Groppi; Tania Clucas; Tara Rowan; Ted Brown; The Bridge Family; Thomas Beauvais; Tim Uruski; Timo D. Zingg; Timothy Callahan; Tobias S. Buckell; Tony James; Tophat3D; Topher Hughes; Travis M. Dunn; Vincent Meijer; Vladimir Duran; Von Welch; Walter Bryan; Warlord Katrina; Yaron Davidson; Yoshio Kobayashi; and Zen Dog.